DAN KOONTZ

The I.P.O.

Made in the U.S.A.
Beverly Ann Publishers
ISBN 978-0615879932

Cover Art by: Gerome E. De Villa

www.dankoontz.net

To the loves of my life:
Kyla, Emily, Ashley and Claire

CHAPTER 1

His eyes snapped open as if spring loaded as his head shot up from the thin foam pillow. Despite the chill that permeated the orphanage barracks half an hour before sunrise, he threw off his covers and sat straight up, sweating and out of breath, tenting his scrawny arms on the cot's metal frame.

A quick look around the converted gymnasium confirmed that all the other kids were still asleep. Good. He knew from experience that this night's sleep was over. At least he'd have the shower to himself before the hot water ran out.

A little over three months had passed since the day Ryan Tyler, Jr. had spent every subsequent day trying to forget. But as he stared down at the shower drain, warm water tumbling off his hair in sheets, he found himself returning yet again to the last memory he had of his parents, on their way to pick him up early from daycare on his seventh birthday.

In a matter of seconds, he was all the way back, standing beside his teacher just inside the center's glass double doors, searching expectantly through the pouring rain.

An impatient grin materialized on his lips as the form of his dad's Honda Civic gradually took shape through the torrent. A hazy rhythmic flash of orange joined the cone of white light from the headlights as the car slowed, approaching the entrance to the parking lot.

Soon he was able to make out his mother's face in the passenger seat as the light from an oncoming car shined through the front windshield. She had just started to raise her hand to a wave, and a smile had begun to take shape on her face, as she briefly made eye contact with her son.

The light on her face grew gradually brighter, until it almost appeared that the sun was shining, only on her. This was the image he had seen every morning since, just before being jolted awake.

Then she was gone.

A cannonblast, followed by the screech of tires, several rumbling thuds that shook the floor, and finally the mundane static of the falling rain.

Ryan's heart stopped. He reflexly jumped at the door, threw it open and bolted out to the edge of the parking lot.

Wide-eyed and panting, blinking away the rain, he stared fifty yards down the street to the glowing tail lights of a massive Chevy Suburban that dwarfed the unrecognizable remains of his dad's eight-year-old Honda Civic just beyond.

After a brief pause, he forged ahead at a slow, deliberate pace, continuing on instinctively toward his parents, scared to death to see what awaited him – no one could have survived that impact – but compelled to go forward, as if drawn to them magnetically.

Broken glass crunched underfoot as he approached the rear fender of the Suburban. His chest felt hollow. His heart seemed to have slowed to a stop.

Just as he attempted to peer around the back end of the SUV to the mangled mass of metal and fiberglass that had been his parents' car, his teacher rushed in from behind, scooped him up in her arms, and took off running as fast as she could back to the daycare center.

He screamed a desolate scream of desperation, stretching both arms out over her shoulders reaching for his parents, futilely giving everything he had to free himself from her serpentine hold, as he watched his whole world slowly disappear from sight.

"Turn that off! You're going to wake up the whole wing," one of the orphanage nannies hissed. "And what makes you so special that you get all the hot water?"

Snapping back to the present, he quickly shut the faucet off. He hadn't soaped himself yet, but he really hadn't done anything to get dirty the day before.

"Now, get dressed," the nanny added with just slightly more compassion in her voice. "You've got a visitor."

His expression brightened a little at the thought. It didn't register with him that it wasn't even six o'clock yet.

~~~

James Prescott scanned one final email as he slugged down the last ounce of his first coffee of the morning. Before reaching the end of the message, he quick-replied a simple "no."

He didn't care what favor he owed to whom or what kind of sob story a supposedly close friend was selling him about how much he needed this. He wasn't about to do anything that might jeopardize his first IPO on the opening day of an entirely new market he'd spent the last 25 years almost single-handedly bringing to fruition.

"Good luck, honey," his wife called out, still in bed.

"Thanks," he yelled back, adding under his breath, "I won't need it."

James Prescott had long maintained a closer marriage to his idea than to his wife – an idea that had come to him as an undergraduate in economics at Princeton. An idea that would gradually grow to consume him. He had submitted it as his senior project, earning him the only failing grade he had ever received. But that had only hardened his resolve. With time, he'd grown to appreciate the F, which added character to a transcript otherwise weighed down by the monotony of A's.

After graduation, he'd been a standout in a brief stint with Goldman Sachs, building as many wealthy or likely-to-be-wealthy contacts as he could. Then came the hard part – essentially putting his idea on hold for the four years it would take to complete the combined JD-MBA program at Northwestern. But he knew he'd need the credentials.

Four long years later, after countless hours of independent research of the legal, ethical, financial and marketing nuances of his idea, he was finally ready to start. Within a week of graduation,

James Prescott, JD, MBA tactfully turned down multiple lucrative job offers and raised just enough capital to turn his idea into an entity.

He named it Avillage.

As he built the foundation of the fledgling company, gradually adding investors and employees but resolutely refusing to take on partners, he forced himself to take just enough time off to find a wife. To build the popular and political support he'd need to take his project past the developmental stage, he knew that a wife and, eventually, a family would be necessities.

With a very specific target in mind, he sought someone attractive but not sexy, motherly without being homely, intelligent but with no specific career aspirations, conservative but not political, Christian but not a zealot, whistle clean on a rigorous background check and, most of all, desperate for children. His search was quick.

An athletic 6'1" with dark hair, dark deep-set eyes, and a masculine cleft to his chin, offset by boyish dimples that made an appearance each time he smiled – a deceptively warm smile – he was a charmer (to the point that even those who suspected he was schmoozing them couldn't really resent him for it). A clear "catch" by any young woman's standards – or her family's.

He married Jessica Prescott, nee Aronson, in June of 2012, before an audience of the most influential men and women he could figure out a way to contact.

Just prior to their second anniversary, Jessica gave birth to John Prescott, followed less than two years later by Jacqueline Prescott. With a healthy son and daughter, there was just one more step he would need to take to complete his family. The most important step.

While away on a business trip in Los Angeles, unbeknownst to his wife, he underwent a vasectomy.

No longer capable of fathering a child, he took any and every opportunity to gush to his wife and their acquaintances about his strong desire to have more children.

After a year of "trying" to get his wife pregnant, he tearfully and ashamedly confessed to her that he'd gone to see a urologist and had discovered that his sperm count was low – they weren't going to be able to conceive again. This, he explained, was not uncommon as men entered their 40s.

They could, however, consider adoption.

Jessica's emotions were frayed over her inability to get pregnant over the prior twelve months, and her longing to have another child was forged in steel. The timing could not have been planned any better. And planned it was – right down to breaking the news on the day that she should have been ovulating.

Within a month the adoption papers were finalized, and in less than a year the Prescott family was complete, as James and Jessica welcomed their second boy, James Edmond Prescott, Jr. The fact that he'd saved that name for his adopted child would be P.R. gold.

Slowly, in carefully calculated sequence, his bizarre, underground but well-funded operation was introduced to the masses. A multi-faceted and seemingly nebulous ad campaign began pummeling the public from all directions.

In one public service announcement, an imprecisely-named foundation emphasized the number of non-infant orphans in need of homes, while another pointed out that due to our country's lack of investment in our children, the United States was falling progressively further behind China in math, science, and, perhaps most importantly, ingenuity. James Prescott's arrestingly magnetic smile was gradually folded into the PSAs, as his name became associated, and eventually synonymous, with the foundations.

Over the next several years, he and his special interest groups peppered congressmen and influential local politicians with tales of orphans trapped in the dead end that was serial foster care without any chance of eventually leading a productive life.

He then turned his rhetoric to what has worked in America. "Why should our most valuable assets be stuck in government-run agencies?" he posed. "What has worked in this country – what has made this country great – is the private sector. Investment. Accountability. Measurable results."

It was a full-court press political campaign. He smeared his rival – the status quo. He made lofty promises, invoking themes of patriotism, compassion and "change." The only difference between his and a typical campaign was that he had no opponent. No one was smearing him back during primetime programming because no one was funding the other side.

Things were already going better than planned when the news "leaked" that James Prescott, who had to this point fought to keep his private life extremely private, was himself a parent to an adopted child. Even the most cynical critic couldn't have perceived this as a publicity stunt. James Prescott, Jr. had been adopted almost a decade earlier.

Finally, with public opinion overwhelmingly on his side, he lobbied for a new division of the securities and exchange commission. His goal had always been to have his idea operational by the time he turned 50.

Now, two weeks shy of his 50th birthday, he was three hours away from realizing a dream; a passion; an obsession. *His* market opened at 9:30. He directed his driver to lower Manhattan.

~~~

"Mr. J.R.!" Ryan beamed, running into the open arms of his guest.

"That's *Doctor* J.R. to you, buster," Jared Ralston laughed, lifting Ryan up off the ground. "You wanna get outta here and get some breakfast?"

"Uh... hmm... let me think about it for a – Yes!" Ryan shouted. "I could use an Egg McMuffin."

Jared Ralston had been the late Ryan Sr.'s best friend. They had met in medical school, gone through residency together in internal medicine, and were midway through the final year of their cardiology fellowships when the accident had occurred.

Both of Ryan's parents had been only-children, and he'd only had the opportunity to meet one of his grandparents – his mom's dad, who had died in his sleep shortly after Ryan had started first grade. The other three were gone well before he was born.

His parents had left behind more college and medical school debt than they had assets, and their life insurance policies had barely covered what they owed. Mere months away from starting what would have been a privileged upbringing, Ryan found himself with nothing and no one. Except J.R.

"So, what did you do at school this week?" J.R. asked with his standard first question. He kept a booster in his back seat and tried his best to make it in to visit Ryan at least once a week.

"Not much," came the standard reply. It was a stock answer, but it was honest. At the beginning of the school year, like every other first-grader in the country, Ryan had taken the recently instituted Initial Aptitude Test, and he hadn't missed a question – one of only four students nationwide to do so.

J.R. wasn't privy to that information specifically, but he knew Ryan was smart – and that he was stuck in a mediocre public school in

Cleveland Heights that had absolutely no idea what to do with him.

They drove on in silence, both a little groggy from the early hour. But J.R.'s mind was preoccupied with what he had to tell Ryan. He knew it would have to come from him. And he knew he had to do it today.

They each ordered an Egg McMuffin. Ryan got an orange juice, J.R. a coffee. Then they made their way over to a table for two, as far away as possible from a group of senior citizens in an otherwise empty restaurant. A flat-screen TV, tuned to CNBC at a fairly high volume, assured that nothing they said would be overheard.

"How do you like where you're living now?" J.R. asked.

"I love it," Ryan answered sarcastically.

"Look, Ryan, you know I'd get you out of there if I could," J.R. said. "It's just that I'm on call every third night, and I'm working everyday."

"I know."

"And..." J.R. paused, as a lump developed in his throat. He took a sip of coffee, exhaled slowly through his mouth, took a long look up at the ceiling, and then heartily cleared his throat. "You know how you're finishing the first grade this week?"

"Yeah."

"Well I'm going to be finishing up my cardiology fellowship at the Cleveland Clinic. And I've taken a position... in Boston."

"You got it?" Ryan asked, grinning from ear to ear. "Massachusetts General? That's where my dad wanted to go! That's awesome!"

"Thanks. But you know, I won't be able to come by as much when I'm in Boston," J.R. said. "Not nearly as much."

"I know." Ryan kept his gaze down toward the table, picking crumbs off the thin arc of bare English muffin that remained on his grease-stained yellow paper wrapper. "That's awesome for you though."

They sat in silence for a few moments as the TV blared the end of an all too familiar commercial: *Invest in America. Invest in your future. Invest in our children. It takes Avillage.*

"You guys gonna watch that today?" one of the seniors shouted over to Ryan and J.R.

"Nope," they answered, almost simultaneously. Ryan's second to last day of school was about to start, and J.R. was already running late for work.

"You should watch," another old man in a foam-mesh VFW hat bellowed, not the least bit uncomfortable with having to yell to the other end of the restaurant. "It's history."

The other three seniors looked over, nodding approvingly at their friend's suggestion.

"We'll see," J.R. hollered back. Then he lowered his voice and looked back over to Ryan. "We should get out of here."

As they returned to the car, J.R. started back into what he had to tell Ryan. It would be easier in the car where he wouldn't have to look him continuously in the eye.

"I couldn't leave town without making sure you were taken care of," he said, concentrating on the road, peering back at Ryan periodically in the rear view mirror. "Ryan, you're going to be getting out of the orphanage."

"I know," Ryan said softly, trying to maintain a smile, looking up at J.R.'s face in the mirror from his back seat booster. Even though he was the one trapped in an orphanage, soon to be losing the closest thing he had to family, he sympathized with J.R. This was obviously hard on him too.

"No, Ryan," J.R. said with an exaggeratedly upbeat tone. "You're getting out soon – this week. You're gonna be going to a great family."

Ryan didn't know how to respond. He hadn't met or even heard of any potential parents. "Don't kids get to meet their foster parents first?" he asked nervously.

"Ryan, this isn't a foster family. You're being adopted! By a great couple. They want a kid to raise. To teach. To love. They want you, Ryan."

"Well what if I don't want them?" Ryan asked frantically. "Don't I get to meet them? Isn't there like a trial period or something?" The orphanage was bad, but at least it was a known entity. And it was temporary by design.

"Look, I know life isn't always fair for kids, and it sometimes feels like all of the important decisions are being made for you, but these parents have been chosen specifically for *you* – over hundreds of other couples."

"I thought you said *they* wanted *me*," Ryan fired back. "What do you mean they were chosen? Who chose them?"

"It's complicated. But I promise, you're gonna have everything you'll ever need growing up. And I'll still be a big part of your life. Trust me."

Ryan did trust him, but he couldn't wrap his mind around all of this. He was excited about the prospect of getting out of the orphanage, but he was terrified to meet his new guardians (he couldn't possibly refer to them as parents,) heartbroken by the news he wouldn't be able to see J.R. nearly as often, and utterly baffled by the entire process. Other kids in the orphanage (mostly younger kids, since they were the ones most adoptive parents wanted) had met prospective parents well before they were taken home. They weren't puppies! And why were there "hundreds of other couples" vying for his guardianship? He had nothing. It didn't make any sense.

J.R. pulled into the drive at Ryan's school. "I love you, buddy," he said.

Ryan was too confused to respond. He gave an effortful half-smile as he unbuckled himself, grabbed his oversized backpack and climbed out of the backseat.

J.R. pulled slowly away, shaking his head in disgust. He knew he had blown it and left a lot out, but there was no *right* way to do this – in the history of mankind, what was about to happen to Ryan had never happened before, and time was up.

~~~

James Prescott brushed past a pack of rabid financial news reporters without so much as a nod. Today was worthy of nothing less than national network coverage and a select group of news channels with international reach.

He strode into his office and shut the door. His second cup of coffee, piping hot, was waiting for him, along with his vice president Aaron Bradford.

Prescott had met Bradford in his final year at Northwestern. Over the years Bradford had developed into the ultimate number two man. He was 3 years behind Prescott in school, 3 inches shorter and 10 pounds heavier. He had all the work ethic and determination, but he wasn't an idea man, which was not to say he wasn't expert in honing and perfecting other people's ideas.

He wasn't unattractive, but he certainly wasn't striking. His hair was starting to thin on top and recede up front; his nose had never been broken but it looked like it had, deviating slightly to the left; and his effortful smile was as warm as permafrost.

Avillage never intentionally put him in front of a camera unless he was behind Prescott. Most of his work was done behind the scenes, often dancing on the line of ethically acceptable and not infrequently crossing well over it. Even Prescott didn't want the details of exactly what he did. "This isn't seventh grade algebra," Prescott would say. "Get the right answer. No partial credit for showing your work."

Bradford idolized Prescott, but he wasn't a yes man. He cherished his number two role in the company and was very well compensated for it.

"As you know, RTJ's set to open at 3," Bradford said. "I've heard some analysts going as high as 9 before the close."

"Sounds a bit high to me," Prescott said disinterestedly, sifting through some intra-office mail. "But I'm not worried about this one; he's a slam dunk. Have you got the next two nailed down? We're gonna have to keep our momentum up. I want JQJ second."

"Yeah, about that. Something's come up," Bradford said wringing his hands. "Turns out there may be a biological father in Newark. He's apparently gotten himself a lawyer and is pretty close to getting paternity testing."

Prescott's secretary cracked the door. "They're ready for you in makeup."

"Can you make it happen?" Prescott asked.

"Of course," Bradford said. "I just don't know if he'll be ready next month. We'd obviously have to disclose any loose ends. There are a couple other candidates we could..."

"Try," Prescott said firmly as he walked out the door.

~~~

Ryan watched J.R.'s car disappear down the street and then took off in a full sprint with no idea as to where he was going. Tears streamed across his cheeks and trickled behind his ears as he ran. It was the first time he had cried since his parents' funeral.

Finally running out of breath, he slowed to a walk in front of a Wal-Mart, one of the few stores already open for the morning. It would be a good place to get his thoughts together. And as long as he kept within reasonable distance of a similarly-complected adult, he probably wouldn't draw much suspicion – certainly less than wandering alone on the sidewalk in a semi-urban neighborhood.

As he loped behind a mom who was too busy trying to corral her petulant toddler to notice she was being tailed, an escalating fear of the unknown gripped his heart and began to squeeze. What he needed was an advocate – someone who loved him – to hold him and make him believe that everything was going to turn out ok. A grown-up unquestionably on his side who could make sense of this avalanche of life-changing information he'd just been hit with. He needed his parents.

But he knew no matter how hard he wished, no matter how hard he prayed, they were never coming back. Ever. Finality was yet another concept he had picked up earlier than most of his peers. And it was excruciating.

The toddler he was tailing finally had a full scale meltdown, prompting her mother to speed off toward the checkout, leaving Ryan all alone in front of the electronics department, where dozens TVs of every size, all set to maximum brightness, all tuned to the same channel, beckoned him to stay. He meandered over to the largest screen, nearly as tall as he was, and happened to catch the introduction for the CEO of Avillage, Inc.

He could hear the old man's voice from McDonalds echoing in his head, "It's history."

~~~

Nearly 500 miles away, James Prescott nodded to a group of media members and a handful of traders who had gathered on the floor below his podium.

"Welcome to the opening of the Avillage Exchange," he declared with a slow presidential cadence, eliciting uproarious applause. A large digital clock counting down behind him had just passed the two-minute mark. Prescott had no plans to say anything substantive or address any controversy; there was no reason to at this point.

"Welcome to the dawn of a new type of investing," he said. "One that will benefit not only the investor, but also our country, our society, and our children. Today is a proud day for me, my supportive wife and my three beautiful kids; a proud day for the amazing employees at Avillage; a proud day for the American people, whose indomitable spirit has never settled for 'good enough.'

"But what I'm most proud of today, is that I – or I should say – *we* get to help a young boy in an orphanage, who the odds say would have had almost no chance – a boy who would have been more likely to end up in prison than in college."

~~~

Out of the corner of his eye Ryan saw the mom he'd been following talking to a police officer and pointing in his direction. He covertly slipped into a small side aisle of the electronics department and wedged himself between two smaller TVs on a lower shelf, hoping to escape notice, still transfixed on the program broadcast in high definition on every screen. He had to find out what was going to happen to this orphan.

Elite test scores and spotless medical records flashed up on the screen behind Prescott as he touted the limitless potential of this exceptional but underprivileged orphan. Then Prescott described the boy's family.

~~~

"Our initial public offering is a little boy who lost both of his parents in one tragic night three months ago," he started in a somber tone. "Both physicians, his mother was a pediatric oncologist-in-training set to join the staff at Boston Children's Hospital and his father, finishing his cardiology fellowship, had just been offered a position at Massachusetts General Hospital, Harvard Medical School.

"This young boy has been languishing in an orphanage for the past three months with no family, virtually no stimulation and, the sad reality is, no hope.

"That will change today!" Prescott paused to let the applause die down.

~~~

"No!" Ryan whispered, his heart pounding harder than it had during the whole run from his school. *They're talking about me!* His eyes were transfixed on the screen, round as saucers, so entranced by the story that he hadn't even noticed the police officer approaching – until he was picking him up to carry him out.

"Wait! That's me!" Ryan shouted, struggling to wriggle free.

~~~

"It takes money to raise a child. It takes morals, ethics and intelligence. It takes love. And, sometimes, it takes A village.

"Our initial public offering will be traded under the symbol RTJ." As the clock hit zero, Prescott tapped the opening bell with an antique wooden mallet.

~~~

A nameless, coarsely pixelated copy of Ryan Tyler, Jr.'s 1st grade picture appeared on the screen, as a white 3 at the bottom left of the screen almost immediately turned to a green 4.25, then 5, then 5.75, then 8.

"RTJ! That's me!" he yelled frantically, straining to see the TV. The last image he caught before the officer turned down the center aisle that led to the exit was a grainy photo of a man and a woman who must have been in their late 20s or early 30s, standing outside a large brick house in what appeared to be a quiet suburban neighborhood.

The green number at the bottom continued to tick upward 12.21, 12.89, 13.41...

CHAPTER 2

A brilliant white light illuminated her face, enveloping her with an almost angelic aura, serene and surreal in the storm. Her eyes, finally finding his, relaxed, widening almost imperceptibly, while her lips fell together and just started to curl at the corners with the inception of a smile. Her expression softened and her shoulders dropped gently as the tension fled from her muscles. Somewhere in the transition from expectant to elated, her countenance found peace; love; contentment.

CRASH!

He was awake, sitting straight up again, but not breathless today.

Ryan looked up at the clock – six forty-five. Better. Most of the other kids were stirring, and he could hear the faint splatter of the shower echoing from the tiled bathroom.

The first few seconds of every morning were always disorienting, waking up in the middle of a half-heartedly renovated gym instead of his old, cozy bedroom. But surprisingly, nothing felt remarkably different than the day before. Maybe that hadn't been him on TV yesterday. After all, the picture was essentially unrecognizable, and RTJ weren't even his initials. The part about the kid's parents though was what he couldn't resolve. That had to have been him.

After the police officer had picked him up at Wal-Mart and delivered him back to school, he'd fabricated a story about swearing he'd seen his mom in a car that looked just like the one she used to drive. He'd run after it and eventually lost sight of it but found it again in the Wal-Mart parking lot. He'd gone inside to try to find his mom.

His tears were real, and everyone bought the story. The principal was more than happy to turn the case over to the school counselor without doling out any punishment, and the story got J.R. off the hook too.

Ryan took a quick cool shower with the fading remains of the hot water and returned to his small space in the middle of the cavernous barrack, occupied by a heavy trunk and a metal-framed bed. As he was rifling through the trunk that held all of his worldly possessions, the same nanny who had scolded him for taking too much time in the shower the day before appeared beside him.

"You're popular," she said. "More guests today."

"Did you say guests? With an 's?'" He only knew one adult.

"That's what I said. Now hurry up. They're waiting. And your bus is going to be here in 15 minutes."

Eager to find out who had come to see him, he threw on a T-shirt and shorts, slipped on a pair of white tube socks, and grabbed his shoes. As he was pulling the laces tight on his second shoe, kneeling on the floor behind his trunk, he turned his gaze toward the window to the lobby, where he caught a brief glimpse of a man and woman just turning to face him.

He'd seen them before!

Pale-faced and expressionless, he dropped all the way to the polished concrete floor, pretty sure he hadn't been spotted, suddenly disturbingly aware of his heartbeat pounding from his chest into his head. It was the couple from the grainy photo he'd seen standing in front of the brick house on the TV screens as he was being dragged out of the store!

The windows in the converted gymnasium were all at least 20 feet off the ground and the only other way out was through the lobby. There would be no escape. Still, he had to buy some time to think.

"Now where is he off to?" he heard the headmistress say, leading the couple ever closer to his space. "He is going to be so thrilled. We do our best to give the boys everything they need here, but we know it's not home."

He silently slid himself under his bed as the footsteps passed by. He'd have maybe a minute to figure out how to handle this. His eyes darted back and forth, looking for approaching feet as his mind raced. He had no idea what an initial public offering was, what J.R. had meant about his parents' having been chosen for him, why the old man had said that the opening of Avillage was historic, and most of all why or how *he* was integrally involved. And he was desperate for answers.

The footsteps stopped at the opening to the bathroom.

"Ryan? Are you in there?" the headmistress called.

The echo of her voice was the only reply.

"Hmm. Tell you what, I'll just to go fetch one of the nannies to check."

"Or I could just..." the man's voice started.

"I'm sorry," the headmistress interrupted, her thin lips struggling to maintain a smile. "Our policy strictly forbids non-employees from entering the children's bathroom – for our protection... and yours. I'll just go get one of the nannies." Ryan listened as her heeled shoes clacked quickly back toward the lobby.

Maybe he could get some answers out of the man and woman who had apparently come to claim him. They had to be in on this somehow. That would be a big gamble though. Once he'd revealed his hand, he couldn't possibly undo it.

Alternatively, if he appeared oblivious for the time being, he could always divulge any or all of what he knew at some point down the road. Plus, he thought, he had to find out if he could trust these people. The one guy he did trust had to have known at least *something* about this. J.R. had somehow known he was going to be adopted this week. He'd try to talk to him first.

A loud creak from the frame of the bed interrupted his thoughts as the mattress sagged in the middle, lowering the springs close to his face. He turned his head to the right and then quickly to the left, but he couldn't see anyone.

"Hi!" came a woman's voice from his right.

Startled, he yanked his head back to the right and saw the upside down smiling visage of a woman who appeared to be in her early 30s hanging her head off the bed, her sandy blonde hair just sweeping the floor next to him.

"Hi," he said, blushing behind a guilty smile, suddenly much less anxious.

"I'm Sara. Wanna come up and talk?"

~~~

James Prescott sat in the armchair opposite his host and casually crossed his right leg over his left. A stagehand deftly slipped her arm over his shoulder, affixed a small microphone to his lapel, and scurried away.

"And we're on in 3, 2, 1..." came the producer's voice from off set.

"Welcome back to A.M. America. I'm Blake Everton," the host crooned with a voice like silk, resting an empty mug on a homey coffee table in front of them. "With me today is James Prescott, founder and CEO of Avillage, Incorporated." He turned toward his guest, and the two exchanged cordial smiles.

Prescott, without any pretense of confrontation, maintained an unbroken eye contact with Blake – just long enough to effect the slightest unease in his host, quickly establishing that although he was the interviewee, he was the one in charge.

"Yesterday was a big day for you and your exchange," Blake continued. "Now, for those of us who may not be familiar with what you do, could you give us the 'Avillage Exchange for Dummies,' if you will?"

"I'll try," Prescott said with a chuckle. "Blake, we all know that America has been suffering from an ever-widening wealth disparity – for decades now. And with that wealth disparity has come an *opportunity* disparity. What we're attempting to do at Avillage is funnel some of that all-too-plentiful Wall Street money down to Main Street by allowing investors to put some of their savings behind some really special, but disadvantaged, young children. Now, that's not to say investors don't have a chance to benefit financially – of course they do. That's what really makes this the quintessential win-win situation."

"And how exactly do investors profit from these... these children? Last I checked, raising a kid ain't only unprofitable, it can put you in the poor house!" Blake joked to the camera, trying to inject some levity into the vapid morning show.

"Well, any profitable company is built on capital, as you know. Now, that capital could be cash reserves or, more commonly, it can come in the form of credit. Many companies, especially young ones, operate at a loss for several years but still have plenty of money to spend on operations, development and research – so long as investors continue to see an opportunity for profit in the future. I'm sure you've seen the occasional stock whose price soars after announcing a quarterly *loss* because it has strong forward-looking projections?"

Blake nodded dutifully.

"So, these children initially benefit from the capital that shareholders have invested in them – or, they're costing a fortune, as you put it. But because of their strong 'projections', if you will, for profitability later in life, they represent value to the investor," Prescott explained. He tried not to sound as if he were reading from a script, but he'd gone over this so many times, it was difficult.

"So the profit comes when the shareholder sells the stock?" Blake asked, furrowing his brow and continuing to nod, reaching back for his empty coffee mug.

"That's one way to make a profit, but that's more of a *trading* strategy than the strategy that I hope people will choose to employ, which is *investment*. Once these children are grown and enter the workforce, a portion of their income will be appropriated to the board of directors, similar to a tax. The board, which will be chaired, at least initially, by an Avillage executive and will also include some of the larger-volume shareholders, will then direct how much of that money is reinvested in the child – well, at that point, man or woman – and how much is paid out to shareholders in the form of dividends."

"My head is spinning. Folks, this is why I let professionals handle my finances!" Blake exclaimed to the camera. Then he turned back to Prescott with a playful smirk, "Now, I know that you probably won't tell us, but the question on everyone's minds is, 'Who is RTJ?'"

Prescott raised one eyebrow and held up an emphatic index finger. "If I told you, I'd have to kill you," he said sternly before finally cracking a smile. They both shared a boisterous laugh over the hackneyed turn of phrase. The inanity of the morning show, along with the wide reach of its viewership, was precisely the reason Prescott had picked this as his first post-opening interview. Low risk; high reward.

"But seriously," Prescott continued. "The SEC has outlined very rigid privacy laws for our children, similar to the HIPAA laws that govern a patient's right to privacy in the medical arena."

"I notice you're very careful not to refer to these children as 'commodities.' Why is that?" Blake asked, lobbing Prescott a softball.

"Thank you for noticing that, Blake. As you know, I'm a dad to an adopted child myself, and these kids – without a home, without role models, without a family – are my number one priority. They're the reason I've been able to keep going, pushing for the massive policy changes that have had to take place over the last 2 decades to get this market off the ground."

"Alright, so we don't know who RTJ is," Blake whined with a fabricated frown. "But what's going to happen to him next? Where does he go from here?"

"We've placed him with a highly qualified mother and father, chosen specifically for him, to help maximize his strengths, develop his weaknesses, and raise him to be the productive – no – the exceptional man he has the potential to be.

"RTJ's new mother has a masters degree in child psychology and has almost a decade's experience teaching gifted children of all ages at a prominent, nationally-rated magnet school. Her husband is a financial executive with a remarkable educational background and, shall we say, more than a stable income."

"Pardon me for interrupting, but how would one of our viewers at home become a parent to one of these extraordinary children?" Blake asked.

Well Blake, your lobotomized viewers at home would never stand a chance of even being introduced to one of these kids, and they're exactly what we're trying to prevent these kids from becoming, Prescott thought before answering. "We have access to prospective parent profiles from all of the reputable adoption agencies. So all of these parents were looking to become parents *before* they considered becoming an Avillage parent. And we have a division of full-time employees whose only job is to match each orphan up with the perfect parents *for that individual*. Don't call us. We'll call you," Prescott said, turning to the live camera with a grin and eliciting a hearty guffaw from Blake.

As Blake began to segue into a commercial break, a screen featuring the scowling face of Bloomberg's Britt Herndon started its slow descent from the top of the set between Prescott's seat and Blake's. Prescott's smooth smile belied his irritation at the sight of the unexpected guest, who happened to be one of his most outspoken critics. The questions were about to get significantly more pointed.

~~~

Sara Ewing couldn't contain her smile as she fought the urge to stare. This was the first time she'd seen him. His frazzled dark wet hair fell boyishly down almost into his fawn-like brown eyes. A few faint freckles dotted his nose, and ran down his cheeks toward a hesitant smile that was conspicuously missing two teeth, one on top and one on the bottom. (Sara briefly wondered if the tooth fairy visited places like this.) His faded blue T-shirt was a couple sizes too large, which accentuated his childish appearance and almost fully concealed his shorts. On the surface he was everyboy, but Sara knew the extraordinary potential that lay behind those bright eyes.

She was a bona fide child-whisperer by profession, but all of her training was currently locked far away in her superego; in this moment she simply couldn't contain her joy. She finally had a child.

Despite every means known to 21st century medicine she would never be able to experience the magic of being handed a newborn baby in the delivery room, but it couldn't have exceeded what she was currently feeling.

Her husband Thomas, less expressive, couldn't quite hold back a single tear which he hastily erased with his knuckle. Then he firmed up his expression and gave Ryan a confident man-to-man nod, which Ryan seemed to appreciate.

"I'm Ryan," he said, feeling the need to say something to break the silence, yet knowing full well that they already knew his name.

Giggling and sniffling and smiling, Sara attempted to compose herself. "How would you like to get out of here?" she said, stooping to his height, taking no shame in the joyful tears that remained on her cheeks.

"Where?" Ryan asked guardedly, not sharing her enthusiasm.

"C'mon. We'll show you," she said, offering him her hand.

Ryan looked up at the headmistress, on her way back from the lobby, who smiled and nodded as if to tell him it was okay. Then he looked down at his bed and his trunk before taking a long last look around the barracks.

Hesitantly, he extended his hand to hers and followed the two complete strangers out of the orphanage, unsure if he'd ever return.

He didn't know what to feel at the sight of his departing bus, as he continued to follow his new caretakers through the pick-up area and on toward their shiny silver Lexus SUV, with the entirety of his former life packed neatly into his backpack. This was really happening.

Ryan leaned his forehead against the rear passenger-side window and stared out at the houses going by, which seemed to grow progressively larger as they traveled. After about twenty minutes, the car came to a stop on a short stretch of red brick road.

Thomas and Sara gave a familiar wave to a uniformed guard, who nodded respectfully and triggered the slow opening of a heavy wrought iron gate. Ryan lifted his head off the window for the first time, craning his neck toward the middle of the car to get a better view as they passed through. He didn't know places like this existed. And he couldn't help but be impressed.

A spotless white bike path snaked through the lush emerald-green grass, so perfect he had to squint as they drove by to convince himself it was real. Islands of deep black mulch, outlined by brilliant red, white and purple pansies surrounded Bradford pear, Japanese maple, and flowering weeping cherry trees in each yard. Even the sky seemed bluer inside these gates. And set in the back of each lot at the end of a long driveway was a colossal custom house, each more impressive than the next.

But halfway down the second cul de sac, Ryan was rocked by another unsettling wave of *déjà vus* as he caught sight of the brick house he'd seen on TV. He wasn't actually surprised this time, but he wasn't prepared for it either. He leaned back with a pit in his stomach, slumping into his top-of-the-line booster seat. One of the four garage doors opened as they pulled into the drive.

Sara and Thomas led Ryan on an abbreviated tour of the 8000 square-foot mansion, focusing on the playroom, basement and office, which featured a miniaturized mahogany replica of

Thomas's desk for Ryan. They finished the tour on the second floor.

"And this is your room," Sara said, nudging the door open with the back of her forearm.

Ryan's eyes widened, and his expression brightened as he scanned the room. But he quickly checked himself, hit with a twinge of guilt for allowing himself a moment of happiness in his parents' absence. He owed it to them not be content with this house; this room; these people.

"Go ahead," Sara said, sensing his hesitation. "It's yours."

He loosened his grip on his backpack, allowing it to fall gently to the ground beside him, as he walked timidly toward a bed in the shape of a pirate ship in the corner. He stopped at the bow to peek up a ladder that led up to a crow's nest which featured a round table in the middle with miniature built-in seating all around. At the stern was a knotty treasure chest loaded with unopened toys. In the opposite corner stood an L-shaped desk with a computer, a tablet and a smartphone.

A large closet stocked with more clothes and shoes than he'd ever seen in one place abutted an adjoining bathroom – his own private bathroom. No more fighting for space or hot water in the shower.

"Sorry about all the clothes," Thomas said, slipping his arm around Sara's waist. "Our families got a little excited when they heard you were coming."

"There's one other thing I want to show you," Sara said, walking over to the ship and pressing a button at the base of a digital frame next to his bed. "I'm hoping we can add a lot more memories to these in the years to come."

Ryan ambled over, keeping his gaze fixed on the frame, as a slideshow of pictures of him with his birth parents began to play. He stood there entranced as each new picture appeared. When the fiftieth and final picture faded back into the first and the cycle started over, Ryan climbed into the ship and lay quietly on his side facing the frame, continuing to watch as his new parents slipped inconspicuously out the door.

~~~

Prescott discreetly glanced down at the phone peeking out of his right pants pocket to check a text he'd gotten from his VP Aaron Bradford before the cameras went back live: `just landed in newark - researching JQJ issue.` *Perfect.*

"And we're back," Blake beamed, oblivious to the tension in the air. "Joining us now is Britt Herndon, chief financial correspondent for Bloomberg News. Always great to see you Britt."

Herndon nodded sternly.

Prescott's smile grew noticeably brighter as he nodded back, knowing that the cheerier he appeared, the more exasperated Herndon would become. Public opinion often had less to do with one's position on an issue than with the appeal of the person espousing it. If he could paint Herndon as an angry old man bent on stonewalling progress, this could be a good thing.

Blake got things rolling. "Mr. Prescott, some of your critics would say that you are planning on hand-picking only the most talented and most intelligent children for your market. How do you respond?" he asked, tilting his head slightly, cradling his coffee mug in both palms.

"Well, we do preferentially choose children who are most likely to provide return for our investors, Blake. Look, I wish that we could help every child who needed it. I sincerely do. But at the same time, even if we were able to help, let's say, even one out of every thousand orphans in this country, wouldn't that be better than not helping any at all, which is what we as a society have been doing – until yesterday?"

Herndon looked like he was going to vomit and couldn't resist jumping in. "You love to cite statistics that show these kids are more likely to end up in jail than in college," he said. "Yet you hand pick the ones who are obviously not on that track, and saddle them with a life of indentured servitude."

"Now Britt," Prescott chuckled with a glint in his eye. "I'm just going by statistics that we have for unselected orphans. If you have more specific data, I'd love for you to share it with us. And as for your claim of indentured servitude, well, that's just absurd. That's like recommending against a student's going to college to avoid being saddled with all of that debt they'll eventually be forced to repay."

Shaking his head, Herndon barked back, "If you look at the roughly one thousand living people who have at one time or another been part of the Forbes 400 – the wealthiest 400 people in the world, mind you – 25 of them were adopted. Two point five percent! That's an *over*-representation of adoptees among the wealthiest people in the world! I could say that you're hand-picking from a population that's *more* likely to overachieve!"

"Now here's where we do have more specific data, Britt," Prescott said without pause. "Of those 25 people you referenced, 17 were adopted as infants, which we don't touch. That leaves eight who were adopted later in life. Seven of those were adopted by extended family members and one by a close family friend. Only one spent any time in an orphanage, which was purely transitional and only for a few days. All of our kids, by law, must have spent a minimum of three months in an orphanage prior to joining the program. So if you look at the population we're drawing from, they represent precisely 0% of the Forbes 400."

"Corporations are going to be making decisions about the way these kids are raised with future profitability as their only motivation – with no concern for their happiness!" Herndon seethed.

"Britt, two suggestions. One, look over our mission statement. Two, try some decaf." He turned over to Blake, snickering, pointing a sideways thumb at Herndon's image on the monitor. "Of course I'm only joking, Britt. But we are very aware that successful adults are the products of happy childhoods. They come from strong families, they have friends, and they're involved in diverse extracurricular activities. I'd also like to point out that short-selling on the Avillage Exchange is explicitly and permanently forbidden, so every investor will only have an interest in these kids' values going up."

"Ok, well why don't you tell the people at home who the true legal guardians are? Is it the 'mom' and 'dad' you referred to?" Britt asked, making quotation marks with his fingers as he spoke, leaning in almost on top of the camera.

"This is an entirely new paradigm where the legal guardians are not the parents but the corporation. I know that's become dirty word, but let's be honest. No investor would put a single cent into one of these kids if there were no legal bond. And if you allow yourself to get past the media buzzword 'corporation,' I don't think that's such a bad thing. The truth is most parents don't know what they're doing a lot of the time. They really don't – myself included. We parents often wind up making emotional decisions without a lot of thought to the long-term consequences. I hear parents say all the time, 'There's no handbook on how to raise a kid.' Well, I'm hear to tell you there is. Sort of.

"We have developed actuarial tables over the last 20 years that cover an amazing array of variables. For instance, Blake," Prescott posed, deliberately ignoring Herndon. "Did you know that only-children have a 57% chance of choosing a profession in the field of their same-sex parent? Or that lifetime earnings of piano and violin players is

73% higher than that of children who played any other instrument growing up? Or that there is a direct correlation between lifetime health quality and educational level?"

"Fascinating," Blake commented.

"I've got literally thousands of those," Prescott said, back in coffee table chit-chat mode with Blake.

Herndon was nearly boiling over. "Anytime you've got a system where a group of wealthy people *owns* another human being, that is a form of slavery, and I am shocked and ashamed that this is going on in the United States. It's an abomination!"

"Britt, I respect your opinion on a lot of issues, but you're way off base here," Prescott said calmly. "No one *owns* these people. Granted, while they're minors, they don't have the right to make all their own decisions, but no child does – their parents do.

"Then once they're grown, they have a financial obligation to the shareholders who've supported them and put them in position to be successful. But they can choose to pursue whatever career their heart desires. Plus they gradually accumulate shares themselves, so that they have an opportunity to buy out the shareholders by the time they're 50 – or earlier in some instances. By SEC regulation they'll own 100% of their shares by the time they're 63. It really isn't that different than having the military pay for your college and then owing them 4 years of service afterward. Our arrangement is longer, but it's actually much less restrictive."

"Yeah, except they owe 90% of their after-tax income to the shareholders!" Britt yelled, nearly hyperventilating.

"Come on, Britt. You're better than that. That's the highest appropriation level, which only applies to the portion of their annual after-tax income over one million dollars – those kinds of numbers would apply to less than one percent of the population," Prescott said, his heart rate at an even 60.

"One final question," Blake said, winding the segment down wearing his familiar morning-show smirk. "Who's next?"

"Sorry, folks. Looks like we're out of time," Prescott said with the same casual demeanor he'd kept throughout the interview, all-in-all satisfied with how the spot had gone.

~~~

Ryan slowly opened his eyes and looked over at the clock. He'd been asleep for almost 2 hours. The pirate bed was infinitely more comfortable than his old metal-framed bed, and the room was incomparably quieter than the orphanage.

Despite its short duration, the nap was the best sleep he'd had in months. Finally waking up refreshed, he realized how chronically exhausted he'd been.

He climbed out of bed, walked over to his desk and picked up his new smartphone, not entirely sure how to use it. J.R.'s number was already programmed into it. With one quick tap, he heard the phone start to ring. And ring. And ring. No answer.

"Mr. J.R., it's Ryan. Don't worry. I'm ok. I just have a couple questions about the thing you were telling me about after we ate at McDonald's yesterday. Can you call me back? I'm not sure what my number is. Thanks."

He then picked up the tablet, a medium with which he was very familiar, and decided to try to do a little research on his own. His search for "RTJ IPO" yielded a treasure trove of information. With tabs open for the dictionary, Wikipedia and several finance pages, he started to piece a few things together. He was extraordinarily bright, but this was almost all new terminology for him.

No relevant information was out there to be found on Sara or Thomas Ewing. But it appeared his real decision-makers were on his board of directors, so he typed in a search for "RTJ board of directors."

The chairman of the board was James Prescott. Ryan never forgot a name – he was the CEO of Avillage. As he scrolled down the list, expectedly, he failed to recognize any of the other names – until he got to the last one.

None of the shocks of the previous two days had prepared him for the lightning bolt at the bottom of the list. It was the name that was now flashing on his vibrating cell phone: Jared Ralston.

CHAPTER 3

"What the fffff...?" Melvin Brown sputtered, spraying the screen of his laptop with flecks of half-chewed Cheerios.

The ESPN homepage he'd been perusing was suddenly being overrun with frame after frame of obscene pictures and videos of prepubescent boys. Each window he managed to close seemed to spawn two more.

"What the hell is going on?" he whispered, as he raced for the phone to call his cable company.

"*Para Español marque dos,*" came the cheery recorded voice on the other end of the line, followed by a long pause. "We are currently experiencing higher than average call volumes. Your estimated wait time is... eighteen... minutes."

"I can't wait no damn eighteen minutes!" he shouted into the phone.

"Your time is valuable to us," the chipper woman's voice answered on queue. "Press one now to leave your name, phone number, and a brief message, and our next available customer service representative will return your call shortly."

Yeah, right. Leave a message that your computer's being overrun by child pornography.

As more and more repulsive images flashed up on his laptop, he tried to shut it down, but his keyboard was frozen. He even tried holding the power button down for what seemed like a full minute – nothing.

Finally he slammed the cover closed.

And that's when the volume came on. Full blast. Godawful sounds from the disgusting videos filled the room.

In full-scale panic mode, he darted over to the window, threw down the street-facing shade and turned back frantically to his computer. Tiny blue lights indicating continuously streaming data flashed relentlessly from the side of the keyboard as he turned the volume of his TV all the way up to try to drown out the vile sounds blaring from his computer.

Then without warning a pounding at the door joined the din. It wasn't the inquisitive knock of a neighbor wondering if everything was ok. Whoever was behind that door was coming in, invited or not.

The flashing blue lights on his laptop maintained their frenetic pace.

"Just a minute," Melvin yelled over the roaring TV. "I'm getting dressed."

"Mr. Brown? Open this door!" came a booming voice from the hall.

"Yeah. Two seconds," Melvin yelled back, heading for the bathroom in a full sweat.

He turned the water on full-force in the tub and then ran back to the living room, where he thought he could hear the jangling of keys from the hall. The super must have been with them.

Grabbing his laptop, he ran for the bathroom, just as he heard the deadbolt release.

"Mr. Brown! Come out here with your hands up. We've got a warrant." They were inside the apartment.

He raised his computer high over his head and then slammed it down as hard as he could on the tile bathroom floor, tossing the remnants into the half-full bathtub. Finally, mercifully, the only noise to be heard was from the blaring TV.

Wearing nothing but a pair of boxers, he looked into the bathroom mirror to see four of Newark's finest over his shoulder, standing next to his superintendent in his living room.

Two of the officers charged into the bathroom and lunged for the mangled laptop. "Mr. Brown, you're under arrest for possession and distribution of child pornography. You have the right to remain silent..."

The words trailed off, as Melvin's attention turned inward, incredulous that this was happening to him. He'd checked out the occasional nude woman on the internet, but who hadn't? He'd never paid for anything. And the sites he'd looked at were more R-rated than X – never even remotely close to kiddie porn.

Could this have been some kind of virus that had hit the ESPN website? That was probably his only hope. But if that had been the case, why were the police immediately breaking down his door? Someone had to have set him up. But who? And why? He didn't have an enemy in the world. He hardly had any acquaintances.

"You think they'll be able to salvage it?" one of the officers asked his partner, inspecting the soaked remains of the laptop.

"Oh yeah. The geeks down at forensics'll have this downloaded by lunch," the second officer answered. Then he turned his gaze to his suspect and sneered, "I wish to *God* this pervert would've resisted!" The statement was loaded with false bravado, made only after Melvin was securely cuffed – and everyone knew it.

Melvin Brown was 6'6" and a chiseled 245 pounds. Bad knees and a string of concussions in his sophomore year were the only things that had kept him from playing defensive end in the NFL. Instead, after a couple of years of college, his scholarship lost and no other way to pay for the remainder of his education, he'd joined his family's meatpacking business.

For the past several years he'd kept mostly to himself, both at work and afterward, spending the bulk of his time watching and reading about sports, unable to kick his unhealthy habit of ruminating over what might've been if he'd stayed healthy – or at least finished college.

His massive shoulders slumped, and his chin hung down to his chest, as the officers led him out. Tears began to well in his eyes as he caught sight of the basketball he'd gotten autographed by the entire New York Knicks basketball team. He'd envisioned the day he would present it to his son. The son he'd just discovered he had. The son who still didn't know his dad existed. The son he'd now probably never be allowed to meet.

"Get some clothes on that monster for God's sake," the officer in charge shouted, looking him up and down. "Pants only. I don't want those cuffs off him until he's down at the station."

Four stories down, on the opposite side of the street, Aaron Bradford removed a small earpiece and powered down his laptop, as he fired off a text to his boss: JQJ is a go.

~~~

J'Quarius Jones swung around the three-point arc to the baseline, pointed heavenward, and took flight off of both feet. The defender in front of him stepped up to try to take the charge, forcing J'Quarius to straddle and then elevate right over him. At the apex of his jump, he met the ball with his fully-outstretched right hand and then hammered it down through the hoop in one fluid motion.

A veritable lightning storm of flashbulbs diffused across the bleachers, as the crowd erupted. He hung on the rim for half a second, allowing himself to enjoy the moment, before gently coming back to earth.

A rising eighth-grader, he was 6'4" with a nearly 7-foot wingspan and a 38-inch vertical leap. He was two inches taller than the opposing team's center, but with the agility to play guard – the epitome of a man amongst boys. He hadn't lost a game in over two years, despite the fact that he'd been forced to change teams three times in that span.

With his team up by thirty and only a minute and a half left to play, number eleven coolly strolled over to Lincoln Junior High's bench, giving a low five to the last kid off the bench who had the unenviable task of replacing him. The crowd was still on their feet, half continuing to cheer and half headed for the exits. Three division I head coaches in attendance jockeyed for position to make eye contact, frustrated that they weren't allowed any more substantial contact with a kid his age.

He took a seat at the end of the bench and leaned forward with a wet towel draped over his head. Sweat and water from the towel mixed on his face and dripped onto the floor below, but no tears. He wouldn't allow that.

J'Quarius had been raised by his grandmother from infancy. He'd been told that his mother had died during childbirth, but his grandmother didn't like to talk about it. And he knew nothing of his father.

Over the course of the past year a gradual role reversal from dependent to caretaker – and from boy to man – had taken place, as colon cancer slowly, mercilessly ate away at his grandmother. He'd been the one to pick up her prescriptions at the drugstore at all hours of the night. He'd learned to change her IV bags when she could no longer eat so she could continue to live at home and not in the hospital. He'd been her psychologist when she'd felt like giving up. He'd taken odd jobs at neighbors' houses to make ends meet when she'd been denied social security disability. He'd stayed home from school on days when the home health aides had called in sick. If it had been an option, he would have quit school altogether.

Two months ago she'd died. Expectedly. But it was devastating. J'Quarius's only other relatives were his great-grandparents in Mississippi who were too debilitated to make the trip to New York for their daughter's funeral, much less adopt a 12-year-old.

He boarded with random friends for a few nights at a time, but eventually he found himself in the state's care at an orphanage, where he quickly discovered that there's a big difference between being blind your whole life and abruptly, permanently losing your sight. The other kids near his age were lifers with no foundation and no direction. They'd been in foster homes for brief stints, but they'd always returned, never really knowing what family was. The orphanage was their home. J'Quarius didn't have much in common with them and didn't want to; he just wanted out – anywhere.

In effect, he was a divorcee looking to rush back into marriage, not because he was on the rebound but because he'd actually been painfully lonely for years. He was desperate to reclaim his childhood before it was gone forever – to be looked after, guided and, hopefully, loved. But he was terrified that no one would take a chance on a hulking soon-to-be 13-year-old in a grown man's body.

~~~

Melvin sat in stunned silence, staring blankly at the table in front of him as his lawyer laid out the charges. "We're gonna beat this," Leonard Weinstien said, with more revulsion than conviction in his voice.

"I've negotiated your release on the condition that you not go within 100 yards of a school, church, daycare facility, or orphanage. Melvin! Did you hear that? Are you listening?" his lawyer asked snapping his fingers, looking for any kind of response. "I said orphanage too. Have you got it? Don't go near it."

"Where do we stand with the DNA testing?" Melvin asked mechanically, his stare unbroken.

"That's off the table right now," his attorney gasped, incredulous at where his pervert client's priorities lay. "That should be the least of your worries."

"Can I go now?" Melvin asked resolutely, standing up but keeping his head down.

"Melvin, listen. These are serious charges," Weinstien said, shaking his head in disbelief. "Your laptop is loaded with files going back years. You might eventually be able to get some supervised visitation if we can..."

"Can I go now!" Melvin asked again, his voice booming behind an eviscerating glare that clearly caught his diminutive lawyer off guard.

"Y-yes. Yes. Sure. Yeah. Legally you can go. I'll, uh, I'll call you tonight."

Melvin turned and left the room without another word, leaving the door open behind him.

~~~

Montay was the oldest kid in J'Quarius's orphanage at 16 and was essentially a prison yard boss in training. He had lackeys, smuggled in contraband, intimidated other kids and confiscated and redistributed most of the gifts that came in. But despite always being the prime suspect whenever something happened, he was never directly caught doing anything of substance by the staff.

J'Quarius had become Montay's unintentional rival from the first day he set foot in the facility. Four inches taller and 25 pounds heavier than the home's heretofore largest resident, he held minor celebrity status for his basketball skills, and he paid absolutely no mind to the orphanage hierarchy Montay had spent years cementing.

On the Sunday of his third week at the orphanage, J'Quarius sat quietly by himself, finishing up a late breakfast in the dining hall.

Montay was always at his most active on the weekends, when staff was thin.

As he approached J'Quarius's table with a few of his friends in tow, he kicked the doorstop out from under the door, sealing off the exit to the dining hall . J'Quarius kept his head down over his tray.

Montay then sloppily slid his tray down, knocking J'Quarius's glass of orange juice off the other side of the table. J'Quarius jumped back onto his feet with lightning quickness and snatched the glass on its way down between his thumb and middle finger.

"Oh no," Montay whined tauntingly. "I'm so *not* sorry."

"No need to be, man. Just a couple drops," J'Quarius said, avoiding eye contact and casually setting his juice back on the table.

Again Montay slid his tray into the glass, more forcefully this time, spilling its contents all over the table.

"Look dude, I'm just trying to finish my breakfast. I'm not after anything you got. I'm not trying to stop you from doing whatever it is you do around here. I don't even know you," J'Quarius said softly, sopping up the mess with a stack of napkins.

"Everyone here *gets* to know me – and answers to me," Montay snapped.

J'Quarius exhaled slowly and shook his head. "Fine," he sighed, taking the last bite of his cereal and lifting his tray up to go. He moped over to the trash can, stepping over the extended leg of one of Montay's lackeys.

"Things can be real easy or real hard in here. It's up to you," Montay said, uncomfortably close to J'Quarius's face. "Now, I see you got two pairs of shoes. The way I see it, no one needs two pairs. I want your high tops."

"No," J'Quarius said disinterestedly, putting his hand on the doorknob to leave the dining room.

Montay slapped J'Quarius's forearm, ripping it off the knob. "I don't think you heard me! I said I want those shoes." His minions were closing in.

J'Quarius grabbed the doorknob in a second attempt to leave. Again Montay's hand slapped down on his forearm. "Where do you think you're going? We're not done," Montay snarled.

This time, J'Quarius's hand held fast on the knob. He lifted his head up from the resigned position it had been hanging in and straightened up his shoulders. Then slowly, deliberately, with Montay's hand still clutched onto it, he raised his arm up to the deadbolt on the dining room door and twisted it locked.

Montay took a quick step back, his sneer fading fast, trying not to let his sycophants see the fear in his eyes. But before he could figure out what was happening, J'Quarius's hand was gripped tightly on his throat.

J'Quarius effortlessly spun him around and threw him into the door. Teeth gritted, tears spurting sideways out of his bright red eyes, J'Quarius unleashed a year's frustration on this petty, insignificant thug who happened to be looking for trouble in the worst possible place at a catastrophically bad time.

With one powerful hand, he lifted him up off the ground by his neck, leaving Montay kicking and flailing his legs helplessly 18 inches off the floor. Veins bulging from his neck and forehead, J'Quarius rhythmically slammed him against the reinforced glass of the windowed door, all the while keeping a maniacally vacant stare fixed on Montay.

Two orphanage workers on the other side of the glass scrambled for the door shouting at J'Quarius to stop as they fumbled with their key rings.

An amalgam of emotions – grief from his grandmother's death, hopelessness that he'd never get out of this place and resentment for having been cast as the town jester playing for the crowd's entertainment on the basketball court, yet going home alone to an orphanage every night – manifest as unadulterated rage.

"You're gonna kill him," one of the lackeys shrieked as Montay gradually stopped struggling and went limp. Thud, thud, thud came the continued drumming of his flaccid body against the door.

Finally, one of the orphanage staff managed to unlatch the deadbolt and pull the door open. J'Quarius gave one more shove, and, with the door no longer there to provide resistance, released Montay, who crumpled to the floor. He lay there lifeless for a few seconds before coughing and gasping himself awake, gulping in the air he'd been starved of.

J'Quarius, suddenly aware of what he'd been doing, sunk to the ground, buried his head in his hands, and sobbed.

~~~

"Melvin, it's Leonard again. Look, if you're there, pick up the phone. We need to come up with a game plan here. You can't just ignore this and expect it to go away. Your court date is in 4 days. If we're not prepared, we're gonna go down in flames. Please..." Weinstien was cut off by the beep of the answering machine, which now flashed "17" new messages.

Melvin threw on a blue tank top and white gym shorts, laced up a brand new pair of white high tops, grabbed a duffel bag and left his apartment, not bothering to lock the door. Down on the street below, he hailed a cab and directed the driver to Greenwich Village.

"This good?" the driver asked twenty minutes later with no specific instruction on where in Greenwich Village his passenger had wanted to be dropped off. Melvin peeled off a hundred dollar bill, handed it to the driver and, without asking for change, exited the cab.

Now on foot, he passed by three blue mailboxes, dropping a letter in each one. Then he ducked into a hardware store, where he bought a sturdy rope, a bolt cutter and a permanent marker, paying with cash. From there he descended into the nearest subway station and took the first train heading north.

As the train rumbled into the Bronx from Manhattan, he moved to an empty car and removed the bolt cutter from his bag. Then just before the train arrived at the last station, he snipped off his court-ordered ankle bracelet.

The train squealed to a stop, and as the doors slid open, Melvin kicked the bolt cutter and the bracelet off the train and sat back down to wait for it to head back south.

A few people straggled into the other cars, but no one boarded his. It was nearing midnight on Sunday.

After a 20 minute wait, the train jostled back to life and hissed loudly, as its doors slid back shut. Melvin closed his eyes and meditated to the rhythmic rocking of the southbound train, going over the execution of his plan in his mind.

For the three weeks he'd been incarcerated, The New York Times had been his only connection to the outside world, and he'd had more time than reading material. What had captivated his attention most was not the sports section, but the financial pages, specifically a new section that had been created, behind the equities, commodities, and currencies, for AVEX – the Avillage Exchange.

He devoured every story about the exchange – the absurdity of it, the legality of it, and the single commodity that was currently on offer. He read daily stories speculating what, or more accurately, who the second listing would be. Rumors had initially sprouted that James Prescott was going to go in a very different direction from his highly cerebral first commodity.

Then, as interest had just started to wane in the fledgling market during the SEC-mandated 30-day hiatus between offering one and offering two, unnamed sources within Avillage had leaked that the next orphan to go public would be an athlete. Unnamed sources were also quoted as saying that the SEC had demanded that the athlete's ticker symbol be changed, so as not to reveal his identity.

Day by day, the pieces continued to fall into place, and it finally dawned on Melvin why he had been set up. His son was already at the top of the middle school All-American lists; he'd even been profiled briefly on Yahoo Sports six months prior. The fact that he was an orphan was a closely guarded secret by the administrators at Lincoln Junior High, but the Yahoo story had touched on his dogged dedication to his terminally-ill grandmother. With the attention to detail that had been ascribed to Prescott, Melvin knew he wouldn't have missed that. J'Quarius was on every high-profile division I school's radar – his initials would become immediately recognizable, if they weren't already.

Melvin had tried convincing his attorney that there was a plot against him, but the computer's data was too overwhelmingly convincing, complete with expertly hacked dates on which he had supposedly downloaded and uploaded data, as well as fabricated emails it looked like he'd exchanged with known pornographers going back 2 years.

~~~

J'Quarius was in counseling when Arlene and Hansford Washington arrived at the orphanage. After two sessions, the counselor had more or less come to the conclusion that J'Quarius had been pushed a little too far by a bad kid. But J'Quarius had to understand and accept the responsibility that came with his size and athletic ability. When a Chihuahua snaps, it gets scolded; when a Rottweiler snaps, it gets put down.

Arlene Washington was 43 years old. A former college basketball standout at The University of Connecticut, she understood the kind of dedication it took to reach the highest levels of athletic success. She was six feet tall, lean but with generous hips, and walked with a limping gait, trying to protect what little was what left of the cartilage in her knees.

Hansford stood a half foot taller than his wife and looked a good ten years younger than his 44 years. He had made some poor decisions early in life and didn't get so much as a sniff from a major college after spending the last 6 months of his senior year of high school in jail for check fraud. But after his release, a local junior college coach made sure he got his GED and then took him under his wing, taught him a little about basketball and a lot about being a man, and eventually got him a transfer to a small four-year school where he earned a bachelor's degree in sports sciences.

With that background, he'd gone on to become quite a coaching success story himself, having directed his inner city Chicago high school team to three state championships, while keeping his players out of trouble with the law and maintaining an astounding college matriculation rate among his players that was three times higher than the high school's average.

Arlene had played briefly in the WNBA, but after meeting Hansford at a local gym, she'd fallen in love, had a child, and walked away from the game for good with no regrets.

Like J'Quarius, the Washingtons' biological son had been a standout in middle school. He even resembled J'Quarius from certain angles. He'd gone on to make the Parade All-American team as a sophomore in high school, but a drunk driver had stolen him from his parents before he'd had a chance to start his junior year. Devastated and too old to start over with a baby, Arlene and Hansford had jumped at the chance to take in an adolescent basketball prodigy from the inner city when Avillage had come calling.

When the counselor opened the door to introduce J'Quarius to the Washingtons, there wasn't a dry eye in the room. Arlene and Hansford didn't care in the moment that they weren't legally full parents. J'Quarius didn't think about how and where his life might be uprooted. They all simply felt an immediate sense of wholeness, satiety for a primal human need for which they'd been starving.

~~~

Just prior to sunrise, with shades of gray evolving to dull colors, Melvin emerged from a public restroom at the corner of Wall Street and Broadway. An impressive suit that had drained the majority of his bank account covered the gym shorts and tank top he'd been wearing the night before. Wingtips replaced the high tops that he now carried in his bag.

Apart from his size, he didn't stand out from any other upwardly mobile young executive getting to work early on an important trading day.

With a purpose in his gait, he walked the two blocks to Avillage headquarters, slid past security with the first wave of employees that came through the lobby and took the unsecured elevator to the 24th floor. From there, he hoofed it up the remaining 22 flights to the roof.

Knees throbbing and out of breath, he threw open the emergency exit and climbed down the small metal ladder to the rooftop, where he quickly shed the suit he'd been wearing. After putting his high tops back on, he removed the rope and marker from the duffel bag and tossed it next to the $600 heap of clothes.

He then laid the thick braided rope down in a straight line on the blacktop before turning back and mouthing the number of paces, as he concentrated on maintaining a constant stride length. When he reached 33, he marked the rope, tossed the marker aside and got busy tying knots.

Once he had securely fastened the end of the rope to the vent cap closest to the corner of the 45-story building, he backed up, slowly, methodically, toward the center of the building.

With his eyes closed, he took in a few deep breaths to clear his mind.

Then he opened his eyes.

The sun was just peeking up over 11 Wall Street to the east. To the southwest he could see Lady Liberty in the shadow of lower Manhattan surrounded by the calm water of New York Harbor, only her torch and crown illuminated.

He then reached down to one of his socks to retrieve a scrap of newspaper that he'd clipped from the back of the sports section six weeks earlier and gently pressed the picture of J'Quarius to his lips. Then he released it to the wind and watched it flitter and float away, climbing the updrafts between the buildings.

When the clipping had disappeared from sight, his expression hardened, along with his resolve.   He bounded toward the edge of the building next to the roof vent. Reaching full speed just before he took flight, he let out a cathartic scream. For the athletic career cut short. For the college dream unrealized. For the son he could never know.

Dozens of faceless suits on the street far below craned their necks toward the leonine roar and then scattered, as Melvin soared 20 feet clear of the building. His rickety knees had conceded one final athletic statement.

With a striking suddenness, his scream went silent as the rope cinched around his neck, choking off his airway.

His lifeless body, adorned in a blue tank top and gym shorts, came careening back toward the top floor of the building.   A full one-story spiderweb took shape in the plate glass on the top floor of Avillage headquarters as his massive corpse slammed into the window of James Prescott's corner office. Clearly visible from inside, through the kaleidoscopic glass, was the number 11 on the back of Melvin's Lincoln Junior High jersey. Above it were the letters JQJ.

~~~

Ticker symbol J opened with even more fervor than RTJ had, as investors leapt at the once-in-a-lifetime chance to get in on the ground floor of the next Michael Jordan or LeBron James, both of whom had reached net worths in the billions. Prescott had deliberately undervalued the listing to re-energize his market, and the idea had worked to perfection. One million shares of J opened at 5, peaked briefly at 34, and then closed at 27. AVEX was the only financial news story of the day.

Melvin Brown's death had been lost in the hype of the opening and had barely made the news the next day. Prescott tried to convince himself that a known sex offender committing suicide outside his window couldn't have had anything to do with him, and he didn't bother to ask any questions.

Meanwhile at the orphanage a man giving the name of Daryl Washington dropped in, looking to pick up anything J'Quarius may have left behind.

"Just one letter that came in today's mail," the headmistress said, handing over the envelope.

"Thanks." Daryl said, his eyes darting nervously for the return address. Then with a suddenly relieved smile he added, "For what it's worth J'Quarius is really happy."

Strolling through the parking lot back to his car "Daryl Washington" placed a call to Aaron Bradford. "You were right. I got the letter. Our source at The Times intercepted the other one earlier this morning."

"Perfect. Bring them to me unopened," Bradford said appreciatively. He wanted to be the one to destroy the letters personally, to know for sure it was done.

He still had a scout in Mississippi watching J'Quarius's great-grandparents' mailbox for a potential third letter, and he'd had Melvin Brown's apartment thoroughly searched – before the police had even positively identified his body. A healthy paranoia pervaded all of Bradford's actions, and it had served him well throughout his career.

A week passed and no third letter was ever delivered. As a token of his appreciation, Prescott had bequeathed the chairmanship of the board of J, along with a 5% ownership stake, to Bradford. J was his now.

CHAPTER 4

Ryan found himself standing in the pouring rain at the rear bumper of the Chevy Suburban that had forever changed his life. Knowing what was coming next, he quickly ducked and looked back over his shoulder, expecting to see his daycare teacher lunging for him.

But she was nowhere to be found.

The facility wasn't there either.

Behind him was only a long, empty road with no clear beginning. On the other side of the tangled mess of metal and glass, the road stretched on beyond the horizon with no turns and no perceptible end.

He straightened up his posture, bit down on his lower lip and, with as much courage as he could muster, *finally* stepped around the back end of the Chevy Suburban. Just as he did, the rain stopped – as if a faucet had been turned off – and the storm clouds melted into a star-filled sky, unobscured by the new moon.

His parent's Honda Civic was tilted grotesquely forward with all four wheels off the ground, effectively molded to the front of the Suburban, the front windshields of the two vehicles nearly touching. Ryan bit down a little harder on his lip and concentrated on the sound of his breathing, shallow and rapid through his nose, trying to stay composed. Nerves taut, he wrapped his fingers over the passenger-side window frame, pulled himself up onto his tiptoes and stretched his neck to try and see inside.

"Ryan?"

Any other sound would have startled him. But this soft, comforting, familiar voice was instantly soothing. Ryan immediately let go – of the car door he was holding on to, of the confidence he was trying to project, of the emotions he'd been trying to suppress, of everything. He ran to his mother, standing at the side of the road with his father, and collapsed into her open arms. Sobbing, with his head still buried in his mother's side, he reached out an arm to embrace his father as well.

"You are our everything, Ryan. You always were – but now more than ever," Ryan's dad said quietly, ruffling his hair the way he had every time he'd said goodbye to Ryan.

His mom gently nudged his quivering chin upward with the side of her finger to look him in his tear-filled eyes. "Make a difference," she said. "Love. Be loved. And be happy." She leaned down and gave him a kiss goodbye on the forehead just like she had everyday she'd dropped him off at school.

Ryan knew he couldn't stop them, but as the tears trickled continuously down his cheeks, one by one, he bit back down on his lip and managed to whisper, "Please, don't go." For the first time, he felt a twinge of real pain in his lower lip. "Don't go," he whispered again. He could feel himself waking, and the harder he fought it, the shallower his sleep became. "Don't go," he heard himself whisper aloud. He was awake.

"You okay?" Sara asked, peeking her head in the door.

"Yeah," Ryan answered, his voice cracking just slightly.

Pretty sure everything was not okay, Sara cautiously entered his room and knelt at the edge of his bed. "Honey, your lip is bleeding," she said worriedly.

"I was just having a realistic dream, and I bit down on it. It's ok."

"Are you sure?" she said reaching for a tissue. "Let me see."

He studied her face as she stared down at his lip with genuine concern, tenderly dabbing it with the tissue. "I'm sure," he answered.

Once she was satisfied with her nursing job, Sara glanced back up to find Ryan looking her directly in the eye. "You sure you're ok?" she asked with a confused, almost self-conscious expression.

Then Ryan did something he'd never done before in his four weeks at the Ewing household. He wrapped his arms around her and gave her an unreserved hug, resting his head on her shoulder.

"Finally," she thought as she hugged him back, her heart soaring inside her chest. She had been so sure for so long that it would happen, but she'd just started to allow herself to question, *"What if it didn't?"*

Ryan loosened his embrace, but Sara wasn't ready yet. She continued squeezing him, blotting the corner of her eye with the tissue she still held in her hand.

For the past month she'd stood up to the Avillage board. He wasn't ready to start his education, she'd told them. They couldn't push him.

Over the last several days her stand had only gotten harder, as she'd felt even more alone in her fight. Thomas, frustrated by their lack of progress, had begun to make the argument that maybe they should consider starting the board's plan. They couldn't possibly start making *less* headway with him. "Do you want them to take him?" he warned. "They can. And they will." Thomas had slept on the couch that night.

But on this nondescript Tuesday morning, when she'd least expected it, Ryan had proven her right. In every way this was a breakthrough.

~~~

"Welcome, everyone. I'd like to call to order the first meeting of the board of directors of RTJ," Prescott announced formally at precisely eight o'clock, the history of the moment not escaping him.

The first meeting was held in the Avillage board room two doors down from the office of James Prescott, who now stood at the head of a long, sturdy oak table with a panoramic view of the financial district as his backdrop. Seated around the table were the nine other board members. Six were early investors in Avillage – business executives mostly in their sixties and seventies. Two were chief executives of mid-sized companies. And the last was a baby-faced cardiologist in his first year out of fellowship, who looked almost as out of place in a suit as he did among the company he currently kept.

"The purpose of today's meeting," Prescott continued, speaking without notes, "is to go over some early financial estimates, discuss some of the progress we've made in the six weeks since open, and, hopefully, come up with some strategies to get things headed in the right direction before we release our first quarterly report.

"I've been in communication with the adoptive parents on a weekly basis. Unfortunately, we lost about four weeks in the transition from orphanage to home, but we've now started most of the educational programs we'd prioritized the highest. Our boy's actually already well ahead of where we thought he'd be in math despite the setback – he's picking up concepts amazingly quickly.

"His tutor is billing out at 45 dollars an hour for 10 hours a week, and we're picking that up. We've also got him working with an English tutor for 4 hours a week, primarily working on writing. That seems to be paying early dividends also, and she bills at the same rate.

"His mom is out of the house for four hours a day, leaving him with a Mexican-American nanny we've chosen, who's got an exceptional track record for teaching conversational Spanish. He's doing very well with that, and she only costs us 20 dollars an hour for 20 hours a week. We'll keep the nanny until he's fluent, but we won't need the math or English tutors during the school year.

"His adoptive mother is playing games of strategy with him for about an hour a night, which I'm told he enjoys, and his dad is introducing him to the basics of the financial markets, obviously avoiding AVEX. Those services are of course free to us, and his parents have waived the parental stipend.

"We're picking up the family's healthcare by contractual obligation, which is about 900 a month, and he'll be starting school at the Hunting Valley Academy for Math, Science and the Arts, which is clearly the top primary school in Cleveland and one of the best in the country – really a bargain at $24,000 annually.

"That puts our annual expenditures somewhere in the neighborhood of $60,000. Any questions or comments on any of that?"

"Any word yet on grade placement?" one of the executives asked. "60,000 times nine sounds a lot more palatable than 60,000 times eleven."

"Hmm. What you're proposing is a bit of a gamble," Prescott said flatly, trying to conceal his delight that someone else was suggesting a course he fully supported. "Kids don't immediately gain maturity by virtue of skipping a grade. Now of course, RTJ is slightly taller than average for his grade, and believe it or not, that's an independent predictor for success in skipping grades – we have data on that.

"What's harder to predict is how he'd do emotionally. Initially, it's hard on all kids who skip

70

ahead. Then, down the road, some kids have trouble building relationships with their peers, who are all a year or two older, especially around adolescence, but I don't have any numbers to give you on that."

"If we can save 120,000 bucks, I say we do it," J.R. said casually, as nine heads turned in his direction. "Look, more than the $120,000, it's the extra years of productivity, while we still have a high percentage of ownership. We have a very fixed time period during which we can extract a profit. If he gets out of college at 18 or 19 instead of 22, that could be a huge difference in lifetime earnings. Yeah, maybe it'll be a little hard for him to adjust at first, but he's a tough kid. I say we push for 3rd or even 4th grade this year – unless you have good evidence to say that these kids don't do as well financially in adulthood."

All eyes turned back to Prescott. "No," he said pensively. "The data show that the vast majority of these kids do very well financially. The only gamble is that a small percentage – around nine percent – crumble emotionally and end up utter failures. And the majority of those kids who do fail are boys. We could always consider skipping a grade *after* we see how this year plays out."

"He'll be fine!" J.R. blurted out, unaccustomed to the standard decorum of a board meeting. "His dad skipped first grade." Aside from Prescott, no one else in the room was aware that J.R. knew Ryan personally.

"Dr. Ralston had a close relationship with RTJ's birth family," Prescott quickly interjected, not entirely pleased that the information was now public. "And he maintains a close relationship with the boy, which is one reason we extended him the invitation to participate on the board.

"I really don't think there's a clear 'right' answer on this one," Prescott said in a feigned conciliatory tone. "We'll put it to a vote. All in favor of pursuing a higher grade placement?"

After 7 ayes, the matter was settled.

~~~

By the time Thomas finally built up the nerve to broach the subject, Sara was already convinced. Neither Thomas nor Sara had wanted the other to think that they were giving up on conceiving a child, so they had never discussed adoption. But almost instantaneously, after building for three years, a pressure valve seemed to have been released. Suddenly, neither felt inadequate any longer or wondered if that's how they were perceived by their spouse. Intimacy once again was about making love instead of the emotionally-distant act of "trying to get pregnant." No more charting temperatures; no more doctors; no more "expert" advice from friends; no more procedures. But they still didn't have a child.

From the day of their engagement, they had been subjected to friends' and family's gushing about how adorable and smart and athletic their children would be, which had only served to create a picture in their minds of what *their* child's potential would be. So, in addition to desperately wanting a child to love, they'd cultivated a strong desire to guide this extraordinary child they'd both been imagining toward realizing his or her potential.

Consequently, they wound up registering with the most restrictive adoption agency they could find, which meant that while they would be required to provide more information about themselves, they would also have access to more information about the prospective child.

Reams of paper documenting every year of their lives pre- and post-marriage were notarized and mailed and faxed back and forth. Rigorous background checks, including fingerprinting, reviews of tax returns, and detailed interviews with contacts from different points in their lives, took them six weeks to complete.

At the end of it all, they were presented with a local boy, who had already significantly separated himself from his peers academically, with biological parents who had both earned doctoral degrees. He had been reading books since age 3, they learned. In kindergarten, he'd been referred to a neuropsychologist and had maxed out the Wechsler Intelligence Scale for Children, the most commonly administered IQ test for kids, after which he was labeled by his public school as "gifted." Sara, a gifted teacher herself, chuckled when she'd read that. "That's like labeling Wilt Chamberlain tall," she'd told Thomas. Then of course there was the Initial Aptitude Test he'd aced in September of first grade. The only concern they had left was whether or not this savant could function in a social setting.

A review of his teacher's report had revealed that toward the end of first grade he had withdrawn socially, but prior to his parents' deaths, the only negative comments he'd ever received were that he was at times too social and could be a distraction to the other kids – the hallmark of an unchallenged gifted student.

All of Ryan's information was delivered to the Ewings piecemeal over a three-week period with his name withheld until the end of his third month in the orphanage. One new tidbit of information would arrive one day without another word for two or three days, followed by three emails in one day. The "Ryan emails" became an obsession. Sara and Thomas both found themselves checking their messages first thing in the morning, all throughout the day, during meals, and even in the middle of the night if they had to get up for one reason or another. The fit seemed perfect, and by the end of the three weeks, they were committed – ready to do whatever it took to bring this incredible boy home with them.

The final hurdle would be an interview with James Prescott, who would personally fly to Cleveland to meet them. Sara had heard of him; Thomas knew the name well. In the financial world, half seemed to think he was a genius, and the other half a sociopath. Oddly, nearly everyone who had actually met him was in the former camp. He was recognized globally as a master fund-raiser and negotiator.

Having earmarked Sara and Thomas's application shortly after it had been submitted,

Prescott had been pulling the strings behind the scenes all along, carefully orchestrating the logistics of the adoption. The couple was perfect, and they were obviously already sold. All he had to have them do now was sign the papers.

The negotiations, however, were far more intense than Prescott had envisioned, forcing him to book a last minute hotel room in Cleveland in order to meet for a second day. The actuarial tables and financial incentives did not impress the Ewings who wanted significantly more parental control. Prescott, on the other hand, wasn't willing to consider giving away any more decision-making capacity than was outlined in the original agreement.

In the end, only one person was unwilling to back away from the negotiating table, and that was Sara. Once both men realized this, the conclusion was foregone.

In the spirit of compromise, and mindful of the need for a positive long-term relationship, Prescott conceded a few minor points that had to do with vacation time and giving Sara and Thomas durable power of attorney for healthcare.

Within a week, Ryan came home.

~~~

"We've got a few other minor issues to deal with here," Prescott said casually. "His parents sent a permission slip for swimming – as legal guardian I signed off on that. And one for soccer, which starts in the fall. I declined to sign off on that..."

"What's wrong with soccer?" one of the executives interrupted. "All my kids played it."

"Repetitive head trauma," J.R. chimed in.

"No!" another member of the board scoffed, rolling his eyes. "Seven-year-olds don't get head trauma playing soccer!" Then he turned to Prescott, "Are you just saying no because you can?"

A lengthy pause followed the pointed question.

"Do you have a favorite wine?" Prescott asked contemplatively to no one in particular yet grabbing the attention of the entire board. He had pushed his chair back from the table and appeared to be staring off at some distant building in the skyline. "Mine's pinot noir, specifically Burgundy. It's a fickle grape – very hard to grow. Winemakers call it the headache grape – nothing to do with hangovers; it's just very difficult to grow."

He stood and began a slow waltz around the table, gradually looping back around toward the head, telling his story as he walked. "To make the perfect pinot noir you first need a great vine from great stock – and the clones from Burgundy are the best. But the best wine grapes don't grow in ideal conditions. Far from it. They need some stress – struggles to overcome! The soils in Burgundy are ugly gravelly clay and limestone with no trace of the dark, fertile topsoil you'd see in a nursery. The weather can be harsh with freezing cold winters, frequent spring hail storms, and hot summers.

"But ahh, those grapes that do survive to harvest, they have *character*. Truly amazing," he whispered, closing his eyes as if he were sipping the wine then and there. "Well, they're full of potential anyway. But they aren't ready. They need age. Perhaps no wine benefits more from age than Burgundy. Finally ten, twenty, even fifty years down the road, the end result can be mind-blowing.

"Gentlemen, we have a great vine from great stock, but if we put him in a nursery with fertilized topsoil, we're sure to get very good grape juice. With some carefully managed adversity and patience, we'll eventually have a world-class Burgundy.

"So to your question, am I saying no just because I can? You could say that.

"But the adoptive parents are the heart raising RTJ. We have to do what they can't. We have to be the mind. Now, are we all agreed that soccer is out?"

Nine ayes.

~~~

It was time. Ryan had to talk to J.R.

Not only was J.R. Ryan's only connection to his former life, he'd also really been nothing but good to Ryan. He was the only visitor Ryan had had for 3 months at the orphanage, and he seemed to have played some role in setting him up with Sara and Thomas, who Ryan had rather reluctantly come to realize were pretty great people.

He picked up the phone and hesitantly tapped "J.R.," still his only contact aside from "Home," "Sara," and "Thomas."

"Hello?" J.R. answered on the first ring.

"Mr. J.R.?" Ryan said nervously "it's me, Ryan."

"Hey buddy!" J.R. yelled, completely taken by surprise. "How are you? It's been a long time."

"Good," Ryan said. "Sara and Thomas are nice. You were right about them."

An awkward pause followed the reference to J.R.'s unexplained prescience in their last conversation. Ryan wasn't ready to divulge that he now knew about AVEX and that J.R. was on his board of directors. And J.R., from his perspective, didn't want Ryan to think of him as an insider – or anything other than a trusted family friend.

"Have you ever met them?" Ryan asked.

"No, I haven't gotten a chance to," J.R. said. "But the headmistress at the orphanage told me *all* about them. So what have you been up to?"

"Not much," Ryan answered out of habit. "Well, actually that's not really true any more. I've been doing a lot. My nanny's teaching me Spanish, I'm taking swimming lessons, and I'm learning *fourth grade* math!"

"Awesome!" J.R. said enthusiastically.

"Yeah, things are a lot better," Ryan said, relieved he still had J.R. to talk to. It was comforting – whatever his role was with Avillage.

"You looking forward to school this year?" J.R. asked.

"Yeah. I guess. But I'm not going to know anyone."

"So what grade are you going to be in this year?"

"Second! You knew that!" Ryan exclaimed, unaware that his meeting with the school counselor that had been rescheduled from that afternoon to the following day was to finalize his grade placement.

"That's what I thought," J.R. answered defensively. "I just hadn't heard yet."

Hadn't heard yet? Ryan thought to himself. That's a weird thing to say. Another awkward pause followed.

"Well buddy, it was *great* to talk to you. I've missed you. I'm gonna let you go. Let's not make it so long till our next talk," J.R. said, trying to wrap things up.

"OK," Ryan said softly, now more certain than ever that his relationship with J.R. could never be what it had been. J.R. was hiding too much from him. Was he trying to protect him? Looking out for him behind the scenes? Hoping to profit from him? Ryan almost wanted to call him on it right then and there and live with the consequences – either an honest friendship or nothing – but he couldn't bring himself to do it. He had another idea.

"And Mr. J.R.?" Ryan said.

"Yeah, buddy?"

"Thanks. For everything," Ryan said with a sincerity and a finality in his voice that suggested this might be his last chance to say it. Whatever J.R.'s motives were, things were going better than he'd imagined they could a few months ago; he wanted to thank him for that.

He then held the phone down slightly and yelled out, "What?... OK. Be right down." He brought the phone back up to his ear and said, "I gotta go. Got soccer practice."

"Soccer?!" J.R. blurted out, unnaturally alarmed.

"Talk to you soon," Ryan said and hastily hung up the phone.

Sara and Thomas had been unable to give a coherent reason why he had been forbidden from playing soccer in the fall. And the idea to play in the first place had been all theirs. They were absolutely resolute with their decision, yet they seemed almost more disappointed than he was that he couldn't play. Something hadn't seemed right.

When the phone rang a few hours later, Ryan was indulging in the thirty minutes of TV he was allowed on weekdays. The caller ID popped up on the screen, "Private Caller: New York, NY."

This is it, he thought.

Adjusting the TV volume just slightly down so as not to draw attention, but to increase his chances of overhearing something, he crept out of the living room and tiptoed toward the cracked door of Thomas and Sara's room.

Inside he could hear a voice that was clearly Sara's, but the words were too soft to make out. As the conversation continued though, her tone changed, and her voice grew louder.

"What?" he heard her snap indignantly. "No!... What are you talking about?... He *should* be playing. He's going to a new school where he isn't going to know a soul, but you wouldn't sign the permission slip, God knows why!"

He could have heard most of that from the couch.

It wasn't the one he wanted, but, slinking back to the living room, he had his answer. At least Sara and Thomas were firmly on his side, but it seemed they were the only ones. And they didn't appear to have much more power than he did.

CHAPTER 5

"Happy birthday to you," Sara sang blissfully off-key as she backed into Ryan's bedroom, balancing a breakfast tray in front of her loaded with a three-inch stack of pancakes planted with 5 flickering candles, a gravy boat of warm maple syrup and a tall glass of orange juice. Thomas followed closely behind, camera at the ready, and managed to rapid-fire several unflattering pictures of a bleary-eyed Ryan just waking from a sound sleep.

Ryan celebrated two birthdays each year. One, his traditional birthday, was in March to mark the day of his birth. The other was in June to commemorate the day he'd come home from the orphanage to live with the Ewings. For lack of established celebratory vocabulary to mark the occasion, they had settled on calling this one simply his "other birthday."

"Thanks, Mom," Ryan said groggily to Sara, eyeing the breakfast tray. "And thanks a lot, Dad," He sneered at Thomas. "That's gonna be a keeper."

"No problem, bud," Thomas smirked. "I tried to get your good side."

Ryan blew out the candles, as his sleepy eyes were blinded by another flash from Thomas's camera

"Now hurry up and get dressed," Thomas said, trying not to laugh at the pictures he was scrolling through on his digital camera. "Our tee time's in 45 minutes."

Sara peered over Thomas's shoulder. "You have *got* to put that one on the digital frame!" she snickered, as they turned to leave Ryan's room.

Ryan sat up in his bed and ate his breakfast as he watched the pictures scroll on his bedside frame.

Joyful pictures of his early years with his birth parents gave way to somber pictures of a melancholy 7-year-old who seemed to have aged far more than the three months that had passed between his two homes. But gradually, as the photos continued to roll on, his smile returned.

His eighth birthday had been a family affair with Sara and Thomas and both sets of grandparents in attendance. That was followed by his first "other birthday" blowout that saw his entire extended family in attendance. Ryan's beaming face fronted a sea of first and second degree relatives, arranged by height and age behind him, curling all the way up the grand staircase of the Ewing's foyer.

As an eight-year-old, he was pictured smiling sheepishly in a Speedo with his swim team, taking his first golf lessons (with the board's blessing,) and soaking up the sun with his parents on vacation in Mexico. At nine, he posed behind an oversized $35,000.00 check from the E.W. Scripps Company made out to Ryan Tyler Ewing, the youngest winner in National Spelling Bee history. He had been told the money would be going into a college fund, but he figured most of it was probably heading to the Avillage board. It hadn't really bothered him; he had way more than most kids, and that wouldn't be life-changing money for him anyway. What had bothered him deeply though was that he'd been forbidden from defending his title the following year, without explanation.

At age ten, a series of pictures marked his two months in Singapore as an exchange student at a Chinese-language immersion program at one of Hunting Valley Academy's sister schools, followed by shots taken all over China on vacation with his family. He'd pleaded with his parents not to send him overseas by himself, and he'd overheard bits and pieces of their arguing with the board on his behalf, citing his understandable predisposition to separation anxiety. But the Avillage board had refused to budge. And it turned out he'd actually enjoyed himself once he'd gotten over there.

Age eleven saw a gradual shift toward more pictures with friends and fewer with his parents, although he did pose proudly next to his dad as co-champions of the Father-Son Invitational Golf Tournament at their country club.

After a single picture from his twelfth birthday party, a new picture he'd never seen before popped up in the frame, featuring a sheet of plain white paper with a hand-written message in pencil: "Check out your mom's purple shirt." He didn't get it.

In the final shot before the loop restarted, he was lying on his stomach on top of his sheets, the back of his Cleveland Browns boxers prominently featured, craning his head up and back to squint perturbedly at his parents as they entered his room.

His dad must have already wirelessly uploaded the photo from just a few minutes prior. Ryan couldn't help but laugh. But that was *not* staying on the frame.

After finishing up his breakfast, he reached over and hit the sleep button on the frame, stood up to stretch, and then took a long nostalgic look around his room. The pirate bed had been replaced by a mundanely conventional queen-sized bed. The desk and chair were no longer kid-sized, the huge closet, stocked with far fewer clothes, seemed even bigger in its emptiness, and the color of the walls had changed. But for a brief moment he could see the room just as it had appeared that first day. The unique smell that every house has, which he'd become so accustomed to that he hadn't noticed it in years, came back in a wave, and he sniffed it in with a long deep breath, gently closing his eyes as a lump began to develop in his throat.

He shook his head, embarrassed by his emotions, forced a half-smile, and headed for the shower.

Ryan still hadn't told anyone what he knew about AVEX ticker symbol RTJ, which was now hidden in an alphabet soup of symbols representing former orphans on the half-full back page of the New York Times Business section.

Strict rules restricted the press from revealing the identities of publicly-traded minors, but it had dawned on him after watching his stock price rise five percent the day after he'd won the spelling bee that his identity was not an especially well-kept secret.

A week or so later, he'd convinced one of his friends at school to request a prospectus on each and every symbol on the exchange, to avoid having the material show up at his home address.

In his sparse free-time, usually after his parents were asleep, he'd begun to track down other orphans. Some were easy – like J'Quarius Jones. Others were harder. Some seemed downright impossible. One poor orphan he was never able to locate had been relegated to penny-stock status after her prospectus had revealed that she'd been diagnosed with "an aggressive hematologic malignancy." Never having learned her identity, Ryan could almost feel her struggle as her stock price bounced around under ten cents a share for the next two months. His heart had sunk one morning when he noticed SUZ had dropped off the exchange altogether.

So far, he had a list of close to a hundred names matched with their probable symbols. None of them were in Cleveland, and he had yet to try contact any of them.

"Ready?" Thomas asked, as Ryan deposited the breakfast tray on the kitchen counter next to the sink.

"Time to go back-to-back!" Ryan said, looking forward to the defense of their father-son golf championship. "Bye, mom," he yelled to the living room. Then he turned back to his dad with a perplexed expression, "She's not wearing a purple shirt. What were you talking about?"

"Uh... I have no idea," Thomas said, looking every bit as confused as Ryan.

"Yeah, right. Those pictures you uploaded this morning?"

"I don't know anything about any pictures," Thomas answered with a sarcastic grin, but still not fully clued in. He had only uploaded one picture.

"Whatever," Ryan said rolling his eyes. He still didn't get it.

~~~

Dillon Higley knew something terrible was about to happen when the power went out in the Boston townhouse he lived in with his dad. The mid-September weather was picture perfect, and their house was equipped not only with a backup generator, but a separately-housed backup to the backup generator. And his dad religiously checked the fuel status of each one twice a week, whether they had been in use or not.

Dillon crept over to the window and peeled back the lower corner of the curtains to see if the traffic lights were out. No. And the lights were still on at the bike shop across the street.

As his gaze shifted away from the bike shop, out of the corner of his eye, he just caught sight of an oblong black object about the size of a soup can hurtling toward him. A fraction of a second later the sound of glass shattering was followed by a heavy thud, as the black pill-shaped object struck the living room floor and began to spin, spitting out a thick cloud of caustic smoke.

Coughing, wheezing, tearing, Dillon pulled the collar of his shirt up over his nose and ran for the back of the house, yelling for his dad as he caromed off furniture and walls nearly blind, helplessly trying to blink away the irritants.

Just as he finally reached his dad's bedroom, a battering ram punched through the back door, splintering the wood around the bronze door knob, which fell to the floor next to his feet.

Before he could get the door to his dad's room open, he was snatched by a masked FBI agent in full assault gear and carted off to a field unit half a block away to have his eyes irrigated with sterile saline.

The next time he would see his father, they would be separated by an inch of plexiglass and fifteen years, minimum. His father would be convicted on every count brought against him, ranging from piracy in his early days to more recent (and far more serious) theft and distribution of classified United States government documents.

Aside from being a closeted anarchist, Horace Higley had actually been a pretty great parent. Dillon's mother had left without so much as a goodbye to either of them when Dillon was six months old, so Horace was the only parent Dillon had ever known.

Horace genuinely loved his son, and he'd done everything he could to try to give him a reasonable, *almost* typical, childhood. He'd signed him up for soccer on his sixth birthday, since that seemed to be what other six-year-olds were doing. He'd even brought the post-game snacks and drinks once per season for the two seasons Dillon had stuck it out. But after wasting a dozen fall and spring Saturday afternoons sitting on the sidelines of the soccer field, Dillon on the bench, Horace in a lawn chair, they quietly bowed out, accepting the obvious fact that sports weren't Dillon's thing.

Next he tried music. But it took only two months of formal piano lessons and regular at-home practice on the small keyboard that Horace had bought him to convince Dillon, his father, and his piano teacher that music wasn't where his talents lay either. It was really by exclusion, environment, and quite possibly genetics that Dillon ended up following his dad into computer programming.

Horace had tried his best to shelter Dillon from his more clandestine interests, but there were only two of them in the house, and they shared a rare gift for coaxing computer-based systems into giving them what they wanted. By the time Dillon was ten, Horace had unintentionally taught him most of what he knew, not only about programming but also hacking. Dillon had even occasionally proven himself useful with fresh perspectives on what had been persistent problems for his dad.

Horace had always tried to tone down his anti-government, anti-military, anti-corporate rhetoric in front of Dillon, who already saw him as overly bitter. Dillon was too young to be indoctrinated with such cynicism.

But that all changed when Dillon's doting father was suddenly taken out of his life by federal agents, and, through a cruel irony, Dillon was placed in the state's care. Horace confidently assured his son during one prison visit that an unassuming introvert with a laptop and no designs on recognition or fame could be a very powerful foe – even for the most powerful country on the planet.

An orphan at the age of 12, Dillon was blessed with patience – and a poker face. After a year under close surveillance, he dropped off the FBI's watch list.

In the orphanage, he'd spent most of his time quietly and independently developing innocuous apps for smartphones and tablets. He was even making a little money at it.

Eventually, one caught the attention of a junior Avillage associate in the Orphan Identification Division.

His father's criminal history had been dubbed a red flag by the higher-ups, but Horace's testimony had convincingly absolved Dillon of any suspicion regarding knowledge of or involvement in any illegal activity. Plus he had a two-year track record of being an all-around good citizen at the orphanage. His age was another strike against him – nearly fourteen at the time of identification, but a set of prospective parents was already in the Avillage queue, seeking a technologically gifted teen, and the bigwigs at Avillage were sold on the risk/reward ratio of grooming the next Bill Gates or Steve Jobs or Larry Ellison or Larry Page or Sergey Brin or Mark Zuckerberg – the list of high-tech billionaires went on and on.

In the end, to heap insult onto Horace's injury, Dillon was taken out of the state's custody and adopted. By a corporation.

~~~

The defending champions walked confidently up to the 18th green needing a birdie to win the best-ball format tournament outright and avoid a playoff. A gallery of ten other father-son pairs trickled down the slope from the clubhouse patio to watch, debating which ball they'd play. Ryan's lay just off the front of the green and would leave them a relatively straight fifteen foot uphill putt to the hole. Thomas's shot was significantly closer, but would break down and to the right – a tough putt for righties.

Without any discussion, Thomas strode onto the green and snatched his ball.

"I'll get it close, and you sink it," Thomas said with a wink, walking back down the green to where Ryan's ball lay. Sure enough his putt rolled to a stop eighteen inches short of the hole. That would be a gimme.

Ryan then stepped up behind his dad and placed his ball back down on the fringe of the green. He'd tracked his dad's putt the whole way; there was no break.

"No pressure, Ryan!" yelled one of the dads who'd long been out of contention, well into his fourth beer.

Standing to the side of the ball, his mind cleared of everything and everyone around him, Ryan took two carefully measured practice swings. He then shuffled a few inches forward, his head now directly over his ball. He glanced up at the hole, then back to his ball, then the hole, and again his ball, picturing the speed and trajectory of his dad's putt. Slowly he drew his putter back, exactly as he had with each practice swing. The head of the putter slowed to a momentary stop at the peak of his backswing, and then, with the identical forward momentum of his two previous swings, he swung through the ball. He barely felt the club make contact with the ball, keeping his head down and softly closing his eyes. He didn't need to watch. He knew it was in.

As soon as he got home, he uploaded the new photo of himself and his dad raising their second consecutive father-son trophy. Except for the fact that he was another inch and a half closer to his dad in height, it looked almost identical to their first picture.

He then scrolled back one frame and, slowly shaking his head, deleted the picture of him in his boxers from earlier in the morning.

"Check out your mom's purple shirt," read the message left on the frame.

His dad had seemed genuinely confused when he'd mentioned the picture earlier that morning, and the handwriting in the photo didn't look like anything like his dad's. What's more the surface under the plain white sheet of paper certainly wasn't to be found anywhere in their house – maybe laminate countertop or a particle-board table.

What does that mean? he thought, trying to squeeze some secret meaning out of the message. As he was thinking, the pictures continued to scroll. He couldn't remember the last time he'd seen his mom wear purple. Maybe one of their neighbors within Wi-Fi range had the same kind of frame, and the photo had mistakenly gotten uploaded to his frame. But the picture still didn't make any sense; why would that scribbled-on piece of paper be worthy of uploading to *anyone's* frame? And no one in their pretentious neighborhood would have had laminate countertops.

As he continued to ruminate, a flash of purple from the frame grabbed his attention, just before the picture scrolled forward again. He snatched the frame from the bedside table and frantically pushed the back button.

On the display was a picture of him riding his first two-wheeler, with his birth mother running right behind him, just letting go of the back of his seat. She wore a radiant smile – and a faded purple shirt. Ryan remembered that soft, worn purple shirt vividly. It had been her lounging shirt. She had changed into it almost every night when she got home from work and often slept in it. As Ryan continued to stare at the shirt, he noticed what appeared to be microscopic black print on the sleeve.

But that shirt didn't have writing on it. He would have bet his life on it.

He placed his thumb and forefinger directly over the tiny black letters and spread them slowly apart. As the frame zoomed in, gradually the text became legible: "www.amazon.com/tp-roll/dp/S890=f238000"

Ryan grabbed his tablet and immediately keyed in the URL exactly as it appeared on his mom's shirt. An item on the Amazon Marketplace loaded, featuring a picture of a half-full roll of toilet paper offered by a user with uniformly unfavorable customer reviews. The text read, "This is more of a social experiment than anything to see if there's avillage (sic) idiot out there would actually pay $18.76 for half a roll of toilet paper. Anyone going to prove me right? I bet you will."

The item had been posted just before midnight the night before. Ryan's price at the market's close that day had been 18.76. He had to pursue this. Without any further deliberation, he ordered it with the "bill me" option, selecting next-day delivery to the house next door. He knew for a fact his neighbors were going to be out of town through the weekend, because he was feeding their cat and collecting their mail while they were away.

For the sake of the seller, he marked the shipment as a gift with the card to read, "Here's to social experiments. I am one. Love, RTJ"

~~~

Dillon had figured out that he was an Avillage listing before he'd even come to live with his adoptive family, and he harbored a deep resentment for it. While he tolerated his adoptive parents, he stayed on a cool first-name basis with them. There was only one person he would ever call "Dad," and in just under 13 years, he expected to be reunited with him. He'd also made it perfectly clear that he was born with the last name Higley, and that's the name he would die with.

Avillage wasted no time in getting him on a comprehensive computer-programming education regimen, seemingly intent on grooming the computer prodigy who would eventually destroy them, he thought. But they also allowed him significantly more free time than most of the other orphans, since he needed "creative time" for producing his popular apps.

In the history of the exchange, ironically, Dillon was the fastest to return a profit for his shareholders. His dad probably would have disowned him on the spot if he'd been aware, but Dillon had his eye on longer-term goals, and he knew he would need two things to overthrow a titan like Avillage: capital and a team.

The profits he kept from the apps would provide the capital, he figured. The team he had in mind was himself and his father, better than before with his added years of experience and his father's heightened motivation, but that plan was about to be dealt a crippling blow.

"Dillon? Are you in there?" his adoptive mother asked, late one fall afternoon, tentatively tapping on his bedroom door.

"I'm busy," he answered back indifferently, rapping away on his computer keyboard.

"Dillon, there's something I need to talk to you about," she said. The clacking of the keyboard continued uninterrupted. "It's about your dad."

With that, Dillon shot off his chair and flung the door open. "What?" he asked with genuine fear in his eyes.

"Dillon, why don't you come downstairs and sit down so we can talk about it."

"WHAT?!" he shouted desperately, the blood draining from his already pale face. "Tell me!"

"Well, your father's case is being reopened. There are new charges – serious ones. I don't know much more than that right now..."

Dillon slammed the door in her face, and raced back to his computer to see what he could find. Two years into his sentence, it appeared, his dad was being charged with *terrorism*. Dillon felt like he'd been punched in the stomach.

Apparently a radical Islamic terrorist had visited his dad's website to learn the classified location of US troops the day prior to detonating a bomb in their midst in Kuwait. From time to time his dad had posted information about the position of various legions of troops throughout the Middle East, but his purpose had only been to uncover lies he claimed the pentagon had been feeding the American people to try to minimize America's presence in the region.

If there was one thing Horace Higley hated more than a lying government, it was religious radicalism. He never would have knowingly worked with terrorists. At the same time, the information he'd distributed was classified, and its use did aid a terrorist, and American soldiers' lives were lost. There would be no chance of successfully defending the case in the court of law or in the court of public opinion.

Dillon's thoughts quickly jumped to *why* someone would dig this up, two years into his dad's sentence and over four years after the bombing. His suspicion, of course, immediately turned to Avillage.

From that moment on, he worked on nothing but gaining access to Avillage's network. He immediately created a continuously-running dummy program to give the appearance that he was working on programming a new app, in case he was being surveilled, but he stopped working on apps altogether, made excuses as often as he could for missing both school and Avillage-directed education, and ignored his adoptive parents to the point that entire days would pass in which they wouldn't see each other.

After three months of near constant effort, he finally made it into their system. But everything was coded. It took him another month to find his personal files, which were all password-protected. Then another six weeks passed before he eventually hit the jackpot.

A directive had been issued after the first board of directors' meeting to look for creative ways to keep Dillon's father away from him, as he was seen as "a potential barrier to profitability." A few weeks later someone had dug up something "substantive."

On October 10, a letter with no return address had been sent to both the FBI and the department of homeland security, detailing the accessing of an anti-government website from Kuwait the day before a major terrorist attack, complete with explicit directions on how to verify the information. The new charges had been brought on October 17; Dillon's stock had soared 7% that day.

It didn't appear that anyone at Avillage had doctored anything; someone had actually discovered the information, so Dillon had no leverage legally. Still, from his point of view, their motive for profit would be the reason he would likely never see his dad again. That was an unforgivable offense.

Capital and a team, he thought. *Back to developing apps. For now.*

~~~

As he crossed onto his next door neighbor's lawn, Ryan noticed a package on the front doorstep. Having deliberately misspelled his neighbors' last name on the online order form, he knew this one had to be for him.

He dumped a little dry food into Mr. Purrfect's bowl, changed his water, and gave him a couple strokes on the head, which turned out to be all the affection either he or the cat were looking for that day. Then he got busy with the package.

Inside was another box, packed in a mess of tongue-in-cheek toilet paper. On the outside of the inner box was written, "No charge. Really. Truly. Justly."

Using the front door key as a blade, Ryan sliced down the seams of the smaller box. Wedged inside was a used copy of *Dinosaurs and Aliens*, a disastrous flop of a multi-player role playing game that had been released about ten years earlier. Along with the game were detailed instructions on where and when to meet up with a warrior by the name of VillagePariah.

Ryan recognized the game title. An otherwise successful software company had produced it and had regretfully, in their original packaging, committed to running the web version of the game for online play for a full ten years. As soon as they'd recognized that the game was a bust, the company had tried to pull the plug on the site, but a few disgruntled players had taken them to court to have the site put back up, and they'd actually won the case. In retaliation, the company stopped online sales and removed all copies of the boxed game from store shelves, drying up game play on the site almost completely.

The ten-year deadline was approaching in a matter of days, and the company was itching to take the game offline permanently and purge all of their data. This was as secure a mode of communication as the sender could come up with on short notice without revealing his identity or creating any permanent log of their conversation. After this, if things went well, they'd have to figure something else out.

That night Ryan loaded the game onto his computer and entered multi-player mode. Per his instructions, he created a princess character by the name of Hot4Higs and entered the cheat code he'd been provided to gain access to the higher levels.

After navigating around the ridiculous game for half an hour, killing dinosaurs and aliens with the invincibility afforded him by his cheat code, he finally stumbled upon the The Time Traveler's Portal, which was the designated meeting point.

And there he waited. At first he could hardly contain his excitement. But his anticipation gradually turned to boredom as he waited for VillagePariah to show. Every few minutes he glanced down at the bottom left corner of the screen to see how many other players were online. Each time, the answer was the same: zero.

After nearly an hour had passed, the number of other online players suddenly blinked to 1. Ryan sat up straight in his chair. Then, from the right edge of his screen he saw a burly armor-clad warrior approaching, the moniker above him flashing "VillagePariah."

"VillagePariah is requesting to chat. Do you accept?" read a message in the center of his screen. Ryan anxiously looked back at his bedroom door, making sure it was still closed, and clicked yes. A text box popped up at the upper left corner of the screen.

```
VillagePariah: Hello
Hot4Higs: Hi
VillagePariah: Can you please
delete    the    picture    of    the
handwritten  note  on  your  digital
frame?
Hot4Higs: Done.
VillagePariah:   Good.       one
more  thing.   the  black  writing  on
```

your mom's purple shirt that gave you the amazon address... it's actually the photo AFTER the one with her teaching you to ride a bike. I superimposed it with an animation effect. I can't actually edit or delete photos remotely – can only add them. can you delete that one too?

Hot4Higs: Done.

VillagePariah: Thx. those frames have no permanent memory. when you delete files, they're gone – unlike text messages or emails. This game sucks doesn't it?

Hot4Higs: Big time. I guess there's a reason only 2 people on earth are playing it. what's this about?

VillagePariah: I think we may have something in common. what do you know about Avillage?

Hot4Higs: Its a stock exchange for orphans – like I used to be

VillagePariah: Like WE used to be

Hot4Higs: You're on the exchange too?

VillagePariah: Yep. I'm glad you already know about it. that makes this easier.

Hot4Higs: Let me guess... Dillon?

VillagePariah: Why do you say that?

Hot4Higs: I've tracked down about half the exchange. you're — i mean Dillon is a computer guy. and look what you made me name my smokin hot princess character

VillagePariah: Not bad. that was supposed to be an inside joke to myself. anyway, I have ALL the names matched with ALL the symbols on the exchange. I want to end Avillage — get rid of it. not just for me. for everybody.

Hot4Higs: Why?

VillagePariah: They're evil. they're manipulating things behind the scenes. taking away our freedom — and of course our money

Hot4Higs: They definitely manipulate things, but I'm not sure they're evil. I've actually got things pretty good

VillagePariah: That's what a neutered dog in a fenced in yard would say too. trust me. I've been all through their private intranet. there's nothing concrete, but there's smoke everywhere. I need you with me, Ryan

Hot4Higs: Why?

VillagePariah: Because you're the poster child. you're the initial IPO. and you're smarter than me

Hot4Higs: smarter than I – just kidding. And I'm definitely not smarter than you. I couldn't have thought of

VillagePariah: I'm not guessing. I've seen our files... I have a question. did you have any other relatives besides your parents?

Hot4Higs: No. my grandfather died a few months before my parents. he lived on the west coast. I didn't really know him that well.

VillagePariah: Sorry about that.

Hot4Higs: It's ok

VillagePariah: Did he die before or after you took the IAT?

Hot4Higs: ?

VillagePariah: The initial aptitude test you took in september of first grade.

Hot4Higs: Would have been after. I remember it was Halloween night.

VillagePariah: Hmmm...

Hot4Higs: What?

VillagePariah: Avillage has the full list of IAT scores from your year. not sure how they got it. your name's at the top. the file is dated mid-October. don't remember the exact date.

Hot4Higs: My grandfather had pretty bad diabetes. his death wasn't too big of a shock to my parents, if that's what you're getting at.

VillagePariah: OK. do you know what the policy is on orphan adoption? I mean how long a kid has to be in an orphanage before he's available to Avillage?

Hot4Higs: 3 months. it's in their company profile

VillagePariah: Did you ever think it was strange that you lost your parents almost EXACTLY 3 months before the opening of AVEX? Or that they confirmed the opening date of AVEX two days after they died?

Ryan's cursor flashed for a full 30 seconds with no reply. Dillon kept an anxious eye on the lower left of his screen, continuously checking how many other players were online, hoping he hadn't scared Ryan away with such a sensitive topic; the number remained stuck at 1.

VillagePariah: It strikes me as odd. I've dug pretty deep into this. opening day was an absolute make or break for Avillage. Ryan, you were it. there was no plan B.

There was another long pause.

Hot4Higs: We need to meet.

CHAPTER 6

A natural leader with a tireless work ethic, strong motherly instincts, and endless optimism, thirteen-year-old Annamaria Olivera had been invaluable at the orphanage in the 3 months since a catastrophic 7.9 magnitude earthquake had nearly leveled her home city of Colón, a working class town at the Caribbean entrance to the Panama canal. Her district, Rainbow City, had been the hardest hit.

She had been on her way to school when the quake had hit, walking in a small clearing between two more densely populated areas. First, she'd felt a curious vibration beneath her feet, almost as if they were starting to fall asleep. Then before she'd had time to consider what exactly the odd sensation might be, she was hit with a thunderous force that threw her to the ground, split the road in front of her lengthwise and crumbled the rickety bridge up ahead, sending its splintered remains into the swollen, muddy river below.

Rattled in every sense of the word, she turned back toward her home and watched helplessly as the low-rise apartment buildings began to crumble, one after another. Plumes of dust twenty stories high formed a haunting new skyline in their stead.

Two days of round-the-clock rescue work would pass before a Red Cross disaster counselor finally confirmed what she pretty well knew to be the case: no one in her family had survived.

But with more work to do than there were able-bodied people to do it, she never took the time to grieve. She got busy the moment she set foot in the overcrowded orphanage, nursing minor wounds of the other children when the staff didn't have time, warming bottles and feeding the babies when she heard them cry out at night, and routinely helping out with the cooking and cleaning. But her most impactful contribution was her unique ability to soothe with little more than a look, especially when the aftershocks hit.

Her large dark eyes were deep yet bright and expressed a sensitivity and simple sincerity that couldn't be replicated by the harried staff at the orphanage. Her soft, full lips came together in a sweet smile, and her flawless bronze skin radiated warmth. Her beauty wasn't lost on the younger children, who naturally gravitated to her, even if they weren't sure why.

But another quake was about to rock her world. Her appearance – and two recent policy changes at a stock exchange a world away – would soon set her life on a drastically different course.

~~~

After three years of mostly rousing successes, Avillage was slogging through a third consecutive quarter of flat growth when James Prescott, without notice, eliminated the position of vice president of operations in the Orphan Identification Division, and ordered its employees to report directly to his Senior Executive Vice

President/Henchman Aaron Bradford. While the move had dealt a serious blow to the section's morale, its productivity did increase. Temporarily.

As it turned out, the problem really wasn't internal; it truly seemed to be a lack of qualified orphans.

In response, Bradford had pushed through two controversial changes in the Avillage recruitment plan. The first was to offer orphan-referral incentives, by way of a 1.5% ownership incentive for each orphan adopted by Avillage, to be split 70/30 between the referring orphanage and the individual making the referral. The second was to pursue international adoptions, thereby increasing the pool of potential orphans a thousand-fold, effective immediately.

Explicit restrictions on foreign adoption, covering criteria from the marital status of the parents to the number of children already in the adoptive family to the ability of the parents to care for a new dependent financially already existed in most countries, so corporate adoptions never got off the ground in most of the developed world. But other countries, mostly underdeveloped and/or those recently devastated by war or natural disaster, were laden with so many orphans they didn't have the systems in place to take care of them all. A post-earthquake Panama not only permitted corporate adoptions, they rolled out the red carpet for Avillage.

Two weeks after an official memo detailing Avillage's mission (and its incentive program) had been sent out to all Panamanian orphanages, Carlos

Villanueva, a conflicted Rainbow City headmaster, not expecting or even entirely hoping for a reply, had sent a series of digital photos of Annamaria to Avillage, which eventually found their way to the desk of Aaron Bradford. He was instantly mesmerized.

Avillage had had a modicum of success with models in their brief history, but Annamaria was on another plane.

Bradford had forwarded the photos to a talent scout at a major modeling agency, who confirmed Bradford's suspicion, while dissecting her look more scientifically. Her face was perfectly symmetrical with high cheekbones and large dark eyes accentuated by similarly-toned hair, and her full lips and bronze skin gave her a somewhat nebulous ethnic profile – a major plus in the industry. While the full body shots were more difficult to analyze because of the baggy T-shirts she wore, she was clearly tall and thin with a long feminine neck, broad but delicate shoulders, svelte arms and long, runway-ready legs.

Already the chairman of Annamaria's board in his mind, Bradford only had one thing left to do; he needed to see her in person. A couple of other longshot inquiries from Panama would justify the trip, including a thirteen-year-old pitcher with a supposed 85 mile-an-hour fastball. But that was probably a fairy tale. Annamaria was the sole reason he opted to make the trip personally.

~~~

The city of Colón's Enrique A. Jimenez Airport was still closed due to runway damage, so after the five-hour flight from New York to Panama City, Bradford and his assistant were forced to endure another hour and a half in the back of an unairconditioned cab.

Wiping the sweat from his brow with an already soaked handkerchief, he finally peeled himself off of the vinyl seat as the cab pulled up to the orphanage and planted his new Salvatore Ferragamo wingtip in an ankle-deep mud puddle. Jaws clenched and eyes closed, he let out a long audible sigh, well past the point of regretting his decision to come to Panama in July. But as his eyes reopened, his scowl vanished, stopped cold by the splendor of Annamaria's profile. She was even more stunning than she'd appeared in her picture. And taller. She had to be at least 5'9". But as she turned to face him, Bradford's expression tightened back up.

"Breasts are too small," he whispered derisively, leaning in toward his assistant.

"Mr. Bradford!" his shocked assistant huffed back. "She's a thirteen-year-old girl."

"Look, I didn't travel 3000 miles to tiptoe around important attributes," Bradford shot back unapologetically through gritted teeth. "Make. A. Note."

"Yes sir," his assistant acquiesced.

After greeting Mr. Bradford, headmaster Carlos Villanueva called Annamaria over for a brief introduction.

She demurely bowed her head, looking up bashfully toward Bradford with a polite smile, and extended her long slender arm, offering him a dainty hand. She had heard that someone from America would be coming to see her.

"Nice to meet you," Bradford said, gently shaking her hand, contorting his mouth into a soulless smile.

Lacking confidence in her English, Annamaria just continued to smile and nodded respectfully.

"YOU ARE A VERY PRETTY GIRL," Bradford shouted, as if her inability to carry on a conversation in English implied that she was also hard of hearing.

"Thank you," she said softly with a thick Spanish accent.

The headmaster released her back to whatever it was that she'd been doing and invited Bradford and his assistant inside.

Carlos Villanueva's office was a converted utility closet, furnished with a foldable card table that served as a desk, an overflowing filing cabinet and two metal chairs – enough to push the cramped space close to maximum capacity. The walls were covered floor-to-ceiling with faux wood paneling, except for a tiny window that looked out over the yard, and the floor was unpolished concrete.

The headmaster snaked between the card table and the filing cabinet to reach his chair, where he plopped down and gestured with an open hand over to the other one. Bradford quickly grabbed the remaining seat, leaving his assistant standing in the doorway cradling her legal-sized notepad, pen at the ready.

"I'm sorry," Bradford sighed, looking back toward his assistant with a manufactured grimace, trying his best to look uncomfortable at the prospect of having to tell his assistant to get lost. "Would you mind waiting outside?"

Without saying a word or changing expression, she took a single step back and pulled the door closed in front of her.

"Thank you for sending me those incredible photos. She is beautiful, isn't she," Bradford remarked gazing out the small window at Annamaria, in the middle of a soccer game with a few of the younger kids out in the mud-soaked yard.

"Yes. She is," the headmaster said, almost remorsefully. Bradford didn't strike him as the type of person a child should be entrusted to.

"I think she's got a big future in modeling. I took her pictures to a scout at a major modeling agency in New York who agrees wholeheartedly. Called her a 'can't miss.' I really think this could be a huge opportunity not only for her but for us at Avillage – and of course for you and your orphanage here. I believe you are aware that you and your orphanage would be entitled to a 1.5% ownership stake for the referral?"

The young headmaster nodded hesitantly.

"Carlos, by now I've been involved in hundreds of these IPOs, and they're always difficult to predict, even more so with models, since we're legally barred from showing their pictures to investors. But with the comments I've gotten from the modeling agencies, I'm guessing she would open with a market cap around a million and a half, maybe two."

Carlos's eyes bugged involuntarily.

"So your share of the more conservative estimate would be around $25,000 – if you sold right away. Which, of course, I wouldn't recommend. But I bet that kind of money could go pretty far in a place like this, couldn't it?" Bradford said with a salesman's grin, raising one eyebrow.

"It would be a godsend," the headmaster whispered guiltily, staring vacantly at Annamaria, innocently laughing and bounding after a group of boys half her age.

"After a few minor cosmetic adjustments, we could be talking about *significantly* more than that. I anticipate you could potentially see upwards of $25,000 *a year* in dividends for several years."

"What do you mean by 'minor cosmetic adjustments,' Mr. Bradford?" the headmaster asked nervously.

"Oh, nothing that would be dangerous to her. Don't worry about that. Actually, it would probably help with her confidence. The only thing I could really foresee would be a minor augmentation – she'd need at least a full B cup to..."

"You're talking about a boob job for a 13-year-old!" the headmaster gasped, eyes ablaze.

"I know, I know. I don't like it either. I hate it," Bradford said, shaking his head. "But the modeling industry is extremely competitive. If she's going to be a star, which I assure you she *will be*, she'll need just a little nudge from us. And

113

we're not talking about major surgery here. It's laparoscopic – one tiny incision – two at the most. The procedure has fewer risks and a shorter recovery time than having your wisdom teeth pulled."

"This doesn't feel right," the headmaster said, deeply regretting his decision to have contacted Avillage in the first place.

"Carlos, listen. You're doing the best job that you can down here. Anyone can see that. Don't put this all on you. And please don't look at her as a sacrificial lamb for the rest of the orphans here. She'll be getting the best deal of all. She's going to get a first-rate American education. She'll be part of a family. She'll get to travel the world. She'll have more money than she's ever even thought about. *And* she'll be able to give more back to the orphanage than she possibly could by staying here. You can't match that offer. Look at how much she loves these kids," Bradford said pseudo-empathetically, pointing out the small window. "In her heart of hearts, what do you think *she* would do?"

"She'd do anything," the headmaster said flatly after a long pause, emotionally spent. "I think she would do it."

"*She* can't do it though. *We* have to," Bradford urged, leaning in for the kill and bringing his hand up to his mouth to cover the smile he wasn't sure he could continue to suppress.

Bradford finished up by detailing the next steps they'd need to take. Avillage obviously could not be the ones to sign off on the surgery. The headmaster as her current legal guardian would have to sign the consent forms. Bradford would, however, find "the best surgeon available" and cover the costs immediately with cash. The adoption would occur only after the surgery was complete.

The headmaster opened the door to his office, physically ill but convinced he had to proceed.

~~~

Back on the ground in New York, Bradford slid his finger across the face of his phone to turn "airplane mode" off. As the bars at the top right corner of the display filled in blue, a chime alerted him to a new voice mail. Then another, and another, and another. All marked urgent, all from his office, and all in the last 20 minutes.

He casually tapped his voicemail icon, rolling his eyes, wondering what in the world his secretary was overreacting to now.

"Mr. Bradford, this is urgent! Please call back as soon as you can. J'Quarius Jones is in the hospital!" his secretary stammered, her voice cracking as she left the number to the University of Chicago Children's Hospital.

Bradford's pulse quickened, his eyes widened, and he began to feel suddenly claustrophobic on the plane. J was Avillage's biggest success to date, by far.

A graduating senior in high school, J'Quarius was on cruise-control toward being the first overall pick in the NBA draft, but Bradford had lucrative plans for him even before that.

The three-time high school All-American and reigning national high school player of the year had received scholarship offers from Kentucky, North Carolina, Kansas, Duke, UCLA, and several other basketball powerhouses. But Bradford had blocked all of them by refusing to release his medical records.

There was no doubt in anyone's mind that J'Quarius was going to be the typical one-and-done college basketball star, so Bradford saw no value in his spending a year in college, where he might get injured and he definitely wouldn't make any money.

The NBA had long since prohibited players' from entering the draft straight out of high school though, so Bradford had arranged for J'Quarius to sign an eye-popping 23 million dollar single-year contract with CSKA Moscow to play in both the Russian league and, more importantly, the wider Euroleague.

And while the salary was immense, the biggest draw of going pro would be that it would allow him to start pursuing endorsement deals immediately. If everything went as planned, J'Quarius would be the first player ever to enter the NBA already a global icon. And 90% of everything he made over $1 million in after-tax income would be appropriated to Avillage. As chairman of the board with a 5% stake, Bradford stood to take home annual dividends in excess of a million dollars.

With the high school season finished, J'Quarius had two more games with his AAU regional team before his first major payday.

The first of those games would have just ended, Bradford thought. From the aisle of the plane, he dialed the hospital.

~~~

"Hello, I'm Dr. Bennett. And you must be... Mr. Bradford?" The doctor asked, looking down at his clipboard on his way into the waiting room from the echocardiography lab.

"No," a frightened Hansford Washington said softly, extending his cool, clammy hand to greet the doctor. "I'm Hansford Washington and this is my wife Arlene. J'Quarius is our son."

"Oh," the doctor said, looking perplexedly back down at his clipboard. "The chart says that his legal guardian is an Aaron Bradford?"

"Well, yes, technically, but J'Quarius lives with us. He's been with us for the past five years. Feel free to ask him. He'll tell you who his parents are," Hansford said desperately. "Doctor, did you find out what's wrong?"

Dr. Bennett sighed. "I'm really sorry, but legally I can't share that information with you until I get permission from his legal guardian. All I can tell you is that his condition right now is stable."

"Can't you at least tell *him*? He's got a right to know if there's anything wrong with his own body!" Arlene pleaded.

"I'm sorry. I really am. But he's still a minor. By law I need to talk to Mr. Bradford first."

Just as the doctor completed his sentence, his pager began to vibrate. He plucked it off his belt to look down at the message, and held up an optimistic index finger. "This might be him," he said with a reassuring smile and retreated back into the lab.

Behind the closed door, he grabbed the nearest phone at the nurse's station and dialed the 212 number. "This is Dr. Bennett, returning a page."

"Yes, hello. This is Aaron Bradford. I'm J'Quarius Jones' legal guardian. Is he ok?"

He certainly sounded concerned, Dr. Bennett thought. "First of all, yes. He's ok. J'Quarius is resting comfortably in stable condition.

"Earlier tonight at his basketball game he was walking up to the free throw line to shoot a foul shot when, without warning, he passed out. The trainer in the gym responded immediately and brought out an AED – basically a portable defibrillator. Thankfully, by the time he reached him, J'Quarius was already coming to, so he didn't have to use it.

"As you might expect, J'Quarius was a little confused to find himself on the ground, but he wasn't injured. The paramedics just brought him into the hospital as a precautionary measure.

"Now, we just completed an echocardiogram, which is an ultrasound of the heart, and it did show an abnormality. We've discovered that he has a condition called

118

hypertrophic obstructive cardiomyopathy. 'HOCM' for short."

"Well what's the prognosis? Is he going to be able to play basketball again? Why didn't this show up on any of his physical exams?" Bradford asked without pausing for answers.

"The prognosis is good overall, but I would strongly recommend against his playing basketball – or any other strenuous sport for that matter – ever again, even recreationally. This is something that may not show up on routine exams, which is why some advocacy groups have been pushing for screening EKGs for all kids before starting high school sports. The arrhythmias – abnormal heart rhythms – that this can cause can even be fatal. J'Quarius is a very lucky young man."

"So this doesn't show up on routine physical exams?" Bradford clarified, his mind having already raced ahead to the upcoming mandatory physical J'Quarius had to undergo before signing with CSKA Moscow.

"Nope. This wasn't an oversight of any of his pediatricians or anything they could have possibly predicted. Nobody did anything wrong here," Dr. Bennett said, incorrectly inferring where Bradford was going with his line of questioning.

"So what would the odds be of something like this, or worse, happening if he were to play basketball again?" Bradford probed.

"The risk that this would happen again is high. The American Academy of Cardiology has published a guideline that participation in sports be stopped immediately," Dr. Bennett said definitively.

"But wouldn't that decision ultimately be left to the parents?" Bradford asked, keyed in on the fluidity of the word 'guideline.'

Dr. Bennett was aghast. "Mr. Bradford, did I not make myself clear that this is a potentially *life-threatening* condition? He might get away with one game or two or even ten, but it's Russian roulette. Yes, technically the decision is up to the parents, but there's no decision to be made here. Now, do you want to break this news to him, or do you want me to do it?"

"I will!" Bradford blurted out. "He hasn't heard anything yet, correct?"

"That's right," Dr. Bennett said. "For now, would you mind if I at least let the Washingtons know what's going on? They're scared to death."

"Actually I would. What I would expect is that you comply with the law and keep all of this information private. Thank you," Bradford said, hanging up his phone. This was potentially disastrous, but if he could just get him through one more game and then the Russian team's physical in 2 weeks, he could at least turn a substantial profit before shutting him down.

~~~

"Olivera?" the nurse called out impersonally through the swinging double doors, failing to recognize that there was only one patient seated in the waiting room.

Annamaria slowly rose to a stand, self-consciously holding the back of her hospital gown together to make sure she was fully covered, and hesitantly shuffled toward the door. She had already been through the most thorough physical of her life, and her upper arms were throbbing from all of the vaccinations she'd received. She couldn't imagine what else they could have planned for her.

The previous day, she had dutifully boarded a cab for Panama City after a morning of tearful goodbyes to the other children and the staff at the orphanage. The headmaster, unable to come up with a sensitive way to break the news to her, had essentially run out of time, so, despite his best intentions, he'd broken the news to her that she'd be leaving the day before it was scheduled to happen. And the only part of it that he could find the words to express was that she was being adopted by an American couple. Nothing else. Certain he would never be forgiven, he only hoped she wouldn't hold it against the orphanage.

Annamaria hadn't wanted to leave, but she hadn't fought it. Told in a nebulous manner that she could help more by leaving than by staying, she had readily agreed. But her heart was broken. It had taken everything she had to keep her chin up and give comforting smiles to the whimpering preschoolers, as she lugged her backpack to the cab. Once inside though, she had sobbed the entire 90-minute ride to Panama City.

Multiple times throughout the day, she had regretted her decision to leave the orphanage and had been able to reason her way through it, but lying there alone on a gurney, as a 20-gauge needle connected to an IV line sunk into a vein in her right arm, she hit a breaking point. Her eyes nearly bulging out of her their sockets, her chest gripped with fear, she screamed, "Stop! What are you doing to me?"

But before her scream had even finished echoing off the pale blue-green tiles of the pre-op room, she felt her heart rate begin to slow. And she was enveloped by a mysterious warmth.

Overwhelmed by the urge to sleep, she felt herself being wheeled through another set of doors, where a shining stainless steel tray covered with glistening surgical tools stood out on a drab green cloth. She still didn't know what was happening to her. But with her IV running, she didn't care

Nurses on either side of her clumsily lowered the rails on the sides of the gurney with a loud clang. The last thing she remembered was a man in hospital scrubs and a surgical mask tugging on her gown, leaving her exposed from the waist up. But in her unnaturally relaxed state, even that didn't seem to merit maintaining wakefulness.

~~~

"My chest hurts," Annamaria quietly moaned, gradually coming to. "And my stomach."

A nurse hurried over to hush the agitated beeping of her IV pump, and within thirty seconds, she was peacefully back to sleep.

CHAPTER 7

"At six feet, ten inches, power forward, J'Quarius Jones, *cum laude*," the principal shouted, his voice building to a crescendo that couldn't come close to matching the volume of the amped up crowd, who easily overwhelmed the high school gym's basic sound system and drowned out the mention of the academic accolade.

A beaming J'Quarius, wearing a Magic Johnson-like smile, floated across the stage in his double-XL black gown, which barely stretched down to his knees, and gave an appreciative tip of his cap to the crowd, squinting into the stands, trying to pick out his parents as he walked.

After a hearty handshake from the principal, he waved one last time to the crowd before quickly descending the steps on the far side of the stage cradling his diploma. As proud as he was, he didn't want to take the spotlight off the graduates behind him. The *next* time he was called on to a stage though – when the NBA commissioner was the one waiting to shake his hand – *that* he would take time to savor.

Twelve rows up at center court, while his wife struggled to get a decent angle on a picture, Hansford Washington stopped clapping, just long enough to brush a tear from his eye. This had been a long time coming. He hadn't walked at his high school graduation because of some stupid decisions he'd made, and his biological son had had his opportunity tragically ripped away by a drunk driver two years shy of his graduation ceremony.

When all was said and done, this probably wouldn't end up ranking in the top fifty of J'Quarius's biggest accomplishments, but the moment couldn't have meant more to Hansford. He went on clapping right through the next graduate's announcement, until J'Quarius finally spotted him in the crowd. Matching his son's smile, he nodded and signaled a proud double-thumbs-up across the gym.

Later that evening, as was tradition the night before a game, Arlene Washington cooked the family a big pasta dinner. Tonight it was spaghetti with meatballs – J'Quarius's choice.

"You're gonna miss these in Russia, JQ," Arlene said, piling a fourth massive meatball on the heaping mound of pasta that would be his typical first serving.

"Yeah," he said dispassionately, keeping his gaze fixed down on his plate. "There's a lot I'm gonna miss."

"Come on, now. It's only a year, and we'll be over there on every break we get during the school year," Hansford said. Then he lowered his head, and with his jaws clenched together and his eyebrows mischievously raised, he covertly mumbled without moving his lips, "And sun of those fretty Russian girls night vee very haffy to neet you," intending his wife not to hear. The sharp smack that jarred his whole head forward, almost into his plate of spaghetti, indicated that she had.

J'Quarius laughed, as his dad rubbed the back of his head. Then he went right back to picking at his pasta.

"You're not worried about tomorrow night are you?" Arlene asked, sensing something more was bothering him. Normally he'd have been be on his second helping by now.

"A little," he said, as he mechanically sawed off a couple slices of bread and passed one over to each of his parents.

"Mr. Bradford said that was just a one-time deal what happened at the last game. A freak thing," Hansford said, brushing it off. He and his wife had told J'Quarius all about Aaron Bradford and Avillage when the college scholarship offers had started rolling in.

"Yeah, but I don't know if I really trust him," J'Quarius said meekly.

"Well, I know I don't," Hansford replied. "But I also know that that man plans to make an awful lot of money off you, and he's not about to do anything that would put you in danger."

"I guess. But that didn't feel right waking up on the court," J'Quarius said shaking his head. "It felt like I was waking up from a full night's sleep. But when I opened my eyes, I was on the court looking up at a bunch of complete strangers in the stands, just staring at me. I can't explain it. It was like a nightmare or something. It just didn't feel right. I don't want to go through that ever again."

"Well, we've just got to make sure you get a good night's sleep tonight, honey. Stay away from caffeine and drink plenty of fluids before the game," Arlene said.

"Maybe take it easy for the first quarter and see how things go," Hansford chimed in. "That Ohio team has a couple guys who can play, but they can't hang with you guys for four quarters."

"Losing the game is one thing I'm *not* worried about," J'Quarius said with a confident smile.

"Well, get to bed early tonight," Arlene said. "We've gotta be in Cleveland by one, which means we have to leave around 6:30 in the morning. And don't count on getting any sleep on the bus."

"Leaving the Land of Jordan for the city where LeBron got his start," Hansford mused delightedly. "Fitting for your last game as an amateur."

~~~

Leonard Weinstien slowly turned the key to his empty Newark law office just before 10PM on Friday night. He had until noon Saturday to be completely moved out before the final inspection.

Where had the time gone? Five days ago, it seemed he had all the time in the world. Now he was staring down an all-nighter just to get everything out.

At sixty-eight with a dwindling client list and increasing rent and employee costs, he felt like he was being forced into retirement. He'd fought it the best he could for the better part of a year, but the inevitability of the collapse of his practice hadn't been lost on his secretary of 23 years. So when she'd ashamedly submitted her two-week notice, having accepted a position at a bigger, younger firm for significantly more money, he'd finally decided to throw in the towel.

Weinstien moped through the empty area where his clients used to wait for him and cast a nostalgic gaze up at the wires protruding from the wall where the office's small TV had been mounted. By force of habit he took a circuitous path to his office, veering around the empty space where his secretary's desk had stood for the past two decades, and gave his door a nudge. A stack of collapsed cardboard file boxes inside stopped it before it reached halfway open.

Organization had never been Weinstien's strong suit. Towers of unsorted papers, all protected by attorney-client privilege, rose from his desk and the surrounding floor. Legally these couldn't go in the standard trash, and the commercial shredder had been removed from the office that morning. He was going to have to take all of this home, which, with a 1-series BMW as his only mode of transportation, meant he'd be making several trips.

With the luxury of procrastination officially spent, he finally forced himself to dive in. A few papers went into a file box; then a name would catch his eye and trigger a memory. Ten minutes later, he would find himself immersed in a document, reliving a fairly mundane case from a decade earlier.

An hour into his packing job, with a box and a half filled and at least twenty more to go, he promised himself a coffee break if he could just finish up the second box.

Having met his goal within fifteen minutes, and eager to claim his productivity bonus of a cup of coffee, he headed for the door carrying two deceptively heavy file boxes. But on his way, his foot dislodged something from one of the stacks on the ground. Just in front of him lay an unopened envelope, addressed by hand, with no return address and a postmark from five years earlier. His curiosity piqued, he picked it up and set it atop the boxes he was carting out. A mystery. It would provide some entertainment while he sipped his coffee.

Weinstien left his car running in the driveway, dropped the boxes off just inside the front door of his house, and set a course for a 24-hour diner he frequented midway between his home and office.

"Hey, Mr. Weinstien," the waitress droned as he sidled up to his standard stool at the bar.

"Black?" she asked, already pouring the coffee.

"No, I think I'll try your soy latte skinny Chai caramel mochaccino," Weinstien deadpanned as the waitress slid the steaming mug of black coffee in front of him without breaking stride.

"Thanks," Weinstien said, running his office key down the side of the sealed envelope and removing a letter written in blue ink on unlined white paper.

Dear Mr. Weinstien,

By the time this gets to you, I'll be gone. First off, I want to thank you for your efforts in trying to help me connect with my son.

I don't know if you'll ever believe me that I was set up. I doubt I would if I were in your shoes, but I think we can at least agree that I no longer have a reason to lie. I don't have the computer background to prove it, but I give you a dying man's word: ALL the charges against me are false.

I know my life would have been a little easier (and probably a lot longer) if I'd never heard about my son, but I'm glad I got the opportunity to know of him. I never got the chance to meet him, but I love him. And as stupid as it might sound to you, I can't live without him.

I promise you that he is being adopted by Avillage. Somewhere around the time you receive this letter, he's going to be introduced as the second offering on their exchange. I'm asking you just one thing. <u>Please make sure he's taken care of.</u>

I thought about sticking around and trying to fight for custody, but sitting there by myself in jail and then at home with nothing to do but think, I came to two conclusions: 1. We were never going to win the case against me. 2. He's better off without me.

That first Avillage kid went to live with an educated mom and dad in the suburbs with all kinds of support and money to spend on raising him the way he deserved. I'm a single guy with a more-than-full-time job, a one-bedroom apartment in the worst school district in the state, an unreliable car, and no prospects for anything better. For me to adopt him (even if I could) just because I love him, would be selfish.

Tell him about me if you ever think the time is right – I want him to know he was loved – not abandoned. And again, <u>please make sure he's taken care of.</u> I'm sending you this letter because I trust you. Sorry I couldn't stay and fight with you.

Sincerely,
Melvin Brown

Along with the letter he'd enclosed a brief medical history from his side of the family so

J'Quarius would have it for his doctors, a player photo from his college football days, and a smaller sealed envelope the size of a thank you card with the name J'Quarius written in cursive across the front of it.

Weinstien was frozen to his stool with his mouth agape. The feelings of utter shock from the day Melvin had died came coursing back through him, sending chills throughout his body. At the time, he'd taken Melvin's suicide more as an admission of guilt than anything. Now the guilt was all on him.

If he'd gotten this letter five years earlier, around the time it had been mailed, he probably would have added it to Melvin's closed file, blocked it from his mind and gone on with another typically hectic day. And he still wasn't entirely convinced that Melvin was innocent. But after spending the last several months leading up to his retirement, with little to do but reflect, experiencing a gradual shift from self-congratulation for his successes to self-flagellation for never really making a difference, he couldn't produce a defensible way to ignore this.

Leaning over in the direction of a man seated next to him intently watching the NBA playoffs on the TV above the bar, he casually asked, "Have you heard of this J'Quarius Jones kid?"

"Yeah. Sounds like he's the real deal. Rumor has it he's going to play in Moscow next year for over 20 million bucks," the man said without taking his eyes off the TV.

"He's in Moscow?" Weinstien asked disappointedly.

"Not yet. His last AAU game is tomorrow in Cleveland. I think they scheduled it on an off day for the playoffs on purpose – probably more people want to watch him than the NBA right now."

Weinstien threw a couple bucks on the bar, ditched the nearly full cup of coffee, rushed back to his office, haphazardly threw all the remaining papers into boxes, and piled the boxes up just inside his front door. After three breakneck round-trips home, he was done.

He forced himself to log a couple hours of sleep before getting back in his car. On his way out of town he made a brief stop at Kinko's, swung through the McDonald's drive-thru for a large coffee, and at 4:15 AM started the 8-hour trip to Cleveland.

~~~

Sara jumped as the sudden blast of a car horn shrieked through the Ewings' great room, nearly causing her to spill her tea.

Ryan raced through from the kitchen, grabbing his backpack off the floor. "See you tomorrow," he yelled on his way to the front door. Out in the driveway, his friend Jasper was waiting in the new Prius he'd gotten for his sixteenth birthday.

"Do you have your phone?" Sara asked, rushing over to intercept him.

"Yes!" he huffed indignantly keeping his hand on the front door without turning around to face her.

"And it's on?"

"Yes." His shoulders slumped. *The same routine every time.*

"And it's charged?"

"Yes!"

Finally satisfied, Sara rocked up onto her tiptoes and gave him a kiss on the top of his head, which she could still just reach. "Bye. Have a good time."

Ryan enjoyed significantly more independence than the average twelve-year-old. Having just completed his sophomore year, he was at least three years younger than anyone else in his class, and with the free-form curriculum at his school, he was actually taking most of his classes with even older kids.

There were certainly disadvantages to being the youngest kid in his grade, but the biggest advantage, from his perspective, was having friends who could drive. His parents didn't share his point of view, but, conceding that he had virtually no opportunity to make friends his own age, they had reluctantly granted him permission to ride along with a select group of boys whose families they knew well on the condition that he keep his phone on him at all times.

His parents were then able not only to track his location continually with the GPS function on his phone, but also to call at random times, just to make sure he was ok. It really was more out of

133

worry than lack of trust, and Ryan knew it. But he still resented it.

To become eligible for the privilege of spending the night at his friend Jasper's house, he'd woken up that morning at six and started his day by running four miles in just under 30 minutes. He then came home for a shower and breakfast, practiced Japanese for an hour with his tutor in Kyoto on Skype, moved on to piano for another hour, and then spent the remainder of the morning re-evaluating his small but growing stock portfolio in the online trading account his dad had set him up with a few months earlier. After lunch, he'd powered through what was supposed to be two hours of homework in twenty minutes, thus completing his school-, parent- and Avillage-directed activities and leaving himself free to spend the balance of the weekend as he pleased.

He opened the passenger door of his friend's Prius and hopped in. The plan for the day, as he'd described it to his parents, was that he'd be going over to Jasper's house to work on a school project, maybe see a movie if they finished early, and then spend the night there. But his actual plans were very different.

"Hey, Jasper. Thanks for picking me up. And thanks for agreeing to do this. I owe you big time."

"You don't owe me anything," Jasper snapped as if he resented the comment, but he couldn't help but follow it up with, "So, did you start that project for Mr. Gilliam's class?"

"It's done," Ryan said, patting his backpack.

Jasper laughed involuntarily, shaking his head with an incredulous smile. "How in the world did you finish that so fast?"

"It wasn't that hard. I'll show you tonight," Ryan said matter-of-factly. "Can I see your phone?"

Jasper handed it over. Ryan popped the backs off of both his phone and Jasper's, switched out the SIM cards, and then gave his phone to Jasper.

"You can answer this if it rings. It'll work just like your phone, but *please* stay at your house. My parents can track the location of my *device* – not my SIM card. If they're looking, and my phone's not at your house, I'm screwed."

"So, what if your parents call *your* phone?" Jasper asked, not following him at all. He and Ryan were friends, but intellectual equals they were not. "And what the hell is a SIM card?"

"It's a subscriber identity module... card. Kind of redundant. Anyway, it's what makes this mass-produced phone yours. It pretty much ties your phone number and personal account info to your device.

"And now I've got my SIM card in your phone, so if my parents call my phone, I would just answer your phone, which I'll have with me," Ryan said, opening the door as Jasper rolled to a stop at the street corner adjacent to the easternmost Cleveland RTA station. "Look, I doubt my parents are watching me that closely, but if you don't mind, just stop through the nearest fast-food joint to here

135

on your way home, so it looks like we had a reason for going this way."

"Dude, you're paranoid," Jasper needled with a grin.

"Come on. I'm just trying to cover all my bases. I'm up against a one strike and you're out policy," Ryan said nervously. "Now hurry up, so it doesn't look like we stopped for an inordinately long time. I'll see you right back here at eight."

Ryan slammed the door shut, as Jasper over-acted a suspicious glance to both rearview mirrors, sunk down in his seat, pulled the bill of his cap down and sped away. Ryan shook his head and allowed himself a quick chuckle as he sidled down the hill to the station.

Just before *Dinosaurs and Aliens* had been taken offline for good, Ryan and Dillon had planned this day for their meeting.

Dillon had already made plans to come to Cleveland for an app-development workshop being held at The Renaissance Hotel, which was adjacent to the downtown basketball arena, where the other big event in town happened to be going on – the AAU basketball game. It would be no big deal for him to sneak over for at least an hour or two. Ryan faced a bigger challenge making it downtown, but he was confident he could pull it off, and they both liked the idea of a crowded arena as the meeting place.

But there was another, stronger motivation for choosing an over-hyped high school basketball game as their rendezvous point. If they were going to stand any chance of chiseling away at the overwhelming positive public perception of Avillage, Ryan and Dillon knew their cause would need a face – someone relevant and recognizable, with mass public appeal. J'Quarius Jones was really the only choice. But at this point they had no idea if he'd be a willing participant. And it wouldn't be easy to get to him. After he left for Russia, it would probably be impossible.

So far their improbable plan was running right on schedule. Ryan boarded the downtown-bound train right at 3:00, taking the seat directly behind the driver with his head resting against the window facing the inside track, his backpack occupying the seat next to him, and his heart racing 120 beats a minute.

~~~

Aaron Bradford gazed up at the arrivals board hanging above baggage carousel five at Cleveland-Hopkins International airport, then impatiently looked back down at his watch for a twentieth time in as many minutes. Their flight landed thirty minutes ago, and they'd already cleared customs in New York! The game started in half an hour. Where were they?

Finally at 3:30, three expressionless businessmen with eerily similar steel blue eyes, close-cropped brown hair and square jaws marched off the elevator in unison.

Bradford tried to produce a cordial smile that fell even flatter than usual. It was not returned. And no apologies or explanations were offered for their mysteriously late arrival, but the overpowering stench of cigarette smoke on the men suggested their tardiness could have been prevented.

They strode over as a unit to claim their CSKA Moscow-embroidered suitcases, which were the only parcels left on the now dormant conveyer belt, and then stared in synchrony at Bradford, as if they'd been the ones waiting all along.

With crimson cheeks darkening toward violet, Bradford struggled to maintain his smile. The fact that he would be screwing them to the tune of 23 million dollars with damaged goods was the only thing that kept him from absolutely losing it.

Bradford waved the Russians outside where his driver, having been parked in a loading zone for half an hour, was locked in a heated argument with a homeland security officer. Unless someone was pointing a gun or a taser at him with real intent, he wasn't about to take a chance on not being at the curb when Bradford walked out.

Noticing his boss's arrival, he left the low-level officer screaming into thin air and scurried over to the Russians to collect their bags and help them into the back of the limousine.

"*Please* tell me you have the tickets..." Bradford sneered with one leg in the car, glaring at his driver. The color ran out of the poor driver's face as he struggled to find words, while Bradford's sneer slowly morphed into a grin. He held the tickets up and fanned them out to show that he had all four. Although he did take some degree of pleasure in pulling one over on his driver, what really delighted him was the power he wielded over his pathetic minion's emotions.

"I do have the parking pass, boss," his driver stuttered, taking a deep breath to collect himself as he shut the car door.

"Gentlemen," Bradford started, leaning in toward his guests who sat stoically in the rear-facing seats closest to the driver in the passenger cabin of the limo. "It's a pleasure to have you here in the States. Welcome to Cleveland. You are in for an absolute treat tonight. Have you seen J'Quarius play before?"

"No," answered one of the triumvirate emotionlessly. "Not in person."

"He is something to behold. YouTube doesn't do him justice," Bradford continued. "He's a *solid* 6'10" – maybe not even done growing, but he plays a small forward. Now, I know he's only considering a one-year contract right now, but keep in mind, you guys aren't encumbered by a salary cap like teams in the NBA are, so if things go well next year... who knows beyond that? I'm sure you'll want to make a strong first impression with your offer."

"Our offer is firm," another of the stone-faced Russian retorted, unimpressed by Bradford's sales pitch. "Tell us what happened at his last game."

"Sorry?" Bradford asked, feigning ignorance and not about to volunteer anything.

"We heard he was taken to the hospital."

"Oh that? That was nothing. A little dehydration. Maybe a touch too much Stolichnaya the night before? Eh?" Bradford said with a hopeful grin but getting nothing from his guests. "No. Of course he doesn't drink any alcohol." *When was this ride going to be over?*

"When were you going to mention this to us?" one of the Russians asked, studying his facial expressions like a KGB interrogator.

"I'm not sure I was, to be honest with you. He's starting today's game. It really isn't an issue," Bradford said casually.

"It is an issue!" the Russian in the middle snapped, for the first time demonstrating some form of emotion.

"Gentlemen, let's just relax," Bradford said, leaning back in his seat, fully aware that his telling them to relax would have the exact opposite effect. The outburst actually put him more at ease. Emotion loosened inhibitions.

"We haven't signed anything..." one of the Muscovites started angrily.

"Neither have we, gentlemen," Bradford interrupted smoothly but decisively, sensing the opportunity to seize the upper hand. "Neither. Have. We. I can see you appreciate directness. So I'll do my best to accommodate you. You are my guests here, and I plan to take good care of you, but don't forget, I'm not asking you for any favors. You aren't helping me out by signing J'Quarius Jones. The demand for this kind of talent *far* outweighs the supply – especially in Europe. It's 250 bucks a ticket to get into tonight's game! A high school game!"

The Russians silently conceded the point, the obstinance fading from their faces as the anger still smoldered underneath.

"Scouts from the top teams in Turkey, Greece, and Spain will all be in the gym tonight. Now, to this point, your offer has been the best, but those other teams weren't too far off. And some are a little closer to home for him geographically.

"A bidding war would be one way to go I suppose, but I'd like to get this signed and done," Bradford concluded. "How about you?"

"You will allow us to watch the game first?" the man in the middle asked with his first attempt at a smile.

"Of course," Bradford answered, mirroring the Russian's disingenuous expression, as the limo pulled up to the arena.

CHAPTER 8

"Alright guys, bring it in. Let's go!" Coach Wright barked at his players, as they slowly congregated in a rough circle around him in the middle of the locker room.

"This is the last time we're going to play together as a team," the coach said. "Let's finish the season the way we've played all year – as winners! And *as a team!*"

"TEAM!" the boys shouted in unison, their emotions running higher than usual for their final game.

An abrupt silence followed as they all dropped to one knee and bowed their heads in anticipation of the coach's pre-game prayer.

"Lord," he started, "we ask that you would allow these young men to honor you by playing to the best of their abilities – abilities with which you have so richly blessed them. Let us play this game with grace... and ferocity. Let us stay true to our principles... even as we attempt to destroy our opponent. Keep us humble ... even as we crush our opponents' pride. Let these young men soar... even as you keep them grounded in the knowledge of who they really play for: God. Family. Community. Team.

"Please watch over us and the team we're about to compete against. And finally Lord, we ask that you watch over our brother J'Quarius with extra care tonight and keep him safe throughout the game. We give all the glory to you. Amen.

"OK, guys. This is it. One more game to perfection. 'Team' on three," the coach said, as the boys rose to a stand. "One, two, three..."

"TEAM!"

As the circle dispersed, a few of the boys bounced up and down on the balls of their feet, loosening up their legs. Others rolled their necks side to side, simultaneously shaking nervous energy out through their dangling arms, as they inched toward the door of the locker room. The second best player on the team breathed in long deep breaths and then blew out slowly through pursed lips, his eyes closed, meditating to the rhythm of the music blasting from his headphones. J'Quarius hadn't moved from his spot in the middle of the locker room and was back on one knee with his head bowed.

Assistant Coach Hansford Washington gently laid his hand on his son's shoulder. "You ok?"

"I don't know," J'Quarius answered.

"What's going on? Is something hurting you?" Hansford asked empathetically.

"No. Nothing hurts. I just still don't feel right." He paused for several seconds with his head down before looking back up at his dad. "I guess I'm scared."

"Do you want to sit this one out?" Hansford asked, expecting a quick and emphatic "no," but getting only silence in return, as his son hung his head back down. "Look," he said softly.

"J'Quarius, look at me. If you don't want to play, you don't have to."

"Alright guys, let's go!" The head coach said, throwing the locker room's double doors open, allowing the din of the arena to flood in from the tunnel.

"I'll see how it goes in the shootaround," J'Quarius said. He couldn't resist the urge to give his dad a hug before he hardened up his expression and joined his team at the threshold to the tunnel, ultimately unwilling to let his dad, his coaches or his team down.

A blast of black and red confetti at the mouth of the visitor's tunnel announced the arrival of the Chicago AAU team, as they confidently jogged through to an explosive reception from the crowd. J'Quarius didn't play road games. No matter where he played, he was the one everyone had paid to see.

In one corner of the arena, a group of four Russian tourists decked out in CSKA Moscow regalia danced in front of a TV camera, frantically waving a homemade poster that read, "The Dawning of the Age of J'Quarius." In the club level a fan wore an Ohio State Buckeye jersey with the name J Jones printed on the back, holding a sign that pleaded, "It's not too late."

At midcourt a pair of ESPN broadcasters debated where J'Quarius's high school career would rank historically now that it was coming to a close. The press boxes were packed with local, national and international media, while executives from all the major shoe companies cheered as enthusiastically and conspicuously as they could from their various courtside locales.

Unfazed by this type of reception, J'Quarius jaunted over to the ball cart, picked up a ball, took a hop-step back and drained a three-pointer. Ten paces behind him, over on the sideline, his dad whispered in the head coach's ear to try to play J'Quarius as sparingly as possible.

~~~

Outside the arena, Ryan was milling around without a ticket amongst a few hundred late arrivers, a handful of increasingly desperate scalpers and a few media members, vigilantly keeping his eyes peeled for anyone either he or his parents might know. He'd already had a near miss, passing within a few yards of Skylar McGhee, one of his classmates who would have relished the opportunity to rat him out. But he was pretty sure he hadn't been seen.

Just before the game was scheduled to tip, he spotted what he'd been looking for – a local sportscaster setting up a live shoot just outside the main entrance of the arena. He casually slid Jasper's phone out of his pocket, activated the camera, and positioned himself as close as he could to the news crew without distracting them.

Placing the phone on top of a railing to keep it as still as possible, he zoomed in as far as he could toward the reporter's chest where a press pass flipped randomly in the breeze and snapped as many shots as the frustratingly slow shutter speed would allow while the reporter was facing his cameraman.

At the conclusion of his 25-second puff piece, the reporter called it a wrap, and Ryan retreated to the sidewalk to begin analyzing the dozen or so shots he'd been able to get off, hoping at least one would be adequate.

"Hey, kid," the sportscaster called out, his ego inflated by Ryan's taking pictures of the broadcast, thinking this would be a wonderful opportunity to use his celebrity to make some kid's day.

Ryan was immersed in reviewing the pictures he'd taken, his expression meeting each one with a disapproving grimace. *Too far away!* Even though the reporter had been standing still, the press pass was constantly flapping in the wind.

"Hey, kid," the reporter repeated from close range, startling Ryan, who looked up with a guilty half-smile. "I saw you taking pictures over there. How would you like for my real-life TV cameraman to take a picture of the two of us on your phone for your scrapbook?"

Scrapbook? Ryan could almost feel his eyes rolling into the back of his head, but he quickly recognized this as an opportunity. "Would I!" he gushed, handing over his phone.

Ryan forced a smile for the photo, leaning in toward the sportscaster, as the cameraman melodramatically "nailed the shot."

"Have you ever thought about being on the news when you grow up?" the reporter asked.

"That would be a dream come true. I'm down here covering this event for my school paper," he said without batting an eye. "Hey, do you think I could get a shot of your press pass, so I can show everybody at school what a real one looks like?"

"Sure," the reporter said, bloated with pride, handing over his credential. "Now, you stay in school and work hard, and you just might end up on TV one day too."

Ryan centered the press pass in the frame of the phone's display and finally got the perfect shot. "Thanks," he beamed, this time with genuine glee.

"Any time," the self-important local TV man answered, as he headed back to the van.

Ryan walked back toward the arena and sat down with his back against the wall to try to figure out how to upload the picture. Within five minutes he'd done it, leaving himself about twenty minutes to kill before he was scheduled to meet Dillon.

Back in Ryan's bedroom, his digital frame awakened from sleep mode to display its newest picture just as Sara walked in to put away some clean laundry. She studied the picture quizzically – the local Fox station's field reporter's press pass for a basketball game, which would have been starting right around that time at the pro basketball arena. Ryan would have called her if he'd changed plans. This didn't make sense.

She walked over to the closest home phone and dialed Ryan's number.

Surprised by her call, Ryan jumped up and sprinted as far as he could from the sounds of the crowds and city streets, and answered the phone on the third ring, trying not to sound out of breath.

"Hey Ryan, I was just in your room putting some clothes away when a picture of a press pass from downtown Cleveland popped up on the screen. Where are you?"

"I'm over at Jasper's!" Ryan said, leaving the "where else would I be?" implied. He could live with not always volunteering the truth at all times, but it killed him to flat-out lie. "We're working on our project."

"Well what is this picture? And why is it on your frame? You only put like 5 pictures a year on that frame," Sara said suspiciously.

"You know that guy Skylar McGhee from my class?" Ryan responded without pause. "He's been bragging to everyone all week that he was going downtown to some high school basketball game today – like anyone really cares. It's a high school game! And now he texts out a picture to everyone in the class that he's got press access. It's a high school basketball game! Jasper and I thought it was hilarious, so anyway, I uploaded it. It's not like I'm going to *keep* it on there." Skylar was definitely at the game, so at least superficially, his story would hold water.

"Hmm. Ok," Sara responded slowly. Ryan was good, but she had a degree – and experience – in child psychology. And even though he had never given her a reason not to trust him, this didn't feel right. She decided to keep him on the phone as she ran downstairs to her smartphone to track his

148

location. "So what do you guys have planned for the rest of the night?"

"Not much," Ryan said, now sensing something was amiss himself. His mom frequently called to check in, but never to chit-chat. He placed Jasper's phone flat on the sidewalk and hunched over it, so he could continue talking while he enabled its map feature. "We might go see a movie if we finish our project early," he said as he keyed his name into the search box.

Sara dashed into the living room and scanned all the flat surfaces before squeezing her eyes shut, trying to remember where in the world she left her phone, as she kept up the small talk. "That sounds like fun. What are you guys thinking of seeing?"

Ryan was almost certain she was just trying to keep him on the phone at this point. Desperately willing the map to load, he cursed the solitary bar of service he was getting as tiny sweat droplets began to bead on his forehead. "Uh, I don't know," he said, "Jasper was talking about seeing some movie I've never heard of. It's at some small art house theater. He said it was NC-17, whatever that means."

"Hmm, well don't be out too late," Sara responded, completely oblivious to what he'd just said, bolting over to the smartphone she'd finally spotted on the island in the kitchen. The map was still up, and it put Ryan's location on the street just outside Jasper's house. "So you're over at Jaspers working on your project?" she asked pointedly and abruptly, now clearly attuned to the conversation.

Ryan's map was still loading. "Were you even listening to me?" Ryan stalled. "I said we were going to an art house theater to watch an NC-17 movie, and you told me not to stay out too late?" *Load!*

"Oh, yeah. I knew you were joking," Sara answered tersely. "Now what did you say you guys are up to?"

"Well," Ryan drawled having no idea what the location of his phone was, trying to come up with a safe answer based on his best guess, but just at that moment the map mercifully zoomed in on his phone's location – on the street outside Jasper's house. *Idiot! He was supposed to keep the phone on him!* He'd probably left the phone in his car, parked outside his house. "Right now we're outside working on some sidewalk art," he said with the first thing that popped into his mind. "Have you ever seen that before? With the chalk? You can make it look 3D if you're good at it. It's actually pretty cool."

"What does that have to do with your project?" Sara demanded.

"Well... Nothing" Ryan stammered, feigning trepidation about coming clean with what they were really up to. "We were most of the way done, and we just decided to take a quick break. We were just about to go back in. Sorry." He figured even a small confession could potentially pass as the source of whatever had raised his mom's suspicion in the first place.

"Ryan, that's fine," Sara said reassuringly, now convinced by both the content and the tone of his story. "You don't have to be working the whole time you're over there. But you do need to tell me what you're up to, ok? You need to earn the freedom your dad and I have given you."

"I know," Ryan said ashamedly.

"Alright, now enjoy that NC-17 movie," Sara said. "And don't forget your fake I.D."

"I won't," Ryan laughed, hoping he'd just dodged a bullet.

~~~

Half a block away, at the Renaissance Cleveland convention center, Dillon Higley was making plans to split up with his adoptive father who had accompanied him to the app-development conference. Dillon had manned his booth for most of the morning and early afternoon, so he was now free to explore the other exhibits.

"Ok, so I'll meet you back here at 6," Dillon agreed, gesturing to his booth. He then picked up his laptop and his phone and carved out a circuitous route toward the exit, making sure he wasn't followed. The convention center was big and crowded enough that he would never be missed, and the hotel was conveniently connected to the arena through another building, so he wouldn't even have to step outside, but it was still a good ten minute walk, and he had some work to do.

His first stop was the business center in the hotel lobby. Using his room key to pay, he sat down at one of the terminals and plugged in his laptop. In no time at all he'd grabbed the shot of the press pass and several other recent photos of Ryan off of the digital frame. Then with remarkably little effort, he fashioned Ryan a personalized press pass, changing the text and the photo but keeping the Fox reporter's bar code on it. He then printed it out, cropped it, inserted it into the plastic sleeve from his "exhibitor's pass" that he was wearing around his neck, and took off for the arena.

Just as the game was scheduled to start, Dillon arrived at the will call window to pick up his tickets – one in section 230 and one in 213. Then he walked out the northeast exit to look for Ryan.

Ryan was leaning against the rail at the top of the stairs just outside the arena, wearing a Hunting Valley Academy polo shirt, per the plan, when he saw Dillon exit the building.

Dillon looked like he was stepping into the sunlight for the first time in his life. His mop of coal-black hair accentuated the pallor of his complexion, and his gaunt limbs looked like white pipe cleaners with knees and elbows. He was almost three years older than Ryan, but he was a little shorter and actually looked younger. He was dressed in a plain black t-shirt and baggy jeans, hunched forward, struggling under the weight of his overstuffed backpack.

Ryan didn't have time to register, much less modify, the gut reaction of surprise and disappointment that was painted across his face at first sight of his colleague before Dillon made eye contact with him. Dillon's pale white cheeks blushed as the look of determination and resolve on his face gave way to searing embarrassment, and his gaze sunk back to the ground in front of him. He'd seen that look before – so many times. But he'd never gotten used to it – one of the many reasons he preferred to stick with electronic communication.

When Dillon looked back up, Ryan's expression had overcompensated to an unnaturally effusive smile that came across as both condescending and emasculating. Dillon scowled at Ryan as he brushed by, his self-consciousness now turned to anger.

Ryan put it together immediately. He had to go through the same thing at the beginning of each school year, before saying or writing a word. He was the cute little kid with the can-do attitude. He realized he'd just given Dillon the same "Look at you, in the big kids' classroom!" smile that he'd gotten every August at school. And unfortunately, he couldn't take it back.

Just before Dillon turned the corner of the arena, he removed a smaller bag from his backpack, placed it on the ground against the wall and continued on his way.

Ryan started after him, picked up the bag and yelled out, "You dropped your bag!" – just for the purpose of satisfying any potential witnesses. But by that point Dillon had already re-entered the arena.

Ryan unzipped the bag to find a ticket to the game, the press pass, a walkie-talkie and a Bluetooth earpiece. *A Bluetooth-enabled walkie-talkie.* He had to hand it to Dillon, that was a pretty clever way to make sure there would be no record of their communication with each other. He fit the earpiece in his ear, turned the walkie-talkie on, put the smaller bag inside his backpack and headed into the arena. Amazingly their plan was still right on schedule.

~~~

The score was 24-18 Chicago at the end of the first quarter, and the CSKA Moscow execs were getting restless. Scowling with their arms crossed in front of them, they muttered to each other tensely in Russian. J'Quarius Jones had yet to take the floor.

"Ya govoryu po rusky (I speak Russian)," Bradford announced in their direction to try to settle them down with the only Russian he knew, hoping they wouldn't test him on it.

He bit down on his knuckle as one of the Chicago kids scored again. The longer they continued to lead, the slimmer the chances were that J'Quarius would see any action. "You'll excuse me for a moment, gentlemen?" he grinned coldly.

Stopping about halfway up the aisle, he pulled out his phone and fired off a message to Hansford Washington: "GET J'QUARIUS IN THE GAME! NOW! RUSSIANS ARE HERE!" Then he stared intently across the court as he slammed his finger down on the send button to see if his text came across. Hansford's hand went briefly down to his right front pocket, apparently silencing his phone, but he never diverted his attention from the game.

Bradford was seething, but with no other recourse, he sauntered back down the stairs and joined his restless guests in the stands, reassuring them that J'Quarius would probably see "significant action" in the second half.

"Yes!" he whispered, pumping his fist slightly as the Ohio team scored, cutting the lead back to six.

~~~

"Tell me what you know," Ryan said bluntly, wearing his Bluetooth earpiece. Direct and to the point, the statement couldn't be construed as condescending, and it highlighted the fact that Dillon had essential information that Ryan not only needed but was unable to get himself. He hoped it would be enough to erase the first-impression fiasco.

"First of all, hi," Dillon said with a low but cracking voice that was obviously in the process of changing. There was a confidence to his tone that suggested Ryan's play must have worked. "Do you have something to jot notes on?" he asked.

"I don't need to take notes," Ryan said dismissively.

"Listen, you need to know this like the back of your hand. I would suggest you jot some stuff down. If you end up not needing the notes..."

"Look, I – I don't need to take notes," Ryan repeated, more self-consciously than boastfully. "You said you've seen my file?"

155

"Oh. Right," Dillon said, remembering why he'd sought Ryan out in the first place. "So this is what I found. You might already know some of this, but J'Quarius was raised by his grandmother, Verna Jones, who died of cancer. His mother Cheryl Jones died in childbirth, and his father is unknown, but Avillage has always been supremely confident that no one is going to come forward. There's no paper trail as to why they're so confident.

"He was adopted by Avillage and placed with Arlene and Hansford Washington just after he finished 7th grade. Hansford is a high school basketball coach and the assistant coach of the Chicago AAU team. Arlene primarily stays at home and helps out with coaching too. Aaron Bradford is the chairman of his board of directors."

"Ok. Any controversy? Any dirt?" Ryan asked, unsure how to use any of this bland biographical information in a post-game interview.

"It looks like J'Quarius really had his heart set on going to college, but Avillage wouldn't release his medical records, so no one could offer him an athletic scholarship. He's resigned to go to Russia to play professionally at this point, but I don't think he's too happy about it."

"I wonder if J'Quarius knows anything about his biological father," Ryan wondered aloud. It seemed to him that J'Quarius was doing pretty well with Avillage (like Ryan was himself.) Sure, he was probably miffed about not being allowed to go to college and by the fact that he'd be losing a huge chunk of his pro basketball salary down the road to his shareholders, but Ryan wondered if that would be enough for him to put any effort into joining their cause.

On the other hand, every adopted kid wants to know about his biological parents; that was Ryan's whole motivation for being at a basketball game in downtown Cleveland instead of at his friend's house in the suburbs.

"Dillon," Ryan asked hesitantly. "Do you have any more info on my parents?"

"Yes," Dillon answered curtly. "We can talk about it later. *After* you get J'Quarius to join us."

"It's conditional?" Ryan asked, shocked and somewhat offended. Maybe Dillon wasn't over that unintentional look he'd given him.

"It has to be," Dillon said flatly.

"Well, what if I can't get to him?" Ryan asked, feeling suddenly overwhelmed.

"Then we'll have to come up with a plan B," Dillon said unsympathetically. "This is *very* important."

~~~

By halftime the game was knotted at 46, and the Chicago team jogged off the floor to a chorus of boos. The Russian businessmen clearly weren't the only ones who had noticed J'Quarius's conspicuous absence from the court.

The game had been both entertaining and competitive, but the *only* thing most of the fans had paid to see was the next NBA superstar before he was a star.

Above the entrance to the visitors' tunnel, Leonard Weinstien jockeyed for position with a host of amateur photographers. Then just before J'Quarius was directly beneath him, he unfurled a 72 by 36 inch banner with a neon-orange background that couldn't be ignored. On the left side of the banner in large black print was Leonard Weinstien's contact information along with the statement, "Your father loved you." Taking up the entire right side was a blow-up of the picture Melvin Brown had enclosed in his letter to Weinstien. Melvin was nineteen in the photo and in perfect health with bright eyes and a wide smile, kneeling on one knee in his football uniform. J'Quarius stopped cold just in front of the sign. Aside from the dated hairstyle and thin moustache, he could have been looking in a mirror.

He looked up at Weinstien who smiled reassuringly at him and nodded back down to his contact info printed on the banner, before J'Quarius was rushed into the tunnel by his coaches. Hansford, who'd entered the locker room ahead of J'Quarius, hadn't seen the banner.

Hansford and Arlene had warned J'Quarius that one day someone may come forward claiming to be his biological father. They'd made it clear that whether the claim was true or not, they would never stop being his parents and they'd never stop loving him, but they'd warned him to be skeptical. And he was.

The banner read, "Your father *loved* you" though. Past tense. Was he dead? In jail? Had he stopped loving him? Whatever the case, it would be an ineffective way to start a scam, if that was the intent.

From the opposite end of the arena, Ryan had watched the banner unfurl in front of J'Quarius through his binoculars. He now had his answer. J'Quarius did *not* know about his biological father.

"Weinstien@weinstienlaw.com," he whispered, committing the email address of the man with the banner to memory.

Two sections and twenty rows closer to the court, Bradford had watched the same scene unfold, aghast at the sight of Melvin Brown's picture. He was and should have remained a non-factor. Things couldn't be going much worse. He frantically added Weinstien's contact info into his phone while the banner was down, inadvertently transposing the "e" and the "i" at the end of Weinstien's name.

Back in the locker room, Coach Wright harped on his players about stepping up their pathetic defense and sluggish ball movement, while scattering in just enough praise to keep the team's spirits up. As he ranted, Hansford briefly dropped his gaze down to his phone and read the new message from Bradford.

As soon as the head coach finished his pep talk, Hansford walked up behind J'Quarius to see how he felt.

"Fine," he said. "I've felt fine the whole time. I'm just nervous."

"You think you might want to try and play a little bit?" Hansford asked. "The Russians are here to watch you."

"I guess I've gotta try at some point," J'Quarius said with a tepid smile. "It's probably harder on my heart having to watch the other team make runs on us, being stuck on the bench."

"I'll talk to Coach Wright," Hansford said, patting him on the shoulder. "Now listen. If you feel like you need a sub, you ask for one. Don't try to be a hero."

"I won't," J'Quarius assured him. "Oh and Dad, there's one other thing I want to talk to you about – after the game." With only four minutes until the start of the second half, there wasn't enough time to bring up a subject as complex as his biological father.

"Sure, son."

~~~

The subdued crowd erupted, as J'Quarius finally shed his warm-ups and threw them over to the bench.

Bradford heaved an internal sigh of relief, but glanced at his Russian friends with a knowing smirk, as if he'd never had a doubt. The Russians couldn't help but smile back.

From the opening tip of the second half, the crowd's discontent evaporated. J'Quarius mesmerized the fans, his teammates, his soon-to-be employers and even the other team with highlight-reel dunks, no-look passes, and lockdown defense.

The ESPN announcers screamed out the play-by-play, straining to yell over the crowd.

By the end of the third quarter, Chicago was up by a comfortable fourteen points, and Bradford was seeing green.

Ryan, with his heart pounding out of his chest, made his way down to court level and got in line with a few eager members of the press to gain early access to the visiting team's locker room. At the front of the line, a stadium security officer sat on a foldable chair, mindlessly scanning barcodes and nodding in the direction of the door to the locker room after each pass cleared. They always did.

Ryan looked over at the Chicago bench, shocked at how huge these high school kids were from his new vantage point.

"Kid!" the security guard said impatiently. "Let's go!" He scanned the barcode and then flicked his head in the direction of the door.

Synergistic aromas of sweat, spray-on deodorant and bleach belted Ryan in a full-on olfactory assault as he entered the locker room. Most of the media members were transfixed on the flat-screen TV on the back wall where the final quarter was about to start back up, oblivious to the odor. No one seemed to think anything of the smell – or of Ryan's presence.

"How you feel?" Coach Wright asked J'Quarius.

"Good, coach," J'Quarius said.

"You got a couple more minutes in you?"

"Definitely."

With the outcome of the game more or less decided, Coach Wright drew up one more play for the crowd. After that, the plan was to sub each of his seniors out individually, to allow the fans a chance to show their appreciation and then empty his bench to make sure everyone on the team got some playing time.

The overhead buzzer blasted to start the final quarter, as the ref handed the ball to the home team's point guard. Dribbling it out nervously, he kept a wary eye on J'Quarius who herded him over to the left side of the floor close to midcourt. J'Quarius then gave him a little room to his right, which the point guard took as soon as he saw it.

As he dribbled past, J'Quarius wrapped his long arm around the point guard from behind, poking the ball forward to his waiting teammate. Before his teammate had even secured the ball, J'Quarius was already accelerating toward the other team's basket.

He looked back as he reached the three-point line and sure enough, the ball was in the air. J'Quarius stomped down hard on the free-throw line and then took flight off his left foot as he caught the pass from his teammate. Palming the ball in his fully-outstretched right arm, he reared back, arching his back as he flew. Then just as he reached the apex of his jump, the totality of his motion – torso, arm, hand, ball – shifted violently forward, culminating in a thunderous dunk that brought everyone in the arena out of their seats. The ESPN broadcasters didn't even attempt to comment on what they'd just seen, both for lack of words and for the realization that it would be at least half a minute before they would stand a chance of transmitting over the deafening roar of the crowd.

J'Quarius came back down to his feet, turned toward his bench, and looked straight at his dad with sheer terror in his eyes. Then he crumpled to the ground.

As if a switch had been thrown, the crowd went stone silent.

Ryan, watching from the visitors' locker room, Dillon from high in section 213, Weinstien near the tunnel, and Bradford five rows from the floor simultaneously mouthed the word, "No."

Hansford sprinted out onto the court with a medic trailing right behind him carrying a defibrillator. For the second time in as many games, Arlene Washington rushed down from the stands screaming, "I'm his mother! I'm his mother!" bypassing the security guards.

J'Quarius lay flat on the court, his face, misted with sweat, slowly turning gray. The medic threw the fallen player's shirt up and applied the defibrillator pads. His shout of "Clear!" echoed all the way to the rafters of the eerily silent arena. J'Quarius's chest heaved, as the electricity flowed into his body, but nothing else moved. Hansford couldn't bear to see his wife watch this and threw himself between her and J'Quarius, holding her tightly in his arms.

The medic hit him with a second jolt. Again nothing.

A group of blue-uniformed paramedics materialized from the far end of the court, running over with a stretcher and as much equipment as they could carry.

One applied a mask over his mouth and nose and squeezed oxygen-spiked air into his lungs by bag, while another applied EKG leads hooked up to a portable monitor. It didn't take a medical degree to recognize the flat line on the display. One of the paramedics loudly announced that he'd gotten an IV established, as his colleague handed him an ampule of epinephrine, which he quickly jetted into J'Quarius's vein. Still nothing.

With a man at each corner of the stretcher, four paramedics lifted him off the floor, allowing the collapsible wheeled scaffolding to lock into place underneath him, and raced toward the ambulance to the sound of cautious applause from an apoplectic audience not quite sure how to respond. All the while, the paramedic at J'Quarius's head continued rhythmically squeezing the bag, inflating his lungs against no resistance.

Within seconds of hitting the emergency room, after 21 minutes of CPR, 17-year 11-month old J'Quarius Jones was pronounced dead.

~~~

Back at the arena, Ryan and all the other media members, had been quickly ushered out of the locker room to give the Chicago team some privacy.

Ryan placed the Bluetooth earpiece back in his ear. "Did you see that?" he asked, in utter shock.

"Yep. Figures," Dillon answered disappointedly, as if something had happened directly to him. "This whole thing was for nothing! We were so close!"

"I hope he's ok," Ryan said, not even considering the possibility that this youthful embodiment of physical fitness was already dead.

"Me too," Dillon said. "But even if he is, I don't have any idea how we're gonna be able to make contact with him at this point."

"I tried," Ryan said, holding out hope that Dillon would still give him whatever information he had on his parents.

"Well, we'll have to try again. Think. And I'll be back in contact with you – somehow."

"Wait," Ryan pleaded. "What about my parents?"

"Sorry, I can't give away my only leverage," Dillon said heartlessly. "I need you."

"What?" Ryan snapped back angrily. "If you think telling me whatever info you have is going to make me *less* committed to your cause, I don't need it. Don't contact me again!"

"Your dad's friend Jared Ralston is a minority owner of your stock," Dillon blurted out. "And he's been on the board of directors since day one."

Ryan shook his head and gritted his teeth. "I already knew that!" *What a waste of time.* He reached up for his earpiece disgustedly. He had to get back to the train station to meet Jasper.

"But he never purchased any shares," Dillon added.

Ryan stopped mid-stride. "Then how did he..." It had been years since he'd last spoken to J.R.

"That's all I can tell you. Really. That's all I know," Dillon said. "I'll get back in contact you when the time is right."

~~~

In the weeks following J'Quarius's death, Bradford, desperate to exonerate Avillage of any involvement in the untimely death of the wildly popular student athlete and under heavy pressure from investors who'd seen their shares plummet to zero, filed suit against the University of Chicago Children's Medical Center for failing to disclose the risks of J'Quarius's condition.

The charges were reviewed by the hospital's lawyers, who determined that Dr. Bennett, the treating physician, had meticulously documented his entire conversation, specifically detailing his warning that J'Quarius "could die with continued participation in sports."

Bradford wouldn't back away from his position that he'd never been given that information though – despite the fact that the electronic medical record supported Dr. Bennett's account. And Bennett's entry was time-stamped just minutes after he and Bradford had talked.

Lawyers from Bradford's team, along with the hospital's side, all urged Bradford to drop the baseless case, but he wouldn't relent. He would, however, be willing to settle out of court, he announced.

Dr. Bennett pushed hard to stand and fight, but as a single physician in a multi-specialty group-practice employed by a self-insured hospital system looking to protect its bottom line, the decision wasn't up to him. Bradford, only interested in winning in the court of public opinion, opened with an offer to settle the case for a ludicrous sum of one thousand dollars, on the condition that the amount never be disclosed publicly. The hospital, looking at the alternative of a legal fight, which they would unquestionably win but that would cost them potentially hundreds of thousands of dollars to defend against a client with Bradford's resources, jumped at the offer.

CHAPTER 9

By 1AM, most of the guests had either departed or were heading for their cars, gradually giving way to a bustling cleaning crew, now diligently but inconspicuously engaged in vacuuming, blotting out wine stains, and shuttling empty cocktail plates back to the kitchen of James Prescott's expansive Southampton estate. But Prescott, in a nostalgic mood on the tenth anniversary of the opening of his exchange, couldn't quite bring himself to call it an evening. By any measure, tonight qualified as a special occasion.

After a quick survey of the dwindling crowd, he singled out Alec Alanson, a media member of all people, to join him in his study for a nightcap.

Alec wrote for the Financial Times and was the rare individual who Prescott believed actually "got" him. If anyone ever set out to pen his biography, Prescott tacitly hoped it would be him, with his style of interview that weighed heavily toward listening. A successful interview, Alec believed, was like a memorable photograph. Of course it had to have a compelling subject, and it had to be successfully framed, but if the one recording the beauty or the evil or the genius of the subject became even the slightest focus of the piece, then it was a failure. Alec's portrayals didn't center around getting answers to "the tough questions."

They involved unobtrusively peeling away layers and, hopefully, reaching the core. Tonight, he wouldn't pose a single question.

The heavy wooden door to the study creaked open from its high arched frame as Prescott ushered his guest in ahead of him. Prescott had actually given his housestaff explicit instructions not to grease the door, as he felt the creak added character to the entrance to this most august room of the house.

Inside, a fire crackled within a cavernous stone fireplace behind a masculine wrought iron gate, flanked on each side by a stack of hand-split oak logs and heavy iron pokers. The opposite wall was lined with rare books that Prescott had painstakingly collected over the years. His most prized possession, an original field atlas illustrated by Audubon himself, lay on a glass-covered pedestal in the center of the room, illuminated from above by a focused beam of white light that somehow left the remainder of the dimly lit room under the influence of only the warm tones of the flickering firelight. Dark wood stretched up the windowless walls to the sixteen-foot beamed ceiling, and a hand-knotted oriental wool rug dating from the late 1800s covered the entirety of the floor. A bare desk at the back of the room and two worn leather armchairs toward the fore were the only furnishings.

Prescott discreetly tugged on the false spine of a three-volume set on one of the lower bookshelves to reveal a simple ovoid decanter and 2 stout crystal glasses. "Care for a drink?" he asked, holding up a bottle of 60-year-old Macallan Whisky.

Just sober enough to realize that another drink was the last thing on Earth he needed but also that this would probably be the only time in his life he'd be offered a drink from a bottle that cost more than his car, Alec Alanson politely accepted.

Prescott handed a generous pour to his honored guest, the most recent member of an exclusive club who'd seen the inside of his study, and he began to pace. He carefully studied a row of books at his eye level, as Alec sat in silence, hypnotized by the honeyed aroma of the whisky mixing with the campfire smells of the burning wood.

"You know," Prescott started hesitantly, "when you're young, your focus is on the question, 'What are you going to do?'"

He plodded deliberately a little further down the row of books before continuing, "Then sometime in your 30s, you pop your head up from your work long enough to ask yourself, 'What am I doing?'"

He paused again, having reached the end of the bookshelf, before starting back, "In your 50s, the question gradually evolves to, 'What have I done?'

"Now," he said, walking back toward the front the room, "as I'm entering my 60s, I've begun to consider how what I've done will be perceived historically – what my legacy will be.

"Are you old enough to remember the 1984 Olympics?" Prescott asked, abruptly changing the subject as he slid down into the armchair opposite Alec, casually crossing his right leg over his left.

Alec shook his head "no," careful not to interrupt the mood with extraneous words, studying Prescott's every move and expression.

"The United States won more gold medals that year than the next five countries on the medal list *combined*." Prescott followed the statement with a period of silence sufficient to ensure that what he'd said had fully sunk in. "This will probably sound simplistic – and it was; I was just a kid at the time – but I saw what America could be that summer. Our 250 million against the world's five billion, and we came out ahead.

"That lit a fire in me that's never really been extinguished – even after I learned of the Soviet boycott.

"My goal from that summer forward became to do whatever I could to keep or, in some cases, to make this country great. Exceptional.

"At eighteen, I'd been offered admission to Princeton, but I had actually planned to delay my admission to serve in the army – not the reserves or ROTC, mind you. I was going to enlist." After stealing a quick peek at Alec to measure his response, he glanced back down at his single-malt Scotch and swirled it reflectively in his snifter, studying the legs of the amber liquid as they slowly stretched down the sides of the glass. He'd never disclosed this to anyone before – not even his wife. After briefly reconsidering, he opted to keep going.

"My dad talked me out of it – and of course he was right. My talents lay in other areas. I had far more to contribute as a civilian. And I needed more of an academic foundation to maximize my personal strengths.

"As a junior at Princeton three years later, I finished a minor in American Politics – with the genuine intention of one day running for office.

"Again, my dad steered me away. 'Governments are run by schmoozers,' he told me. 'Businesses are run by leaders.' Again, he was right.

"Then, later that year, I was hit with a lightning bolt of clarity," Prescott said, his voice rising as he stood back to his feet. "What made this country great – this country with such a brief history and a relatively small percentage of the world's population – in everything from athletics to electronics, medicine to space exploration, entertainment to finance – was a very small number of exceptional individuals. America had always celebrated these men and women – native born and immigrant – and had given them the environment, the opportunity and the incentive to maximize their potential.

"But unlike the olympic development program, where the best of the best were identified early, nurtured, trained and, in due time, celebrated, I saw our country implementing policies focused not on nurturing genius but solely on pulling up those people with no potential for greatness, while the would-be-great seemed complacently contented as bigger-than-average fish in their small ponds." Prescott walked toward the west wall and gazed deeply into the fire. There was no way for him to continue without potentially coming off as callous. *So be it.*

"I freely admit 'no child left behind' has never been my policy. And I could not care less how our average student stacks up against any other country's average student in math or science," Prescott said unapologetically, forcefully stoking the bottom log in the fire, which crumbled into a heap of glowing embers. "Some children are destined to work at the grocery checkout. Some are destined to become automatons in the world's most powerful military. Some may carve out a nice living as an engineer or a doctor or a lawyer. There's certainly no shame in that. We need those people. But they aren't the individuals who make this country exceptional.

"The exceptional are few and *far* between. *They* make an impact. *They* leave a legacy. *They* would become my focus."

~~~

Annamaria Olivera's eyes struggled to half-mast, as she slowly transitioned from a sound sleep to a semi-conscious twilight. A persistent buzzing from the front-left pocket of her painted-on jeans and a continuous throbbing in her head wouldn't allow her to fall back asleep, and the lingering alcohol that had kept her liver working double-time all night prevented her from fully waking up.

A thin web of viscous saliva stretched between the corner of her half-open mouth and a puddle of drool on the magazine cover her head had spent the night resting on, as she slowly pushed herself up off the floor. A veritable newsstand of similar magazines carpeted the opulent hotel suite, her image splashed across every one – Glamour, Vogue, Cosmo, Vanity Fair, and a host of weekly tabloids. How they – or she – ended up there was a mystery that would probably never be solved.

Holding her pounding head in one hand, straining to focus her blurred vision on the cell phone in her other, she mumbled the incoming text message out loud, "We need to meet – Fellow Avillage Orphan."

And with those seven words, she was wide awake – despite the persistent headache.

Annamaria's childhood had officially ended the day that Aaron Bradford had set foot in her Rainbow City orphanage.

For most of the past five years she had traveled the globe with her adoptive mother, an aging model, who was far too envious of her to be any kind of role model, and her father, a photographer who viewed her as no less an inanimate piece of artwork than any of the other photographers she'd worked with had.

When she'd turned seventeen, Bradford and her board of directors had happily signed off on her request to move on without her parents, saving the shareholders a year's worth of parental stipends in the process. And while she hadn't sacrificed any nurturing or love by ridding herself of her toxic adoptive parents, she had given up the last shred of structure she'd had in her life.

Her flawless look and effortless talent allowed her to live by her own rules, and she knew it. As was the case with many Avillage recruits, she resented her work – and the people who were profiting from it – but the money was addictive, and she'd been so deeply indoctrinated with the idea that she had to be successful that she kept going. Plus she knew if she stopped, even for a moment, she might be forced to look at what she'd become, and she wasn't ready to deal with that.

The text message was a complete shock. Aside from her adoptive parents and a small group of people within Avillage, no one should have known that she was bound to Avillage, and as far as she knew, she had never come across anyone else who'd been adopted into the exchange.

She called down to the valet to fetch her car as she changed into a pair of looser-fitting jeans and a baggy sweatshirt and then threaded her impossibly shiny black hair through the back of a Yankees hat that she pulled down low over her eyes.

Her shoot that weekend was cancelled, effective immediately. It wasn't as if her agency could do anything about it. The only threat they could possibly make was that they'd get someone else. But who would they get? The day would inevitably come when she would be replaceable, but for now, there was only one Annamaria Olivera in the fashion world.

Judging from the 617 area code on the text message, she figured she'd be heading to Boston.

~~~

Tenuous allies at best, Ryan and Dillon had at least managed to resolve one of their longstanding issues. Covert communication was no longer a problem now that they were living in the same city. With high-end walkie-talkies, Dillon, a freshman at MIT, could transmit clearly two miles up Massachusetts Avenue to Harvard, where Ryan was a third-year senior majoring in economics.

They had gone back and forth for months over whether or not they should reach out to Annamaria. Dillon was stuck on the fact that she'd become by far the highest-profile Avillage orphan, while Ryan contended that her near 24/7 press coverage was overwhelmingly *un*favorable and that anyone who was regularly referred to as a "socialite" in the tabloids wasn't the face they needed for their cause – no matter how beautiful or famous a face it was.

Dillon, driven by a self-sustaining internal fusion reaction of anger, was running low on patience and was desperate to do something. Anything. Now. On the other hand, Ryan, who was still cautiously trying to distill the truth out of what his obviously biased source was feeding him, argued that they could potentially end up doing irreparable harm to their image if they made the wrong move. They had to be viewed from the outside as sympathetic figures – exploited orphans – not greedy, entitled rich kids who already had way more than the average American (at least partially because of opportunities that Avillage had given them) and were now trying to hoard even more money. Annamaria, whose only marketable talent seemed to be showing skin for the camera, exemplified the entitled rich kid.

Eventually Dillon couldn't stand the inaction any longer, and texted Annamaria from his computer – using Ryan's cell phone number.

~~~

Ryan was an even six feet tall with broad shoulders and a man's build. At seventeen, he wouldn't have looked completely out of place in high school, but he certainly didn't stick out in a lecture hall full of college students in their early 20s. And his casual, confident demeanor further disguised any age discrepancy.

His dark hair was thick but neatly cropped, and his big brown eyes were as clear and bright as they'd been the day he was adopted by Avillage ten years earlier. He was thoughtful and compassionate, but often difficult to read with an expression that tended away from extremes. It was an accurate external representation of his constantly working mind, but one that was occasionally misinterpreted as cold or indifferent.

Although he held celebrity status with a few students on campus who'd either figured out or had been told by their shareholding parents who he was, he maintained a small group of close friends and a wider group of friendly acquaintances, like most of the other kids did. And since the arrival of the first freshman class near his age the previous fall, he'd had no trouble finding dates.

He had yet to find a course that he'd considered a real challenge; the most difficult decisions he faced often centered around which classmates he'd work with on group projects – a sensitive issue in a school of grade-mongers often being graded on a curve.

And even though he had more than enough credits to graduate, he kept up a heavy course load in a wide array of subjects, ranging from mathematics to psychology to history to international law, all while making good money in the stock market. And neither he nor his parents nor Avillage saw any advantage in his graduating before he was eighteen.

Away from the classroom, he'd come up with a way to combine a rough application of an incomplete-information game theory model with his unique ability to rapidly assimilate and recognize patterns in large sets of data to come up with a strategy for trading futures on the Chicago Board of Exchange. Using his method, he was reliably gaining 3% per day on 60% of his holdings, while the other 40% would end up down by the same amount. That led to a modest net increase in his bankroll of 0.6% per day. But compounding that daily over the roughly 250 trading days of the past year – a year in which the commodities markets were relatively flat – he had nearly quintupled his original bank roll, while quietly socking a portion of his profits away into a growing portfolio on the Avillage Exchange.

He was on his way out of a World War II history course taught from the various perspectives of all of the major players, contemplating how he and Dillon were a lot like the pseudo-allied United States and Russia – ideological opposites thrown into an alliance against the bigger and more immediate threat of Avillage's Germany – when he was blindsided by a phone call from New York.

"Hello?"

"Who is this?" came the hushed but determined Latina-accented voice on the other end.

"Who is *this?*" Ryan asked.

"You texted me!"

"What are you talking about?" Ryan scoffed. Then his face sank. *He wouldn't.*

Ryan looked down at his phone and saw the caller's 212 number. He'd only seen it once, several months ago, but he recognized it instantly. He was on the phone with arguably the world's top supermodel.

He wanted so badly to respond with the disdain he'd always held for her, but, finding himself incapable of not picturing her on the other end of the line, he instead felt his pulse quicken and his mouth dry, as he started stumbling for words. *Why couldn't she have just texted back?*

"You said you wanted to meet me?" Annamaria asked forcefully, as she grabbed her keys and slid on her Cartier sunglasses on her way to the hotel elevator.

"Yes. Yes, I did," Ryan stammered, cursing himself for coming off as such a starstruck dweeb. "When are you available?" *Ugh!* He sounded pathetic. *He* should be dictating the terms!

"I'm in New York. I'm just getting in my car now. You are in Boston, no?" Annamaria asked.

Dammit! She even sounds sexy! "Yes, I'm in Boston," Ryan answered mechanically in a full sweat, futilely trying to relax. "It'll take you about 4 hours to get here. I'm not sure if you know the city. Maybe we could meet at a coffee shop or restaurant?"

"I know the city," Annamaria answered bluntly. "But I can't just show up at a restaurant. I *will* be noticed."

"We could meet at the Widener Library," Ryan said. "Everyone pretty much minds their own business..."

"Don't you have an apartment or something?" Annamaria interrupted. "I assume you want to keep this private too?"

"Uh..." and with that, Ryan came officially unhinged, with a lump in his throat so big it rendered him temporarily mute. She'd completely taken control of the conversation, and he couldn't believe he was reacting this way. "I guess we could meet at my place," he managed. "Just put the intersection of Massachusetts Avenue and Dunster Street in your GPS, and call me when you get close. I'll direct you from there."

"OK," Annamaria said resolutely. "I'll see you in about three hours. I drive very fast."

"Bye," Ryan said, just as his phone beeped to indicate the call was over. And finally, his shoulders dropped and the blush started to fade from his cheeks. He could breathe again.

After a quick pause to collect himself, he whipped out his walkie-talkie. "Dillon! Come in! I know you're there!" No answer.

~~~

Annamaria parked her convertible Mini Cooper on Dunster Street and brushed right by the meter on the curb behind her rear bumper, not giving the first thought to paying it.

As she hurried up the red brick sidewalk toward Massachusetts Avenue, she caught her first glimpse into Harvard Yard. The timeless, classic brick buildings on the periphery circumscribed a yard of bright green grass that was speckled with towering oak trees and streaked with black walking paths, crisscrossing at sharp angles in every direction. She'd traveled all over the world and had gained access to places most people would never see, but this still impressed her. Growing up in small-town Panama, most people hadn't heard of Stanford or Yale or Princeton. They all knew Harvard.

And while she had more money in the bank and a higher future earning potential than 99% of the students bustling by her in both directions on the crowded walk, she felt somehow out of place, self-conscious even.

Ryan had spent the better part of the past three hours scouring the internet, reminding himself why he'd never had any interest in contacting this hollow social butterfly and convincing himself that it was not he who should be intimidated. Especially on his home turf. This time he was prepared for her call when it came.

"Yeah," he answered.

"It's me," Annamaria whispered into her phone, almost demurely. "I'm at kind of a triple archway on Massachusetts Avenue at the entrance to Harvard Yard. Do you go here?"

"Yeah," Ryan said coldly. "Stay there. I'll be down in a few minutes." Click – he hung up his phone, leaving the prima donna no time to protest. *Now that's how it's done*, he thought.

Ryan slowly descended the steps of his dorm, exited out onto the yard and strolled at a deliberately lazy pace toward Mass Ave, fighting the urge to peek toward the arched gate. As he walked through, he found Annamaria sitting cross-legged on the sidewalk with her back resting against one of the brick archways.

"I'm Ryan," he deadpanned. "Follow me."

"Nice to meet you," Annamaria smiled, jumping up to a stand. "This place is amazing. I've never been here before. Any chance you could give me a quick tour on the way back to your place? And maybe we could just pick up a little snack? I'm starving."

"You eat?" Ryan sneered.

"I'm not that skinny!" Annamaria shot back playfully.

"No, certainly not everywhere," Ryan said, looking her up and down, convinced that she'd had some work done. "You are definitely uniquely proportioned," he muttered just loudly enough that he hoped she would hear.

They walked on in uncomfortable silence through the Yard for another sixty seconds.

"See that there?" Ryan said condescendingly, pointing toward Widener library. "That's a library. You may or may not be familiar with one of those. It is a place of learning, full of books. One of the books inside is an original Gutenberg Bible. The Bible is a popular religious text that I'm almost certain you're not familiar with."

"What the hell is your problem?" Annamaria snapped. "You contacted me!"

"Someone contacted you on my behalf," Ryan clarified. "I thought it would be a waste of my time – and yours."

"Oh, I see. So you think you know me?" Annamaria asked, her Spanish accent intensifying with her anger. "Please, don't pretend that you know me," she continued without giving him a chance to respond. "*You* get more looks around here than I do. How would you like it if I asked one of these ass-kissers about you, and I based my whole impression of you on that?"

I don't give a damn what you think about me, he thought before thinking better of actually saying it aloud. "You're right," he conceded half-heartedly. "I don't know you."

He pointed out the statue of John Harvard and a few buildings of interest as they continued the awkward tour toward one of the science buildings where they ducked in to grab a snack before doubling back to Ryan's dorm on the south end of the Yard.

Ryan's "single," a privilege of upperclassmen, was on the third floor of Wigglesworth dormitory. The unadorned walls were coated with thick white paint that had been caked on progressively thicker over the decades. A few of the beams of the original hardwood floor were just starting to buckle upward, but the floor was clear of clutter and his twin bed neatly made, an unusual state for his room – one which he'd argue to his death had more to do with the fact that he had *a* guest than with who that guest may be. A microwave rested on top of his perpetually empty dorm fridge at the foot of his bed, and his black wooden Harvard chair was pushed up tidily to his desk under the room's lone window that looked down on the peaceful Yard below.

Ryan unlocked the door and invited Annamaria to have a seat wherever she liked, as he mulled over how much he wanted to reveal to her. From the doorway he could see that his laptop was still open, displaying a picture of a bikini-clad Annamaria on the cover of some trashy tabloid, toting some sort of fruity alcoholic drink across some generic tropical beach while flirtatiously smirking at a throng of salivating suitors. The headline teased "Off Again?" suggesting that her currently-rumored relationship with her Hollywood boyfriend *du jour* had ended.

Annamaria gazed over to the laptop with a hint of disappointment on her face as Ryan rushed over to close it. She shed her hat and her sweatshirt, under which she wore a form-fitting plain white T-shirt, and sat down on the side of the bed, curling one foot up underneath her as she popped open a can of Coke.

Ryan sat facing her in his black wooden chair, thinking about where he should begin (and grudgingly admiring the fact that she didn't drink diet) when she completely disarmed him by speaking first.

"Tell me about your parents," she said, sliding off her sunglasses for the first time, and looking him straight in the eye, as if the argument they'd just had had never taken place. The sincerity in her eyes was undeniable, and the depth was hypnotizing – like a bottomless volcanic lake in the dead of a moonless night.

The tabloid covers instantly vanished from his mind, and he was forcefully struck with the realization that the two of them shared a terrible, powerful, character-defining history.

He hadn't talked about his birth parents to anyone for years, but not a single day had passed that he hadn't thought of them.

"My dad runs a hedge fund," he started, with a last-ditch effort to evade her question.

"Your *real* parents," she interrupted, still staring directly in his eyes intently – but tenderly.

"They were both doctors," he said, turning toward the window as tears began to well on his lower lids. "I remember every moment I spent with them from the time I first started to form memories."

His voice stayed steady as an occasional tear trickled down his cheek and Annamaria listened. "My dad was a huge Cleveland Browns fan. Every

Sunday at 1:00, without fail, we would park ourselves on the couch, eat popcorn, and watch the game together – the whole game – no matter how bad the score got. He told me when he was finally done with all of his training and making a real doctor's salary, we were gonna go to a game and sit at the fifty yard line, no matter what it cost.

"My mom was busy, but she never let me feel it. She'd work on Saturdays if she had to to make it to my school so I'd have someone there on days parents were invited. She taught me to read and how to ride a bike.

"When I was scared or sick, one of them would come and stay in my bed with me and then go to work at the crack of dawn the next day on essentially no sleep. They loved me. Unconditionally.

"I was an only child. When they died, I was completely alone – devastated.

"I was seven, and..." he drew in a deep breath before continuing. "I saw it. I saw it happen. For the next few months I woke up with nightmares of that scene every morning." He shook his head slowly. "It was terrible.

"But honestly," he said, turning to Annamaria, "it was even worse when they stopped – when the images weren't as vivid, and the pain wasn't as intense. My parents didn't have anyone else in the world either. I was their entire legacy, and as hard as I tried not to, I could feel myself... forgetting them – at least emotionally."

"My dad worked security at the Canal," Annamaria jumped in, sensing he was reaching his

186

limit. She hadn't talked about her family for years either – since she'd left Panama. "And my mom stayed home with my little brothers. We weren't poor by Panamanian standards, but we didn't have much. I shared a room with my two little brothers, and we'd converted our living room into a third bedroom for my grandmother.

"They all died in a massive earthquake when I was thirteen."

Ryan reached down for her hand and squeezed it gently.

"For a few days I was overwhelmed with guilt for not being with them when it hit. But then I was thrown into an overcrowded orphanage with a bunch of other new orphans, mostly younger and even more confused and heartbroken than I was, and surprisingly, I was ok.

"I had a purpose. Those kids loved me. They needed me. And I needed them." Her voice trailed off as if she were just realizing this for the first time.

"And that's when Bradford stepped in?" Ryan asked, reaching for a box of tissues.

She pulled out a few tissues and nodded her head with a polite smile, too choked up to continue speaking. Ryan sat down next to her on the bed and gently wrapped his arm around her just as her trembling shoulders slumped forward, and she buried her face in her hands.

When the sobs finally stopped, she raised her head and looked at Ryan with red, swollen eyes that were infinitely more endearing than any photo shoot she'd ever done. "Do you know why I got my reputation as a party girl?" she asked

"Uh, are the all the tabloid stories true?" Ryan asked cautiously.

"Yes," she answered flatly.

"Well..." Ryan started to squirm. His arm around her shoulder suddenly felt awkward, and he wasn't sure what to do with it.

"I asked, 'Do you know *why* I got my reputation?'" she repeated gritting her teeth, silently pleading with him – begging him to get her.

"I was trying to get pregnant!" she finally blurted out. "I wanted to have someone I knew I could trust in my life; someone whose love I never had to question; someone that I could love without worrying about what I might find out about them later on – or what they might find out about me.

"But I guess it wasn't meant to be."

She opened up the laptop cover and looked at the girl in the tabloid photo with equal parts shame and sympathy. "Whatever anyone has ever thought about me, I promise you I've thought worse. The alcohol is pretty much the only thing that makes it tolerable," she mused.

"Two days after Bradford left, I got those," she said, pointing to her sparsely covered chest on the computer screen.

"Wait!" Ryan exclaimed, jumping to his feet. "You got those *after* Bradford came to the orphanage?"

"Of course!" she gasped. "I was thirteen!"

"No, I mean *right* after?"

"Yeah."

"Do you know dates?" Ryan asked.

"I couldn't forget that day if I tried. It was exactly two weeks before I was adopted. But I don't even know which hospital I was in – somewhere in Panama City."

"If that was before you were adopted, then who paid for the surgery? And who gave consent?" Ryan asked, his mind whirring.

"I can only assume the headmaster at the orphanage did," Annamaria said, shaking her head disgustedly. "He was the one who met with Bradford; he must have made some deal with him. He sent me to the hospital alone – I'd never even been in a hospital before. No one told me what I was there for, and I woke up still all alone, with terrible pains in my chest and my stomach I'll never forget."

"Your stomach?" Ryan asked. That didn't make any sense.

"That's how they get the implants in without leaving any obvious scars. I've got one right here," she said lifting her shirt a few inches to reveal a tiny scar just inside her belly button. "And two right here," she added, flipping her waistband down to reveal two more tiny scars, one on each side."

Ryan's face went white as a sheet. "That's not how they put implants in," he whispered.

"Maybe not in the U.S., but I woke up with those three scars and these," she said cupping her augmented breasts, "at the same time."

"Annamaria, I'm so sorry," Ryan said softly. "But I think I know why you've never gotten pregnant."

CHAPTER 10

"You ok?" Ryan asked after a full minute of silence.

"No," Annamaria answered tersely, her heartache drowned under a roiling sea of anger.

"It was probably a tubal ligation," Ryan whispered, proceeding with extreme caution. "Those can usually..."

"You said someone contacted me on your behalf," Annamaria said, her eyes ablaze. "When we were walking outside. You said it wasn't your idea to contact me. Whose was it?" she demanded.

Given the opportunity to drag Dillon into this, Ryan didn't hesitate. "It was this geeky computer guy at MIT. He hacked into Avillage's system and got the names and contact info of all the orphans. He's actually one of us."

"Does he know anything more about me?"

"I'd guess he probably does, but he's pretty tight with it. I'm not sure why."

"How far is MIT from here?" Annamaria asked, her speech still pressured.

"Mile and a half?" Ryan guessed.

"Let's go!" she said, reaching for her hat and glasses.

~~~

Dillon's whole body jerked, startled by the abrupt banging on his door.

Trying to make as little noise as possible, he tiptoed over to the door and peeked into the peephole. Nothing but black. Whoever was out in the hall must've been covering it up. "Who is it?" he asked with a low but self-conscious, cracking voice that just screamed computer nerd.

"Open the door," Ryan demanded, continuing to bang away.

Dillon timidly unlocked the door and cracked it a few inches to find Ryan standing in the hallway with an angry yet disconcertingly satisfied look.

"I tried to call you..." Dillon stammered.

"Hmm, that's weird. Because I had my walkie-talkie on me all day yesterday and today, and I never heard a thing." Ryan stared him down, inching progressively closer to the doorway.

"Oh. I was must've been on the wrong channel." He was pretty sure Ryan would never resort to physical violence, but the shred of doubt that remained was enough to shoot his heart rate into the 130s.

Ryan gave him one more glare and then brusquely shoved the door wide open, to reveal a still seething Annamaria standing to his right.

Dillon staggered back a few steps, his eyes like saucers, suddenly feeling light-headed. Annamaria's face, meanwhile, visibly sank, as if Ryan had just exposed Oz from behind the green curtain. *This* was their source? He was about five-four, skinnier than Annamaria, and didn't look a day over fourteen.

Dillon held his gaze on Annamaria just long enough to register her first impression before his eyes darted sheepishly down toward the floor. A deep blush replaced the usual pallor of his cheeks – yet another face-to-face encounter he'd be forced to start in a deep hole. *Always the same reaction!* It seemed to hurt more each time.

Ryan walked in behind Annamaria and closed the door. "Can we talk here?" he asked, more to appease Dillon than out of any concern of his own. Dillon had been making great money for himself and his shareholders with his steady release of apps for five years now. No one in their right mind would have continued to surveil him that long without coming up with anything.

Dillon reached over and turned up the grinding, manic-depressive music pouring through his computer speakers. "Yeah, we can talk now," he said nervously, just audible above the music.

"Do you know anything about me or am I just pissing away time here?" Annamaria hissed with the tone of a queen addressing one of her subjects, unable to get over the fact that she was relying on what appeared to be a middle school nerd.

"Yes I know something, and yes, you're wasting your time here," Dillon sneered, shaking his head in disgust.

"Look," Annamaria shot back, her accent picking up. "If you think *I* need *you*, you are sorely mistaken, my little friend. All I need is a doctor to confirm what happened to me, and I'll be on the front page of every paper in the country tomorrow."

"What *happened* to you?" Dillon asked, with no idea what she was talking about.

She folded her waistband down, as Dillon stared at the small scars, equally embarrassed by their location and confused about their significance.

"Oh my God! You didn't even know about it?" Annamaria sighed, rolling her eyes and turning for the door.

"I think Annamaria had a tubal ligation," Ryan muttered quietly to Dillon, getting nothing but a blank look in return. "Tubes tied."

"Whoa!" Dillon gasped, finally clued in. "Wait! Don't go. We need to talk."

"Annamaria, I think you should stay," Ryan said softly. "You came all the way from New York for this."

She squeezed her eyes shut, trying to force herself into a rational decision, when the only thing she wanted to do was run out of the room and never look back.

"Two things I want you to think about," Ryan said. "And I'm not trying to cause you any more pain. One: there were other poor, orphaned teenage girls surreptitiously sterilized after the Panama disaster. I read a New York Times piece on it a couple of years ago. It's happened in other developing countries after devastating natural disasters too. It was a terrible thing that happened to you, but it didn't happen only to you. It might be harder than you think to pin that on Avillage, and I'm sure if they're at the bottom of this, they'd be well aware of that.

"Two: Dillon does know what he's doing. Yes, he's a pain in the ass to work with, but you can't question his commitment. He's been as angry as you are right now for five straight years."

Dillon didn't exactly take it as a compliment, but he also couldn't protest what was a pretty accurate characterization.

Annamaria's face relaxed slightly, as she let out a long sigh and slowly sat down on the corner of Dillon's bed.

"Here's what I've got," Dillon said, snuggling up to his computer. "Your ticker symbol is BUTY, which I'm sure you already knew, and your chairman is Aaron Bradford. He's also the chairman of one of the Yankees' top pitching prospects (also from Panama,) who he discovered on the same trip he met you. The only other kid of note he's been chairman for was J'Quarius Jones, who, unfortunately, is dead.

"Prior to your going public, a partial ownership gift of 1.5% was transferred to a Carlos Villanueva..."

"I knew it!" Annamaria shouted, slamming her fist into the mattress.

"What? Who's Carlos Villanueva?" Ryan asked.

"The headmaster at my orphanage," she said, her lower lip quivering. "He sold me like a slave."

"And he's been making a *lot* of money off of you," Dillon pointed out, trying to fan the flames.

"Maybe," Ryan said. "You were adopted *after* Avillage started offering a 1.5% ownership

194

stake to anyone who referred an orphan that went on to be successfully adopted. What he got would've been standard."

"Still, he referred you, didn't he?" Dillon said, scowling at Ryan. "So when was your... uh... procedure done?"

"Fourteen days before I was adopted," she said, biting down on the inside of her lower lip.

"So 12 days before her IPO," Ryan added.

Dillon was typing and clicking and scrolling maniacally. "Hmm," he said. "It doesn't look like there's any paper trail of any meeting in Panama at all around that time. Bradford's travel plans were well documented, but he either doesn't use computers or he covers his tracks so well that he leaves absolutely no record of what he's been up to."

"Well, he definitely wasn't in Panama at the time of your surgery because that was the day J'Quarius died," Ryan said, putting the dates together in his head.

"Who's J'Quarius again?" Annamaria asked.

"He was another orphan chaired by Bradford," Ryan said. "A lot of people thought he had the potential to be one of the greatest basketball players of all time, but he died just before he turned eighteen of a heart condition, which either was or should have been diagnosed a week beforehand, when he'd collapsed on the court during a game.

"After he died, Bradford sued the University of Chicago Children's Hospital, where he'd initially been treated, for failing to disclose the risks of the heart condition that had caused his death. The hospital ended up settling out of court."

"The amount was never disclosed!" Dillon chimed in.

"Dillon thinks it was all a PR stunt on Bradford's part, and he might be right, but the day the court settlement was announced, Bradford did donate a million bucks in J'Quarius Jones's name to a foundation that identifies and treats kids with the same kind of heart condition he had."

"Get your head out of your ass!" Dillon blurted out. "That was his own money! He talked to the doctors the day J'Quarius passed out the first time. He got the whole story. And then he sat there in the stands with those rich Russian team owners and just watched him die.

"Bradford's not an idiot. You know he had that kid's life insured for more than a million dollars." Then he softened his tone as he turned to Annamaria. "J'Quarius's parents never forgave him. They actually tried to block the piece of shit from being allowed to use J'Quarius's name for the foundation. They were very vocal."

"So how did Bradford get out of that?" Annamaria asked.

"Oh, he was very apologetic publicly. Said he couldn't even imagine what the adoptive parents were going through," Dillon said disgustedly. "Then he kept bringing up that the one thing he could take solace in was that at least he'd been instrumental in picking them as the perfect parents for J'Quarius. The media bought it hook, line and sinker. He's a scumbag. Probably the worst guy in the whole company."

"But he's not your chairman?" Dillon was kind of growing on her.

"Nope. Bradford's second in command at Avillage. My chairman's some mid-level yes-man who's too stupid to be sinister. If he never showed up for work again, it'd probably take weeks for someone to notice."

"What about you?" she asked Ryan.

"Him?" Dillon jumped in. "No, no. Ryan's chairman is the head honcho. None other than James Prescott himself – the founder and CEO of Avillage. Prescott gets shares in all of us, but he's only the chairman for one," he said pointing a sideways thumb at Ryan. "And he's been buying every time the golden boy's price dips."

"Really? What's he like?" she asked Ryan hesitantly.

"I don't know. He's not that bad," Ryan shrugged. "He was a little tough on certain things. Probably a little too intent on making sure I learned that life isn't fair, but nothing compared to what happened to you guys.

"I mean, he didn't let me participate in certain activities or go on certain field trips growing up. Things like that. And the only college he let me to apply to was Harvard. But my life's pretty good.

"He's obviously not as benevolent as he claims to be, but he did set me up with good parents, I am getting a Harvard degree, and I probably *am* better off now than I would've been if

Avillage hadn't adopt me out of that orphanage. It's just..."

"When are you going to wake up?" Dillon butted in, physically sickened by what he'd just heard.

"When are you?" Ryan shot back. "This is our life! Like it or not. Laws were changed – well before any of us were ever orphans. And you've got no *proof* of anything. You have suspicion built on suspicion that only leads to more suspicion. You hand-pick what information you choose to dole out, and it *always* supports your theories. Then you keep everything else hidden. Sorry, but I personally am not that bad off. She needs to hear the whole story."

"Annamaria was sterilized! My dad was put away for life for what should have been a few years at most! J'Quarius Jones is dead! Your parents were murdered!" Dillon exclaimed, his voice rising as he spoke.

"That's enough," Ryan warned, his glare squarely back on Dillon.

But this time Dillon wasn't backing down. "And you're padding the bank accounts of the people who murdered them!"

"My parents were killed in a head-on collision. I saw it," Ryan insisted through gritted teeth.

Dillon cackled condescendingly. "A *fatal* car accident involving *both* of your parents exactly three months before the opening of Avillage? They were *murdered!*"

"Enough!" Ryan shouted, leaning in inches from Dillon's face. Dillon matched his stare for a few seconds, and then tilted his head slightly, raising his eyebrows, tacitly questioning whose side Ryan was on.

Ryan took a couple of deep, slow breaths to collect himself and then turned toward Annamaria. "You see what I mean?

"I've gotta get out of here. Do you want to come with me?"

"Actually," Annamaria waffled, holding her gaze to the floor, "I think I'm gonna stay here a little while longer."

"Oh. Yeah, no problem," Ryan said reassuringly. "Don't worry about it. You've got my number if you want to talk again. Just... don't do anything rash."

"But don't do nothing," Dillon added, looking directly at Ryan.

Ryan took one more sharp glance at Dillon, shook his head and started out the door, trying not to be offended that Annamaria had chosen to stay with Dillon. He did understand Dillon's emotional appeal – especially in the short-term.

Feeling the need to clear his head and organize his thoughts, he headed west toward the Charles River to take the scenic route home.

The brilliant shades of red from the morning's sunrise had been swallowed up by a monotonous gray that blanketed the sky with a single drab tone, neither portending a storm nor showing any sign of clearing. Perfect weather for introspection.

His dysfunctional team had increased in number by fifty percent, but they still didn't have a viable face for their cause. He could acknowledge that Dillon genuinely loved his father, but Dillon was driven primarily by revenge and was in no way, shape or form a sympathetic figure. His dad was a felon, implicated in terror – and found guilty. No one would care *why* he was caught or how that had affected his son.

Ryan himself had started out a tragic figure, having lost both parents at such a young age, but it was hard to feel too sorry for him ten years down the road, nearing graduation from Harvard at seventeen with no debt and with a stable, happy homelife. To an outside observer, he appeared to be the prototypical Avillage success story – which had really been the only point he was planning to make before Dillon started in on his parents' death.

Annamaria was beautiful, clearly preyed upon by a greedy corporation, and had a potentially heart-wrenching story, but she was so overexposed as a soulless socialite in the basest forms of media that most of the country probably would have been delighted to hear she wouldn't be able to procreate.

J'Quarius, even in death, still seemed to be their best hope, Ryan thought. He'd tried reaching out to Hansford and Arlene Washington – and to Leonard Weinstien – after the game, but he'd never heard anything back. Maybe it had been too soon. *Probably time to revisit that,* he thought.

Dillon was right about one thing – Avillage was surrounded by smoke. But Annamaria's scars were the first time he'd actually seen fire. It was time he personally started doing a little digging.

He quickened his pace to a jog as a light mist began to fall. A band of rapidly-rising black clouds on the horizon announced that the sky had finally committed. A storm was coming, and from the looks of it, he wouldn't have much time to get home before it hit.

~~~

"What!" Aaron Bradford finally shouted after the third knock on his door. With the clock nearing midnight, he should have had the office to himself.

"Sorry, sir" Corbett Hermanson said, leaning in close to the door. "But I found something you may be interested in."

"Can't it wait until tomorrow?" Bradford moaned.

"It's up to you, sir, but I thought it was worth checking with you tonight."

Tall and thin with close-cropped fire-red hair and perpetually tired eyes, Corbett wore the same pale blue short-sleeve Oxford shirt, black pants and nondescript black work shoes everyday, no matter the season. He was the first head of IT at Avillage that Bradford had actually approved of – someone as meticulous and paranoid as he was – and as part of his standard security protocol, he routinely monitored a few dozen randomly-chosen files a week for activity, always at different times on different days.

"Fine," Bradford sighed. "Give me a second."

Three minutes passed before Bradford gave Corbett the ok to come in.

"Will there be anything else Mr. Bradford?" his twenty-six-year-old assistant asked right on cue as the door opened, sitting conspicuously formally in an armchair several feet from her boss, cradling a completely blank notepad.

"No, Ms. Williams. That will be all. Good night," Bradford intoned robotically.

"Good night," the assistant whispered as she hurried out of the room, keeping her head down to avoid making eye contact with the IT manager.

"Now *what* is it, Corbett?" Bradford huffed.

"Well sir, it's just that I didn't think that you'd been traveling recently, have you?"

"You've seen me here every day this week! What do you think? Get to the point," Bradford demanded, wishing he'd continued to ignore the knocking at his door.

"I actually didn't think you had been traveling, which is why I found it odd that a few of your files had been accessed by an IP address in Indianapolis earlier today."

"What?" Bradford gasped, his attention now undivided. "Which files?"

"Some of the old J files and a some of the BUTY ones off the intranet. My guess is that whoever this is probably *isn't* in Indiana but is disguising their IP address. And of course I'll look into it further with your permission. You wouldn't have shared any of your passwords with anyone by chance, would you have?" Corbett asked.

"No!" Bradford shot back, insulted at the suggestion. "Now listen. I want you to look into this and find out who's been snooping around, and I want you to report back directly to me! Do you understand?"

"Yes sir. Of course, sir. I'll start immediately. In the meantime, I'd strongly suggest that you change all of your passwords."

"I'll keep my passwords, thank you," Bradford said, wondering just who in the hell Corbett thought he was "strongly suggesting" anything to his boss's boss's boss. "I've got nothing to hide on our intranet – I've never trusted it – and I don't want this low-life hacker to know we're on to him until we're ready to nail him. Got it?"

"Yes sir," Corbett said, backing out of Bradford's office.

~~~

Ryan stared blankly out the window waiting for his laptop to finish booting up, as the persistent pattering of the steady rainfall on the roof filled his dimly-lit top floor dorm room with a hypnotic white noise that beckoned him back to the night of his parents' death. He consciously shook it off; now wasn't the time.

A brief scan of his email's inbox revealed the typical swath of junk – offshore pharmacies, lurid invitations to meet singles in the Boston area, and plenty of the popular "(no subject)" emails from hacked accounts he hadn't yet removed from his contact list.

But as he scrolled down the page, selecting messages to mark as spam, something jumped out at him. One of the junk mails with the "(no subject)" subject line had been sent by jared.ralston@ccf.org, J.R.'s old email account from his time at the Cleveland Clinic.

Ryan still used the same account that had been opened for him at age seven, and J.R. had been his first contact. But he hadn't heard anything from him in years, and J.R.'s Cleveland Clinic account should've been deactivated a decade ago. Was it possible he was back there? Ryan knew he wasn't in Boston any more. A search for Dr. Ralston on The Cleveland Clinic's website returned no matches.

Suddenly a light bulb went off in Ryan's head. He went right back to his email and fired off a message to michelle.tyler@ccf.org, which he inferred from J.R.'s address would've been his mother's old email address. No sooner than the message had been sent did he receive an "undeliverable message" reply in his inbox.

For good measure he then sent another email to ryan.tyler@ccf.org. This time nothing returned. After a quick reload of the page, still nothing. With his heart now racing, he closed his browser and reopened it.

Hovering his cursor over the bookmark to his email, he closed his eyes and hesitantly clicked the left mouse button. After a long, slow, deep breath, he reopened his eyes. Once again there was only one return message – from his mom's old account.

He immediately grabbed his walkie-talkie and began shouting for Dillon to come in.

While he waited, he searched the Cleveland Clinic website for a Dr. Ryan Tyler, on the off chance someone with the same name now worked there. No match.

"What do you want?" Dillon eventually groaned, bracing for another argument.

"I might have found something," Ryan started, ignoring Dillon's sour tone. "I was gonna try emailing Leonard Weinstien again about what he knew about J'Quarius Jones's biological father when..."

"Wait," Dillon interrupted. "Who's Leonard Weinstien?"

"The guy who was holding the poster at the basketball game in Cleveland."

"What? What poster? You never told me about that."

"Yes I did. I told you about it a couple of days after the game," Ryan said confidently.

"You did not!" Dillon insisted.

"Dillon. Really? Come on. You know how these disagreements go."

"You think you're *always* right," Dillon scoffed.

"The conversation took place at around 9:30 PM, two nights after the game, right before you left Cleveland. You couldn't talk long because your dad..."

"Guardian!" Dillon snapped.

"Fine, your *guardian* was only going to be out of the hotel room for a few minutes. I was wearing a Browns T-shirt that day that my mom made me change because it had a stain on the left sleeve from the last time I'd worn it. I had Apple Jacks for breakfast that morning, a chili dog for lunch, and spaghetti for dinner. The Indians played the Angels that day and won 6-4 with a three-run ninth inning comeback. BP announced disappointing earnings before the market opened that morning and ended up falling 2.4%."

Dillon was silent on the other end. He hated when Ryan did this.

"Even back then I knew you didn't know what I was talking about when I brought up the guy with the poster, but you're so bull-headed, you had to act like you did," Ryan said.

"Well," Dillon hedged, knowing full well he was wrong but not about to admit it. "Whatever the case, I don't recall your ever telling me. Just get on with it, and tell me who he is."

"He was a lawyer in Newark from what I could find. He brought a sign to the game with an old picture of a guy that looked a lot like J'Quarius that he claimed was his dad. The sign read 'Your father loved you,' and it had Weinstien's contact info on it. But that's not why I called you."

"Well did you contact him?" Dillon asked frantically, starting to hyperventilate.

"Yeah, yeah. A long time ago. I never heard anything back, so I gave up. I'm gonna try again. But there's something else! I got a spam email from Jared Ralston's Cleveland Clinic account tonight!" Ryan said excitedly.

There was a long silence.

"And?" Dillon finally said, crashing down from his previous high.

"That means his account is still active! I emailed my mom's account and it was returned undeliverable, but the message I sent to my dad's old account never came back! It must be an oversight by the cardiology department.

"If you can hack into those accounts, we might be able to find out how J.R. got his shares without buying them and how he ended up on my board of directors."

"Hmm." Dillon paused. A reluctant smile was growing on his face. He was actually impressed. "I can't imagine it would be very hard. I've got a major project due in a couple of days, but I should definitely be able to get the passwords by the weekend. Give me the addresses."

"One more thing before I give you the addresses," Ryan said solemnly. "You can do whatever you want with J.R.'s email, but promise me you won't look through my dad's emails without my permission. I feel guilty enough looking through them myself."

"Yeah, sure," Dillon said, understanding fully. "No problem."

CHAPTER 11

"I got 'em!" Dillon's voice echoed off the walls of Ryan's previously silent dorm room at two o'clock Friday morning.

Ryan reached a clumsy hand up over his head and groggily patted down his desktop, eventually knocking the walkie-talkie off onto the floor with a jarring crash.

"What?" Ryan mumbled, finally having seized control of his walkie-talkie.

"I got the passwords! Get a pen!"

"I don't need one," Ryan yawned.

"Are you sure? Come on, you don't even sound awake."

"I'm sure," Ryan intoned lifelessly. "I'm pumped. Trust me. It's just late. Or early. Whatever."

"Okay. Jared Ralston's password is CCFpassWord14. No spaces. C, C, F and W are caps. And your dad's is RyanJr0316. The R and J are caps."

"Yep, thanks. Good night."

"Did you get 'em? When are you going to go through the accounts?" Dillon pleaded, hopped up on his third energy drink of the night.

"I got 'em. I'll look at 'em in the morning. Good night. Signing off," Ryan said, turning his walkie-talkie off and closing his eyes, futilely trying to will himself back to sleep.

Five minutes passed. Then ten. Then twenty. He was kidding himself if he thought he was going to be able to get back to sleep. Reluctantly, after half an hour of tossing and turning, he swung his legs off the side of his bed, rubbed his eyes and let out one last yawn, before tugging down on the pull chain of his desk lamp.

Mail.ccf.org was his first guess for the Cleveland Clinic email server, which proved to be correct. Very carefully he typed in the username ryan.tyler followed by the password that Dillon had provided him. And, with surprisingly little effort, he was in.

A bold black number at the top left of the screen indicated his dad's account had 7,734 unread emails, most of which appeared to be system-wide email blasts. For the next 30 minutes Ryan mundanely rolled his mouse back and forth between "Select All" and "Delete," eliminating 25 messages with each cycle, quickly scanning each of the subject lines as he went. The only thing that really stuck out at first glance was that recruiters were still contacting his dad with job offers 10 years after his death.

As the received dates of the emails continued to rewind, an uneasy anticipation began to build. These were private communications between adults. The only perspective from which he'd ever known his parents was that of an innocent child. They were still infallible in his mind, and he really didn't want that to change.

A sinking in his chest met a rising from his stomach as he deleted what would probably amount to the final batch of 25 junk messages, received in the first few days after his parents were gone.

As the next page loaded with another set of 25 emails, his eyes were drawn to the bottom of the screen, where for the first time previously-read messages stood out beneath the bold-type unread ones. There was something powerfully sentimental, almost tangible, about the realization that his dad had sat before a computer somewhere ten years earlier and had clicked on these same messages. The most recent one, received just hours before his parents' death, was from his mom with the subject line, "re: Li'l Ryan's Bday".

With a lump developing in his throat, he clicked on the message. His mom had written: "That's something dads should talk to their sons about ;)" *Hmm.* Didn't make sense without context.

Below the end of the message he found the option to "show quoted text," which he clicked on to reveal the entire exchange in reverse chronological order. She had been responding to his dad's message: "I'm sure he'll get it. I like the idea, but you better be prepared to have a discussion about the birds and bees. You know how his mind works. He'll want to know how that baby got in there."

Ryan's palms grew sweaty as he began to infer what was coming next. Not entirely sure he wanted to continue, but certain he couldn't stop, he scrolled to the end.

The thread had started with his mother's message, "I'm already showing big-time. Sweaters only get so baggy, and it's going to be warming up soon. I think tonight would be the perfect time to tell Ryan. I wrapped up a T-shirt for him in one of his presents that says 'Big Brother' on it. A birthday surprise! You think he'll get it?"

Having trouble taking in a deep breath, he rose to a stand and slowly backed away from his computer. It wasn't his nature to ask fate "Why?" or to dwell on whether or not something was "fair." But this was utterly overwhelming – a knife wound on top of an old scar that had never sufficiently healed.

~~~

Corbett Hermanson peered around the edge of Bradford's half-open door and knocked gently on the frame. Bradford was sitting at his desk, leafing through a thick binder.

He had to have heard the knock, Corbett thought, peeking in, but his attention to the material in the binder remained unbroken.

Now regretting his timid first knock, Corbett anxiously debated whether he should knock again, which could be perceived as rude, or try something else to get Bradford's attention. Ultimately he decided to clear his throat loudly, while standing more prominently in the doorway.

Still, Bradford kept his nose buried in the files in front of him.

Finally, Corbett knocked more confidently on the door itself.

"What!" Bradford demanded. "If you've got something to say, just say it!"

"Sorry, sir. Wasn't sure you heard me," Corbett said, with a nervous chuckle.

"Do you think I'm deaf and blind?" Bradford sneered. "Just get on with it already."

"Well sir, I'm sure you recall our conversation a few days back about the potential unauthorized user in our system? It turns out..."

"Close the door!" Bradford whispered emphatically, waving his arms wildly for Corbett to stop talking and come all the way into his office.

"Sorry, sir," Corbett said, his cheeks glowing an orange-red hue to match his hair. After self-consciously closing the door behind him, he picked up where he'd left off. "It turns out, he's quite good at keeping himself hidden. I was right about his not being in Indiana, but behind that location, his IP address bounces around all over the world from India to Singapore to Brazil to several U.S. cities – all places I believe you've traveled. Had you originally planned to be in Indiana last week?"

"No," Bradford said dismissively, before pausing for a moment. "But my secretary had put it on my calendar. He must be basing his locations on where he thinks I'll be!"

"Tracking down his true location, unfortunately, may prove to be beyond my expertise. If we got the authorities involved..."

"We're not getting authorities involved. This is what we pay *you* for," Bradford barked.

"Well I do have another idea," Corbett said, taking a step closer to Bradford's desk and lowering his voice. "We could set a trap."

Now he was speaking Bradford's language.

"I've set up a half dozen dummy accounts on our corporate email server," Corbett said, handing Bradford a slip of paper with several handwritten lines. "Some time today I would ask you to send an email to those accounts referencing an urgent confidential issue with former ticker symbol J. Along with the message, I'd like you to attach the file that I've listed below the email addresses on that piece of paper.

"He's been coming and going as he pleases anywhere he wants in our system for the past three to four years as far as I can tell, so I'm counting on the assumption he's let his guard down a little by now.

"I've attached a tiny tracer virus to that file I've written down for you," Corbett said, motioning to the scrap of paper in Bradford's right hand. "I'm pretty sure his computer will detect and destroy it fairly quickly. But if I'm online at the time he downloads it, I should have just enough time to pinpoint his location."

"I like it," Bradford beamed, nodding his head approvingly. "I'll get the email out today."

"Make it juicy, but not so much that it's suspicious," Corbett added, smiling along with his boss.

Bradford's expression quickly soured at the suggestion. "I don't need your 'expert' tips,

Corbett. Trust me, I know how to play this game better than you. Now, get back to work."

~~~

As the sun slowly inched above the Cambridge horizon, casting long streaks of blinding light westward down the Charles River, Ryan found himself on the south end of campus, gazing up at the Eliot House clock tower, its hands transposed on top of one another, pointing straight down to six-thirty.

Having spent the wee hours of the morning wandering aimlessly around the mostly empty campus, oblivious to the world around him, he was suddenly reminded that his last final of the semester was coming up in an hour and a half. And maybe that wasn't such a bad thing. At least he'd be able to focus on something else for an hour or so.

But as it turned out, he wouldn't find the distraction he was looking for in the classroom. A mere twenty minutes after taking his seat, he returned the pen he'd borrowed from the professor along with his completed answer sheet from a test that unfortunately hadn't been challenging enough to give his tormented mind any reprieve. He exited the lecture hall with the same hollow feeling that he'd come in with. If anything, it had only intensified.

The previously peaceful campus was now bustling with sleep-deprived, stressed-out students hurrying off to take final exams or squeeze in one last cram session.   Desperate to be alone, he reluctantly headed back to his dorm.

A wave of nausea hit him as he unlocked his door, knowing his computer would be staring him in the face right when he walked in.

Mercifully, the email account had timed out, so he didn't have to relive the experience in its entirety. He nudged the laptop closed and collapsed onto his bed, mentally and physically exhausted from traipsing around campus all morning, and he was dead asleep before he even hit the mattress.

Instantaneously he was transported back to the double doors of his day care center. It had been a long time. As was always the case, he was standing next to his teacher, waiting for his parents to arrive, but this time there was no rain.

A flood of sunshine from the cloudless sky amplified the reds, blues and yellows of the slides and swings in the fenced-in playground off to the side of the front parking lot. Across the street, he could see the bright green soccer field and baseball diamond where he and his friends would spend their afternoons when the weather allowed.

To his left, the narrow two-lane drive in front of the facility stretched past a row of one and two-story concrete office buildings and on toward the entrance of the office park where the road opened up into a busier four-lane highway.

Off to his right, repeated glimmers of reflected sunlight were bouncing off the back of a furiously swaying stop sign from the corner opposite the day care center straight into his eyes. The sign was in continuous chaotic motion, as though the thin pole that supported it may snap at any second. But curiously there wasn't so much as a ripple in the grass around it. And the leaves in the tree next to it were perfectly still.

Then out of nowhere the sky suddenly blackened, and a driving rain began to fall, as his gaze was involuntarily pulled back to his left, where he saw headlights approaching. Emotionally incapable of watching what he knew was coming next, he tried to look away, but he couldn't. He knew he had to be dreaming, but he couldn't manage to snap himself out of it.

Just then, a soft but completely out-of-place chime broke his concentration, disintegrating the dream world, as it dawned on him that it was his phone alerting him to a new email.

"Stop sign," he whispered to himself as he opened his eyes.

Looking over at the clock, he was amazed to find that he'd been asleep for over an hour; it had felt like less than a minute.

There was a four-way stop in front of the day care center. And the day care center was off the main road in an office park that had no through streets. His whole life, he'd been trying to suppress the specifics of that day, not dissect them.

Whoever had hit his parents head on would've had to have floored it from the end of a cul de sac, run through a stop sign, and swerved (or stayed) in the wrong lane. If that driver hadn't also died in the crash, which was likely, he would have had to have been charged with a crime. Either way, there had to be police records documenting what happened.

Would he have any right to them as his parents' only survivor? And if he did, would he be able to access them as a minor?

As he pondered these questions, he grabbed his phone to see who had sent him the well-timed email. His inbox contained only one new message: a reply from Leonard Weinstien.

"Thank you for contacting me," the email read. "I'm sorry I won't be able to tell you much via email. Previous experience has left me distrusting of computers. I would, however, be more than happy to meet with you face-to-face. I'm retired with no one depending on me and (sadly) not much to do. So I'd be quite flexible as to where we could meet. – Leonard."

~~~

Corbett's head and eyelids drooped slowly downward in unison, nearly giving in to an overwhelming urge to sleep, before they snapped back up and started their same slow descent all over again. He had been parked in front of his terminal for 24 hours and counting, the most recent half-hour of which had been a constant struggle to maintain consciousness.

Well beyond any benefit that coffee could impart, he decided to stand up and pace for a few seconds, all the while keeping his bloodshot eyes fixed on his monitor. The hacker hadn't been in the system for 6 days, which was an unusually long

217

hiatus for him, and Bradford's juicy email had been dangling out there on the mail server since just before this marathon session had begun. With only one shot at this, he couldn't allow himself to fall asleep.

Just as he sat back down, considering whom he might be able to trust to watch over his monitor for an hour or so while he caught some desperately needed shut-eye, someone logged into Bradford's email. The IP address was from New York, but it wasn't one he recognized. This was it!

In a matter of seconds the tracer embedded in the email's corrupted attachment gave up the hacker's true IP address, which Corbett furiously scribbled down, and then, just as he'd predicted, it was gone – destroyed by the host computer.

At long last, he could finally let his guard down. He plodded along through thirty more minutes of inefficient work, which normally would've taken him ten, and narrowed the location of the hacker down to somewhere in the Massachusetts Institute of Technology. Finalizing his exact location would only be a matter of time. But, more pressingly, he needed a nap.

~~~

As the shot of adrenaline from the vivid recollection of his former day care center's surroundings wore off, Ryan felt the hollowness that had pervaded his morning gradually creeping back in. And he had no interest in burying this like he had with his parents' deaths for so long.

He had good friends on campus he could talk to – loyal, insightful and trustworthy, but none of them had ever experienced anything even remotely similar to losing a parent, much less a whole family. There were only two people he knew who could possibly relate to what he was going through. One was Dillon, who would probably be twistedly happy to hear about Ryan's lost little sibling so he could use it as more ammo against Avillage. The other was Annamaria.

Hit with a peculiar giddiness at having a legitimate excuse to call her, he reached for his phone. But as soon as he started to dial, his heart began palpitating and his palms began to sweat; self-doubt began to creep in. Did he really need to bother her with this? Where would he start? Why would she care? She hardly knew him.

By the time her name popped up on the display, he couldn't will his thumb down to the green phone icon on the screen to initiate the call.

It would probably be more productive to look a little further into the emails, he decided.

After a few deep breaths, he opened his laptop back up and logged back in as his dad. The junk-to-personal email ratio remained fairly high, as he continued to sift through the messages. In a way he was fortunate his dad hadn't deleted much, but it did make for more work for him.

He decided to scroll back a full year, cleaning up the junk as he went, so he could go through the messages quickly and chronologically.

A pattern began to emerge as he continued back through the year. Relatively few of the more recent emails from J.R. had a curved arrow next to them, indicating a reply, while the farther back he went, the more likely the messages were to be marked with an arrow. Somewhat surprisingly though the frequency of the incoming emails seemed to have stayed relatively constant.

Eventually, he made his way back to the day of his sixth birthday, a full year before his parents had died, and then reversed course, reading through each message in its entirety. While Ryan's dad had sent a fairly high volume of emails to J.R., J.R. seemed to be the originator of every single thread.

One email to Ryan's mom contained the sarcastic subject line "My 'best friend'" and was loaded with complaints about J.R.'s never leaving him alone and his paranoia that they wouldn't end up at the same hospital after fellowship. At the end of the message he wistfully posed the question, "how do you break up with a friend?" To which his wife had responded, "You move. Don't worry. We'll get those jobs in Boston."

On he read, as invitations from J.R. to housestaff get-togethers and pharmaceutical-sponsored dinners were repeatedly declined or ignored altogether.

At the end of January there was an email from Massachusetts General Hospital offering Ryan's dad a spot on the faculty. "I knew it!" Ryan whispered aloud, pumping his fist with a conflicting sense of pride and sorrow at the sight of it. His parents had never told him. Prescott had announced that his dad had accepted a job at Harvard the day

AVEX had opened, Ryan recalled, but he had never known if that was really true until now.

His dad had forwarded it on to his mom with the subject line, "Got it!" The body of the email started, "I guess Little Ryan's going to have to go to a new school next year (and J.R.'s going to have to find a new best friend.)"

A few days later J.R. had sent a message to Ryan Sr., telling him that he still hadn't heard anything back from Harvard, wondering if Ryan Sr. had heard anything, to which Ryan's dad replied, "I got an offer. I'm thinking about taking it. Michelle's still waiting to hear about the job at Boston Children's. Good luck. Would suck to lose my partner in crime."

J.R. didn't send another correspondence for the next week. His next message had the subject "Jobs" and read, "I've been thinking about it, and I really think we should just stay here. I talked to Dr. Easterbrook. He definitely wants us stay. Positions are there if we want them. Think about it." There was no reply.

A slew of email invitations to get together to study followed, mostly rejected but with just enough accepted, so as not to seem rude.

In early March a fairly long thread began with the subject "Location." It started with an email from J.R. to Ryan Sr.: "Hey Ryan, can you turn the 'share location' feature on your phone on, so we can meet up if we're in the same area. I turned mine on."

Ryan Sr. then forwarded it on to Michelle with the addendum "UGH!" The following day, he replied to J.R. that he didn't want everyone knowing where he was all the time, claiming he was worried that he'd probably be tracked down by some crazy patient.

Later that day Ryan's mom had responded, "Do what you want, but it'll probably only be a problem until late June. I got the job at Boston Children's! We're going to Boston! (and J.R.'s not!)"

Meanwhile J.R. was left pleading with Ryan Sr., "You can choose who you want to see it. You could just allow me and Michelle."

Days passed as Ryan's dad tried to kill the issue with a series of claims that showing his location would max out his data usage on his wireless plan, that his phone didn't support the function, and then finally that he just couldn't figure out how to turn the feature on. Each time, J.R. replied with detailed solutions to the "problems," some of which involved a considerable time investment on his part.

Finally at the end of the thread, six days before he died, Ryan Sr. appeared to have caved. "I got it working," he wrote. "My location is no longer a mystery."

The final email chain from J.R. was dated March 15th, the day before the crash. "Hey Ryan, last chance to stay in Cleveland! Dr. Easterbrook is going to finalize those two faculty slots by the end of the week. We could own this town for the next 30 years..."

"Would be awesome," read the reply, "but we're headed to Boston. It's finalized at this point. You'll have to come visit once we get moved in."

"That's a shame," J.R. wrote back. "I'll miss you. You have been a great friend."

Curious that he'd use the present perfect tense, "have been a great friend" – instead of the simple present "are a great friend," Ryan thought. No, not curious. Suspicious.

~~~

A steadily intensifying tingling sensation in his lower legs gradually woke Corbett from a sound sleep. Still sitting upright in his office chair, he rolled his ankles back and forth and then stomped his numb feet on the ground, trying to beat the sensation back into them. His windowless interior office was completely black, providing no clue as to what time of day it was or how long he'd been asleep.

Still somewhat disoriented, he fumbled around his desktop eventually bumping into his mouse, which woke his monitor from sleep mode and illuminated the room. It had only been two hours. But he had a new email from Bradford marked urgent with a file attached.

"You need to address this now!" the message read. Corbett could almost hear Bradford yelling it at him.

He clicked on the attachment to open it and then rotely clicked away the annoying warning message that popped up cautioning him to download attachments only from trusted sources. Just as he did, he was struck with an intense panic – a split second too late. He'd already released the mouse button. The file was downloaded.

A text file opened: "Turnabout is fair play. I would suggest you give up this line of investigation you're pursuing. I'm not working alone. You're in <u>way</u> over your head, and you seem to have just downloaded something that you won't know how to deal with. Bradford isn't going to be happy if he finds out. Of course this could all stop right here. It's up to you..."

It was probably a bluff. But he had no other option than to leave the decision on how to proceed to Bradford.

Was it too much to ask for just one thing to go right? Now instead of being praised for his diligence, once again he was going to get reamed. With a pit in his stomach, he trudged over to Bradford's office.

His knuckles hesitated a few inches from Bradford's door, his eyes closed and his head hanging down almost to his chest as he weighed how he should break the news.

"What are you doing?" Bradford asked loudly, walking up behind him.

Corbett jumped. "Uh, I was just coming over to discuss something with you," he said, unshaven and looking generally disheveled from spending the better part of two days in his office.

"You look like hell," Bradford noted, opening his door. "Come in. You've got five minutes. I have to get to a meeting with Mr.

Prescott." (Bradford was the only person in the company who addressed the CEO by his first name, but when referencing him to another employee, he always called him Mr. Prescott.)

"Oh. Well perhaps I should just come back when you have more time," Corbett sputtered.

"When I say I've got five minutes, that's a *lot* of my time to dedicate to you. Now get on with on it."

"Well, I've got good news and bad news. Mostly good actually..."

"You still haven't said anything! Spit it out! I'm perfectly capable of making a determination of whether news is good or bad."

"Yes, of course. In reference to that email you sent out with the corrupted attachment, well, it was downloaded, and I captured the IP address of the snoop in our system. So far I've narrowed his location down to the MIT campus. I should have his exact location, and hopefully his identity, by the end of the day today."

Bradford smiled as his eyes narrowed.

"Now, to get this information," Corbett continued with a tremulous voice, "I had to sit at my desk, monitoring my computer very closely for more than 24 hours straight with only brief breaks to run to the bathroom."

"Yeah, yeah," Bradford groaned, rolling his eyes. "We all have to work long hours sometimes."

"Well, my point is that I was exhausted. So after I got the IP address, I ended up falling asleep in my chair. Then when I woke up, I saw that I'd gotten an email from your email address about an urgent matter, so I opened the attachment on it, obviously thinking it was from you, and..."

"Damn it, Corbett!" Bradford erupted. "You fell into your own trap?"

"I know," Corbett sighed. "I was just waking up and I wasn't thinking, but now I am, and I don't want to dig the hole any deeper.

"I printed out the text file the hacker attached," Corbett said, handing Bradford a sheet of paper. "I couldn't detect anything suspicious on my machine or on the intranet. I ran a virus scan and didn't pick anything up. I think it's a bluff, but I wanted to leave the decision to you as to how I should proceed."

"Find him!" Bradford growled, crumpling the paper into a tight ball as he stormed out of his office.

~~~

"Ryan. Come in. I want to see you," Dillon called through his walkie-talkie, with his typical corny imitation of Alexander Graham Bell's first phrase transmitted by telephone. But there was an unusual urgency in his voice.

In no mood to talk to Dillon, Ryan almost ignored it. But sensing something wasn't quite right, he answered back with his typical "What?"

"Hey, Ryan. I might be in trouble. I downloaded a file from Bradford's email account that was sent out to six other Avillage employees, who I've since found out don't exist. The file had a tracer on it, and I think it probably gave up my identity.

"They set me up, so they're definitely aware that *someone's* been in their system, and I think there's a good chance that by now the IT security guy over there knows it's me."

Dillon sounded scared – or maybe just nervous – anyway, something outside his typical spectrum of emotions, which ranged from insulted to angry.

"What are you gonna do?" Ryan asked.

"I've got some ideas, but I'm not sure how much they know yet. Let's just say I could potentially be in a lot of trouble. I've spent all morning kind of re-evaluating my goals. Don't worry, I'm not planning on going down without a fight, and trust me, at least on some level I *will* get my revenge.

"Anyway, I have a bunch of Avillage information that only I know, and if I'm taken out of play, that information is gone. You're the closest thing I have to a confidant, so I'm going to share it *all* with you. Nothing picked over or edited this time. I probably should've done it a long time ago.

"I've transferred all my data onto an external hard drive, and I'm mailing it to your home address in Cleveland. I want you to read everything and then destroy the hard drive – really destroy it. Be paranoid for once in your life. Hack it up and dispose of the pieces in different locations. Your brain is essentially a secure hard drive that no one else can access."

"Yeah, sure," Ryan said. "I'll look out for it, but I think you're overreacting. When they find out you're one of theirs, you'll probably get off with a slap on the wrist."

"We'll see, but I doubt it. Oh, and don't waste your time with Jared Ralston's email. It was overrun with spam. All the old stuff's gone."

There were a few seconds of radio silence before Dillon added, "You've been a great friend."

~~~

"Sir?" Corbett said, walking right into Bradford's office. There would be no waiting anxiously outside the door with news this big. "I've got the hacker's identity. And he's one of ours."

"An employee?!"

"No. An orphan. Dillon Higley – ticker symbol DILN. He's a computer programmer and app developer. Actually been quite profitable."

"Who's his chairman?" Bradford demanded.

"Tom Erskine in orphan ID."

"Good. Never even heard of him," Bradford said, staring at his monitor as his index finger stroked the wheel of his mouse. "I don't have a single share. Prescott's got his standard 2%, but he hasn't been buying.

"Leave me his contact info, and I'll take it from here," Bradford said. "Do not tell *anyone* about this!"

"Yes sir."

"And Corbett?"

"Sir?"

"Nice work," Bradford managed, as much as it pained him to do so.

As soon as Corbett left the office, Bradford changed all of his passwords and got to work researching Dillon. He learned that his father was a hacker and that his father's sentence had been extended on a terrorism charge. Dillon had never gelled with his adoptive family, but he was a consistently productive app developer.

A cursory review of his financial statements though showed that the dividends his stock was paying out were far too high for the amount of money the apps brought in. It turned out that almost half the money he was bringing in was in the form of capital gains – from trading other Avillage listings.

Got him, Bradford thought, his sneer morphing into an icy grin, as he typed out an email to Dillon.

Dear Mr. Higley,

I hope you have enjoyed snooping around our intranet. I am quite confident that you did not find whatever it was you were looking for.

Currently I am weighing my options with respect to what my next step should be. Before I go to the authorities, I'd like to give you the opportunity to tell me your side of the story and, possibly, tell me what you might be willing to do to keep this issue out of the legal system.

Let me remind you that corporate espionage is a potentially serious federal charge, especially when the perpetrator profits from it. And I see that you have done remarkably well trading Avillage equities.

As you have probably already discovered, I don't conduct any important business over email. I will be in the Boston area next Friday. We can discuss this in person then at a location of your choosing.

I look forward to hearing from you.

Aaron Bradford
Executive Vice President, Avillage

Send.

He leaned back contentedly in his office chair, imagining the panic that would be coursing through Dillon's veins the next time he opened his email. But his pleasant daydream only lasted half a minute before it was rudely interrupted by the chime of a new email.

It was from Dillon. It simply read, "Northbound rest area Interstate-95 just across New Hampshire border. Noon."

CHAPTER 12

All packed up and ready to move out, Ryan still had almost twenty-four hours to kill before his parents would arrive to pick him up for summer break, and the last thing he wanted to do was spend that time alone, holed up in his even-more-barren-than-usual dorm room. He needed a change of scenery. He didn't really care where. Just some place different.

After running into the bank to take out a few hundred dollars cash, he scampered down the stairs of the T station at Harvard Square and hopped on the red line toward Boston South, where he bought a round trip Amtrak ticket to New York.

Maybe Annamaria would be available, maybe she wouldn't, but after traveling all morning, he couldn't foresee chickening out on at least calling her. Worst-case scenario, he'd spend the afternoon in Manhattan. Either way, it would beat sitting in his dorm.

As the Amtrak express train squealed to a stop into bay 3 at Penn Station just past noon, Ryan finally willed his thumb down to the green phone icon on his phone's touch screen – and then froze. Annamaria answered on the first ring.

"Hello?"

Silence.

Having put all his effort into initiating the call, he hadn't thought far enough ahead to consider what he was actually going to say if she answered.

"Hello?"

More silence. He was about to hang up when he heard her say his name.

"Ryan? Is that you? I can't hear you."

"Uh, can you hear me now?" he stammered.

"Oh yeah. Now I can. Loud and clear," she said casually, obviously not sharing his anxiety. "So what's up?"

"Uh, it's nothing major. But I didn't know if maybe... you might have any time to talk sometime today?"

"Sure. My shoot's about to start back up, but I'll be done in a couple hours. You want to call me back?"

"I could..." Ryan said, his heart pounding. "But is there any chance we might be able to meet up in person?"

"Oh. Well," she hesitated, "I don't think I can make it back up to Boston again this soon."

"No. I... uh... I actually just arrived in New York." He paused, shaking his head. That had to sound weird. "I don't know how you feel about stalkers?"

"I love them. *Love* them!" Annamaria laughed. "Hey, let me give you a call when I'm done. I'm staying at the Peninsula Hotel, if you want to head over that way."

"Awesome. Oh, and if you don't mind, can you just give me your room number? I brought some of my higher-powered telephoto lenses down with me, and I just need to know where to aim them."

To Ryan's relief, she laughed again – a bubbly carefree laugh that reached through the phone and demanded reciprocity. "I'll see you in a couple hours," she giggled. He was feeling better already.

But as he walked out of the train station onto W 31st street to start the 25 block trek toward the hotel, the melancholy seeped back in. The stagnant New York air was thick, holding on to every scent the city had to offer, and the low-hanging sky was a virulent gray that seemed to infect everything it came in contact with, somehow sapping the color from both heaven and earth.

By the time his phone rang an hour and a half later, his mind was once again wholly consumed with what had led him to New York in the first place.

Then he caught sight of Annamaria stepping out of the lobby of the Peninsula. The world stood still for a moment as she walked out in a plain white V-neck T-shirt paired with well-worn jeans and flip-flops, an ensemble that tens (if not hundreds) of thousands of other women in the city were futilely trying to wear like she did.

She made fleeting eye contact with Ryan and then headed north into Central Park, as Ryan followed at an inconspicuous distance.

A hundred yards or so into the park, she veered off the asphalt path toward a large steep-faced boulder with a flat top under a mature elm tree. Ryan tried his best not to struggle as he scaled the nine-foot rock to join her at the top. And at last, they sat side by side, their legs dangling off the front of the boulder, nearly invisible to the rest of the city.

"Nice spot," Ryan said, squeezing his knees together to prevent any potentially misinterpretable touching of their legs.

"Yeah, I found it last time I was here on a shoot. Every so often, I'll leave my phone in my room and walk down here – just to think; stare off into nothing for a little while; cry sometimes. I've never been bothered here. You're kind of away from everything. But I like that I can still hear the city. It's kind of comforting."

He gave her a silent nod that told her he got it. He knew the fine line between solitude and isolation, and he'd found himself on both sides of it at different times alone with his thoughts.

"But you're the first person I've shown this place to," she said with a fragile smile, trying to keep the mood from getting too somber. "So congratulations!"

Ryan took his phone out of his pocket and pretended to take a picture. "Gimme just a sec here. I'm gonna upload this location to my Facebook page and then tweet it out real fast."

Annamaria laughed and threw her shoulder into his, nearly knocking him off the rock. "So how have you been?" she asked with a playful smirk. "Why did you come to visit me?"

He strained to smile back at her, but his expression read more sorrow than joy, and eventually his eyes fell to the ground below.

"What is it?" she asked, gently placing her hand on his shoulder.

"I just found out that my mom was pregnant when she died."

"Oh my God. How do you know?"

"I read an email between her and my dad. They were gonna surprise me with the news the night of the car wreck.

"It's just that..." He paused, staring straight ahead, shaking his head slowly. "I always wanted a sibling."

"I'd give anything to have mine back," Annamaria whispered.

Ryan continued, "And I've started to remember some things that might not be significant, but after hearing what happened to you and listening to Dillon's rants, I'm starting to wonder if Avillage really is behind a lot of this. Maybe Dillon's right. Maybe part of every dollar I ever make will be padding the bank accounts of my parents' – my family's – killers."

Annamaria took Ryan's hand in hers, ready to listen for as long as he wanted to talk.

"This is gonna sound weird," he confessed with a nervous a laugh, "but the most impactful thing my parents ever said to me was after they'd already died. I mean, I know it wasn't really them, but it seemed real. And it's what they would've said if they could have.

"My dad told me that I was their everything – even more so since they were gone. And then my mom told me to do four things. She said, 'Make a difference. Be happy. Love. And be loved.'

"'Make a difference' was first.

"That's always been my biggest motivation – trying to be their legacy. But now I'm almost done with college, and what I'm good at is taking tests and making money. That's not what they cared about."

"What do *you* care about?" Annamaria asked.

"I care about my family." That was a cop out though. Who didn't care about their family? He thought for a while before coming up with a real answer, as if it were the first time he'd ever considered the question. "And I guess I care about us Avillage orphans. Even Dillon.

"I mean, look at us. We're a pretty complex group of... anomalous individuals – outliers, I guess you could say. All of us have come from tragedy early in our lives, yet most of us have achieved or are at least on our way to achieving some level of what society would call success.

"But I think we still resent and fear some malevolent puppet master behind the scenes at Avillage headquarters. And I think most of us have never come to grips with the trauma from our childhoods."

"I know I haven't," Annamaria said. "But I know what I have to do. If I could ever work up the nerve to do it.

"I've gotta go back to Panama. Back to the orphanage in Rainbow City and confront my old headmaster. Then, somehow, find a way to be of some use to those kids again. That's what I care about. And I used to be good at it. Thing is, I don't know if anyone could even take me seriously at this point."

He looked Annamaria squarely in the eye still squeezing her hand firmly, his voice now even and steady. "Annamaria, listen to me. It's incredible that you've been able to get where you are right now with everything you've been through. I'm not saying you're not beautiful. You are. But don't ever let anyone try and convince you that you got where you are on your looks. Your looks nearly damned you. They were an obstacle you had to overcome. And you did it."

She smiled appreciatively, her lower lip quivering.

"And I hate to say it right now, but I actually have to get back to Boston. My train leaves in half an hour. Thank you for talking to me. I know it was quick and I hogged most of the conversation, but you have no idea how helpful it was. And if you *ever* need someone better – or I should probably say different – than your rock in central park to talk to, I'm here. Any time."

~~~

Anxiety was a foreign concept to James Prescott. But right now he was anxious.

From the day he'd turned thirty, he'd never fluctuated more than five pounds north or south of 180. At his last doctor's appointment he weighed in at 170. That seemingly insignificant finding had led to a thorough exam, which then led to routine blood tests and eventually a series of CT scans.

Today, he'd be getting the results. His doctor had politely but emphatically declined to provide them to him by phone, encouraging him to come in to discuss them in person, as soon as possible.

Doctors don't get paid for phone calls; they get paid for office visits, Prescott reminded himself cynically, but he knew deep down that the news couldn't be good.

And so he waited – alone in the bright, airy, teal and stone waiting room of the Executive Health Clinic of New York-Presbyterian Hospital. Too keyed up to sit, he began to pace, intermittently looking over at the receptionist for some indication he might be on the verge of being called back.

Technically, he was still early. But, they had to know that his time was infinitely more valuable than the doctor's. Wasn't that the point of the Executive Health program? That people like him wouldn't have to wait?

Finally reaching a boiling point, he approached the desk with an uncharacteristically disingenuous smile. "I'm sorry, ma'am. It's been nearly fifteen minutes. Is there any way you could page Dr. Timmons?"

Before the receptionist had a chance to respond, Prescott heard the "clack" of the mechanical door to the back of the office unlatch, and the door slowly swung open. Dr. Timmons stepped through into the waiting room and greeted him with his characteristic firm handshake – but not the exuberant, bordering on brown-nosing, smile Prescott had become accustomed to.

They walked in silence, Dr. Timmons in front and Prescott following closely behind, past their customary exam room and down the hall to a small conference room, where two middle-aged women in white coats were waiting, projecting the same deliberate lack of expression Dr. Timmons had. More evidence of bad news in Prescott's mind. These were clearly colleagues, not assistants. And while "multidisciplinary care" had been an enticing feature in selecting this particular health plan, realizing that he would soon be needing it was sickening.

Dr. Timmons introduced his colleagues, a radiologist and a medical oncologist, offered Prescott a seat, which he politely refused, and then started in a soothing tone, "I wish we had better news for you, Mr. Prescott. But your CT scan of the abdomen was abnormal. There appears to be a mass in your pancreas, and it took up the contrast we gave you. Now, we don't know exactly what we're dealing with at this..."

"What do you *think* we're dealing with?" Prescott interrupted.

"Well, what we need to do to figure that out is more testing, which is what I was leading up to."

Prescott was unimpressed. "You could have told me I needed more testing over the phone," he said pointedly. "In your professional opinion, what do you *think* we're dealing with?"

"In my professional opinion – well, in *our* combined professional opinion – the findings would be most consistent with... with pancreatic cancer."

Prescott nodded with no change in expression. He knew among cancers that was a bad one. "And is it confined to the pancreas?"

"There was a spot in the liver as well," Dr. Timmons answered, knowing there was no way he'd be able to get away with sidestepping the question. "But that spot was also non-specific."

"What kind of life expectancy am I looking at?" Prescott asked emotionlessly.

"Mr. Prescott," his doctor sighed. "There's no way to answer that."

"I'll have my assistant look it up before I even get back to my office. Just save me the time. What is the life expectancy for someone with metastatic pancreatic cancer?"

"The five-year survival rate is less than five percent," Dr. Timmons admitted, hanging his head.

One of the women took over from there. "Mr. Prescott, I'm a radiologist who specializes in interventional procedures. The next step toward a definitive diagnosis would be to determine what that mass in your pancreas is for sure, and the only way to do that is by looking at a piece of it under the microscope. It turns out the easiest and least invasive way to get that piece is with a needle biopsy, performed under CT guidance."

"Alright, when can we do it?" Prescott asked, desperate to know exactly what he was up against.

"That's up to you. We can certainly be flexible with your schedule, keeping in mind that we shouldn't sit on this for too long."

"How long does it take?"

"Thirty minutes or so. An hour max."

"Is there any recovery time?"

"No, it's a pretty simple outpatient procedure."

"Alright then, let's go. Let's do it now," Prescott said decisively.

"Well, the equipment probably wouldn't be available right now," the doctor backpedaled, not expecting that response. "And regardless, you'd need to be fasting for the procedure."

"I haven't eaten anything today. And with the money I'm paying the hospital, I'm sure you can solve the equipment availability issue. Now let's hurry up and get to wherever we need to be in this hospital and get this over with."

~~~

Leonard Weinstien exited the baggage claim at Cleveland Hopkins Airport to find Ryan idling at the curb. After receiving the external hard drive in the mail that morning from Dillon, Ryan had spent the last several hours reviewing all of the J'Quarius Jones files. Nowhere had there been any mention of either Weinstien or a biological father.

"Paper files," Weinstien grunted, as he hoisted an overstuffed suitcase into the back seat and then climbed in the front next to Ryan.

Weinstien was five-six with frazzled gray hair that shot out horizontally from the base of an expansive bald spot. He seemed to be in a constant struggle with a pair of thick-rimmed glasses that were perpetually trying to slide down his nose, away from his reddish-brown eyes that were stuck in a continuous squint. He wore a faded brown suit that obviously hadn't been upgraded since well before his retirement five years earlier, and his generous gut hung lazily over his belt.

"Ryan Ewing," Ryan nodded with a forced smile, hoping his skepticism wasn't too apparent.

"Pleasure. Leonard Weinstien. Ok, then. Now that I'm no longer billing by the hour – or even billing at all – we might as well get straight to business. I'm staying at the Hampton Inn by the way, if you want to head that direction.

"First of all a couple of security questions for you. What school did you go to?"

"Hunting Valley Academy."

"Full name please."

"Hunting Valley Academy for Math, Science and the Arts."

"And what was your birth name?

"Ryan Tyler, Jr."

"How old are you?"

"17"

"College and Major?"

"Harvard. Economics."

"Adoptive parents names?"

"Thomas and Sara Ewing."

"ATM pin number?"

Ryan glared over at his passenger to see a wry smile materialize on Weinstien's face.

"OK, well that's all I've got," Weinstien said, slamming a small notepad shut. "If you're not who you say you are, I'll at least give you credit for doing your homework."

"What kind of law did you practice?" Ryan asked, visibly underwhelmed.

"Mostly family law, but I did a little criminal defense in my early years. Now, what can I do for you?"

"Well, as I stated in my email, J'Quarius was the second orphan adopted into Avillage – after me of course. And I was actually at the game the night he died. I happened to see your sign.

"Since that time, I've had the chance to talk with some of the other Avillage orphans out there, and there were some who had... I'll say *unusual* circumstances surrounding their adoptions into Avillage."

"Uh huh," Weinstien nodded with a knowing smile. "So what you're saying is, 'You see, Mr. Weinstien, I've got this friend who...?'"

"Don't get me wrong," Ryan jumped in. "There were some unusual circumstances around my adoption too. I'm not trying to hide that. Right now I'm just trying to collect as much information as I can – not just for my sake, but for every kid who's been put up on AVEX."

"Ok, ok." Weinstien's smirk had disappeared. He could see Ryan was sincere. "I'll tell you what I know.

"A little over ten years ago, in the weeks before J'Quarius's adoption, I represented a man named Melvin Brown. So, he tells me he'd had a relationship with J'Quarius's mom Cheryl Jones for a little over a year at the time J'Quarius was born – he had plenty of pictures of the two of them to support his story. I don't doubt the story at all.

"Now, he claimed that Cheryl's mom never really approved of him and was constantly in Cheryl's ear the whole time they were together, trying to break them up.

"Then one day, when he was out of town for his uncle's – or maybe it was a cousin's? Anyway. Neither here nor there. He was at a family member's funeral – he got a call from Cheryl's mom to tell him Cheryl had had a seizure, been admitted to the hospital with uncontrollable blood pressure, and had *died* of brain swelling."

"Eclampsia?" Ryan whispered.

Weinstien stared at him incredulously. "I thought you said you were studying economics?"

"Yeah, that's my major, but I try to take a variety of classes."

"So, yes," Weinstien continued, "as it turns out, she died of eclampsia, which you already seem to know is a condition some pregnant women get – causes high blood pressure, seizures, and, if untreated, potentially fatal brain swelling."

"But how did Melvin not know she was pregnant?"

"I don't think *she* knew! I saw the pictures.

"I mean, you've seen J'Quarius. You could probably guess he came from a pretty big mom. She wasn't necessarily fat. Just big. Over six feet. And big-boned. Sure, she looked a little heavier in the later pictures, but I could see how they might not have known she was pregnant. And when I got to digging into it a little, I found out J'Quarius was actually born prematurely – almost a month and a half early.

"Well anyway, years down the road when J'Quarius is starting to make a name for himself as a middle school basketball prodigy, somebody asks Melvin if he has an illegitimate son, just joking around with him. Says the kid looks just like him. So Melvin actually looks into it. Turns out the kid was born on the exact date his longtime girlfriend had died.

"And that's when he got me involved. It didn't take me too long to find out J'Quarius was in an orphanage, and within a week we'd started the process of trying to arrange DNA testing. The only problem was Avillage had found out about J'Quarius a few weeks sooner."

Ryan pulled the car into the Hampton Inn lot and waited while Weinstien checked into his room. About 20 minutes later, Weinstien reemerged from the lobby sans the suit coat carrying a small file folder.

Without so much as a greeting, he plopped back down in the passenger seat of the parked car and started right back in where he'd left off, detailing the child pornography charge, the suicide, and his delayed discovery of the letter Melvin had sent him, a copy of which he took out of his file folder and handed to Ryan.

Ryan quickly scanned the letter. "So he didn't want to stay and fight because he thought his son would be better off without him?"

"Yep. But he couldn't stand the thought of living without his son," Weinstien added. "So he asked me to make sure he was taken care of.

"I truly don't remember filing the letter away. I must have. But I don't remember it. I'm not sure there's anything I could've done anyway, but if I could've somehow extricated J'Quarius from Avillage and left him in the custody of the Washingtons... Who knows?"

They sat in silence for half a minute, both staring out the front windshield, before Weinstien was the first to snap back to reality. "Speaking of the Washingtons," he continued, as if he'd never paused, "I did track them down. They're really another casualty of this whole thing.

"Hansford just couldn't come to grips with it. He claims he was the one who talked J'Quarius into playing in that final game. The head coach and some of the other players tell a different story, but he's convinced J'Quarius never would've played if it weren't for him.

"He ended up getting heavy into alcohol, lost the coaching job he'd held for over 20 years, and eventually watched his marriage fall apart. His brother took him in, but he's still an absolute mess.

"Arlene seems to be doing considerably better, working to raise awareness for childhood heart disease and drunk driving, which is what killed her first son. But she told me privately that the only thing that drives her is an interminable sense of guilt, which she knows will never allow her any kind of fulfillment. She puts on a smile for public events and speaking engagements, but she told me she hasn't had a single *good* day since J'Quarius died."

Ryan's eyes narrowed as he continued nodding after Weinstien finished his story. "How would you like to do some pro bono legal work for an Avillage kid?"

"What did you have in mind?"

"Well, my parents were killed in a car crash – a head-on collision 3 months before I was adopted by Avillage. I saw it. The car that hit them was in the wrong lane, going way over the speed limit and, I'm pretty sure, had to have blown through a stop sign. There'd have to be police records from that night. Would you have any interest in looking into something like that?"

"Trust me, I've got *nothing* better to do. Just give me the details."

~~~

James Prescott's secretary must have been on her lunch break. Bradford hesitated just outside the cracked door to the CEO's office. It sounded like he was on the phone. There was no need to interrupt. He usually kept his conversations brief.

"So what did you find?" Bradford overheard.

"And what about the spot in the liver?"

The liver? Bradford squinted his eyes almost shut and leaned in toward the door.

"So will we need to do another biopsy or do we just presume that it's the same thing?

"I see.

"And what kind of treatment options am I looking at?"

Bradford's heart sunk. It turned out the only man he'd ever admired was indeed mortal. But as he stood in the anteroom with his ear as close to the crack of the door as possible without creating a shadow, he couldn't keep his mind from visualizing a new Avillage – an even more efficient one – with himself at the helm.

Prescott was a big picture guy, but he had a tendency to overlook details at times. Bradford didn't. If he were given the opportunity to extend his reach into every orphan's upbringing the way Prescott did, sure, he may have a few more casualties, but the ones who were really fit to thrive would reach even higher heights.

"I didn't hear surgery," Prescott said into the phone. "Are there any other centers in the world that are offering surgery for this?

"I see.

"Alright, bottom line it for me. And I know you don't have a crystal ball, and the numbers that you're giving are by no means absolute, but I have a very important business to run, and I need to be physically and mentally able to run it for as long as possible. Between chemo and palliative care, which one would give me the more *meaningful* time."

Chemo? That confirmed it. It had to be cancer.

"No way. Not a chance. I absolutely cannot miss that much time."

Bradford had been with Prescott for over twenty years. His compensation had gone nowhere but up, and the number of employees reporting to him had increased exponentially, but he could never really be promoted. There was nowhere for him to go. Unless Prescott were somehow no longer around.

"No, Dr. Timmons, *you* don't understand," Prescott said forcefully. "Let me explain something to you. I'm not coming to work everyday, clocking in and out, to earn a paycheck so I can meet next month's car payment or maybe take the family on a nice beach vacation. I haven't taken more than a 3-day weekend off in over ten years. What I do is important. And my physical presence has broad implications for a lot of people's lives – present and future – on an international scale."

That sounded like he was leaning toward palliative care to give him more time at the office, Bradford thought, almost giddy. Then an idea popped into his head. He knocked firmly on the door, intending to strike while the iron was hot.

"Thank you very much. I'll get back to you with my decision in the near future," Prescott said loudly into the phone before hanging up and calling for whoever it was at his door to come in.

"Hey James, you ok?" Bradford asked, walking in with a pseudo-worried expression. "You look a little peaked."

"Never felt better," Prescott replied unconvincingly, obviously preoccupied.

"Well I hope you're still feeling good after you hear the news I've got for you. I just met with the entire orphan ID division," Bradford lied. "And it's worse than I thought. They're telling me our wells are almost completely dry. They keep getting more and more referrals of progressively lower quality, with no trace of a can't-miss prospect in sight. I don't think this'll turn into the worst-case scenario we've always talked about, but who knows? It's bound to happen one day – where we won't have an IPO for a month and a half. Or two.

"And the big Avillage ETF that runs about a third of our volume is already seeing a lag in volume. These next three months could turn out to be the most important quarter Avillage has seen since we opened."

Prescott's shoulders relaxed as his trademark warm smile returned, now certain of what he had to do. "Have we ever backed away from a challenge?" he asked.

"No sir," Bradford said, smiling duplicitously back at his boss.

As Bradford left the office, he dialed Jen Glass, VP of orphan identification. "Jen, it's Bradford. Listen, I want you to send me the full portfolios for your top five orphans and stop all progress on their launches. I just finished talking this over with Mr. Prescott. Your orders are *not* to go ahead with any of these IPOs for now. Is that clear?"

~~~

"Mr. Ewing?"

"That's me," Ryan said rising to a stand, rubbing his sweaty palms down the front of his jeans.

"Follow me," the nurse said with a sympathetic smile. "And don't worry. There's nothing to be nervous about."

But she didn't know why he was there.

She brought him back to an exam room, had him change into a gown and took a quick 12-lead EKG. "You can leave the gown on for now," she said as she walked out of the exam room. "Dr. Easterbrook will be right in."

Ryan gave a polite nod. As the nurse walked away, he could just make out, through Dr. Easterbrook's cracked office door across the hall, the familiar red "*Veritas*" seal on a framed diploma that could only have come from Harvard.

After several reassurances from the nurse that it would only be a few more minutes, Dr. Easterbrook finally hurried in the door. "A young one," he noted with a smile, leafing through Ryan's thin chart. "EKG looks good," he muttered under his breath. "So what brings you in today."

"Well I'm home for summer break from college in Boston..."

"Oh really? Which one?"

"I go to Harvard."

"Really?" Dr. Easterbrook said, lighting up. "My old stompin' grounds. Which dorm are you in?"

"Wigglesworth."

"Ha! That's where I lived my sophomore year," the doctor beamed. "Long time ago. *Long* time ago. Hey, is Grendel's Den still around?"

"Yeah," Ryan said, happy to be putting off his next line of questioning. "I just ate there last week. Cool place."

"You thinking about medicine?"

"No, I don't think so. I'm an econ major."

"Yeah, the world needs business people too, I guess. So what brings a healthy young man like you in to see the cardiologist?"

"Well, I first saw a doctor up in Boston after I passed out," Ryan lied. "I think he actually said he trained here. Have you heard of a Dr. Jared Ralston?"

"Oh yes. I helped train him. Very strong clinically."

"Yeah," Ryan said. "Maybe not the best bedside manner."

Dr. Easterbrook laughed out loud. "I'm sorry. I shouldn't laugh. It's just I'm not surprised to hear you say that."

"Well, I probably would've stayed with him despite all that, but I think he left Boston. You wouldn't happen to know where he ended up would you?"

"No, I really don't. I used to run into him at some of the national cardiology conferences for the first few years after he left Cleveland. Then I guess he stopped going. I haven't seen or heard from him in years." As he spoke, he sunk the head of his stethoscope down the collar of Ryan's gown onto his chest. "Just breathe normally."

"He never had any discipline issues here or anything did he?" Ryan asked.

Dr. Easterbrook quickly pulled his stethoscope away, and glared at Ryan suspiciously. "Now that would be none of your business!" Then, as quickly as his scowl had materialized, it vanished, as it suddenly dawned on him. He was looking at Ryan Tyler.

He quickly did the math in his head. The age worked out.

He placed his stethoscope back onto Ryan's chest. "All I can tell you is that he was one of the best fellows ever to come out of this place. But he was always in the shadow of his colleague, Dr. Ryan Tyler." He paused to listen as Ryan's heart rate immediately accelerated by twenty beats a minute, confirming his suspicions. "I can tell you honestly that Dr. Tyler was *the* best fellow I ever trained."

He looked up to see tears welling in Ryan's eyes. Ryan fabricated a few coughs and reached up to wipe his eyes. "But they pretty much got along, right?" he asked.

"Seemed to. As I said, I'm not at liberty to discuss any disciplinary action that may have taken place at this institution, but if the state medical board ever took any formal action, that'd be public record. And it's permanent. You can do a license check on any doctor ever licensed in Ohio at license.ohio.gov."

Then he smiled warmly at Ryan. "Your heart's in perfect shape."

"Thanks," Ryan said, looking Dr. Easterbrook straight in the eye. "Thanks a lot."

As soon as he got home, he typed "license.ohio.gov" into his computer's browser. For some reason, he felt the need to search his parents' names first. Each page came up with their full name, place and date of birth, and residence on top. "Deceased" was listed next to "current residence" for his parents. In the middle of the page was the license number, credential type and status (active or inactive). And at the bottom was a section entitled "Formal Action." As expected, no formal action existed on his parents' inactive licenses.

He then searched for Jared Ralston. There was only one – born in Richmond, Virginia. That sounded right The age was right. His residence was listed as "George Town, Cayman Islands – Out of State." *Hmm.* And his license status was "Inactive – Expired." *What in the world was he doing if his license was expired?*

At the bottom of the screen Ryan saw, peeking up from the final section, "Formal action exists." He frantically spun the wheel of his mouse to reveal three separate entries. The first was from November five months before his parents died: "CITATION – PRESCRIPTION OF MEDICATION OUTSIDE OF STATE AND OUTSIDE THE SCOPE OF A TRAINING LICENSE, THE FACTS UNDERLYING WHICH INVOLVED HIS PRESCRIPTION OF INSULIN TO AN ACQUAINTANCE, WHOM HE HAD NEVER TREATED, CALLED FROM CLEVELAND, OHIO TO A PHARMACY IN SEATTLE, WASHINGTON ON OCTOBER 30."

The next entry read, "BOARD ORDER: PROBATIONARY TERMS, CONDITIONS, AND LIMITATIONS FOR AT LEAST SIX MONTHS ESTABLISHED. ORDER MAILED 11/15. EFFECTIVE 11/16."

The final entry was from six months later and indicated that the doctor's request for lifting the probationary period had been granted by the state board. *Just in time for him to move to Boston,* Ryan thought, shaking his head and gritting his teeth.

He grabbed his phone and slammed his finger down on Weinstien's number. It went straight to voicemail.

"Mr. Weinstien, I've got one other thing for you to look into," he said, trying to keep his voice steady. "I want you to look into the official cause of death – and any unusual circumstances surrounding my grandfather's death. He died on October 31st in Seattle, Washington, within five months of my parents. I've got a strong suspicion Avillage might have had something to do with that too."

CHAPTER 13

"What do you want for her?" Dillon asked, salivating over the poorly-maintained olive-green '72 Chevy Impala, tucked away in the back corner of Jerry's Affordable Pre-Owned Auto Lot in South Boston. The body of the car was pocked with hundreds of rust spots, some neglected for long enough to have chewed actual holes through the metal frame, and its threadbare white-wall tires looked as though they may spontaneously pop at any moment. Microbubbles pervaded the amateur purplish-black tint job on the side and back windows, rendering them nearly opaque, and the tail pipe hung precariously, halfway between the chassis and the ground.

"If you're willing to take her as is... seven hundred bucks?" Jerry probed almost apologetically, with every intention of taking half of that to rid himself of what was probably the most dilapidated clunker in a lot full of them.

"Sold!" an uncharacteristically ebullient Dillon shouted to the dealer's surprise, peeling off seven one-hundred dollar travelers cheques from his money clip. He wanted the sale to be trackable.

Jerry slapped his clueless customer on the back and heartily congratulated him on his new car.

After a few papers were signed, Dillon slung his backpack into the passenger seat, sputtered off the lot, and set a course for the I-95 New Hampshire rest area. He'd probably be about fifteen minutes late, which didn't give him a moment's pause. That scumbag could wait.

After just under an hour's drive, he pulled off the interstate and parked his car illegally at the curb right outside the entrance to the travel plaza. As he rounded the back bumper on his way into the building, he stooped down to affix a generous amount of duct tape to the loosely hanging tailpipe. Then he strutted confidently into the food court to find Bradford hunched over a half-drunk cup of coffee at a remote table in the back of the seating area.

Bradford looked up from the table to see him approaching and made no effort to mute his expression. He nearly laughed out loud, watching Dillon walk in with some kind of king-of-the-computer-lab bravado. The intensifying glare that fronted Dillon's 110-pound frame only made the scene more delightfully ludicrous.

That's right, shitface. Go ahead and enjoy it – while you still can, Dillon thought.

He tossed his backpack into the booth and took the seat facing Bradford, who could barely contain himself. "*You're* the one who's been snooping around our intranet for the past four or five years?" he taunted. "What? Did you get into hacking when you were six?"

"If you'd taken ten seconds to learn anything about me, you'd know I was taken away from my dad when I was 12," Dillon fumed. "But you wouldn't give a shit anyway."

Completely unfazed, Bradford continued to stare right back at him with bemused disdain. "I'm sorry. This is just unbelievable to me."

Dillon struggled to tone down his glare and leaned back in his seat. "I know about J'Quarius Jones's medical exam before he died," he said, trying his best to project a confident even keel. "And I know about Annamaria Olivera's surgery when she was 13 years old."

Bradford's grin faded just slightly. "And? So what? I mean, is that supposed to scare me? A lot of people know about those things. I had nothing to do with the surgery, and I've been exonerated in J's untimely death."

"J'Quarius!" Dillon snapped. "Don't you dare refer to him as a ticker symbol!"

"Look, kid," Bradford fired back. "You're in no position to be making demands of me! I've got hard evidence against you. You got greedy with your Avillage trades. Frankly, I can't believe the SEC wasn't already on to you. You've got some serious federal charges coming your way.

"The only reason I'm even giving you a chance to try to wriggle your way out of this is that you're one of ours, $D - I - L - N$."

Dillon leaned in to study Bradford's expression. "I also know about the murder of Ryan Tyler's parents," he whispered.

This time he saw something. It was subtle. But unmistakable in its abruptness. Bradford immediately tried to recreate his previous smug expression, but he fell just short in his attempt. His smirk was still there, but it seemed strained now. "I don't have a clue what you're talking about," he said, shaking his head incredulously, but briefly breaking eye contact for the first time. "I've never had anything to do with his account, and his parents were killed in a head-on collision. I certainly wasn't the one driving the car that hit them."

"That's a pretty good memory for something that happened over ten years ago to 'an account' you had nothing to do with," Dillon said. Now he was the one wearing the contented smirk.

Bradford's eyes narrowed. "I came here to give you an opportunity to defend yourself..."

"You came here for extortion!" Dillon yelled, drawing a few glances from the neighboring tables.

"Stupid little shit," Bradford muttered out of the side of his mouth. "You're making a *grave* mistake." He grabbed his coffee, shimmied out of the booth, and stood up to glare one last time at Dillon. "You'll be hearing from the FBI. Soon!"

"Oh, I know," Dillon said, reaching into his backpack. "But it's not gonna be on your timetable."

The color instantly drained from Bradford's expressionless face, as he stared down thunderstruck at the muzzle of a .22-caliber pistol aimed right between his eyes.

~~~

"You were right," Weinstien said just as Ryan's phone reached his ear, not giving him a chance to say hello. "There *were* unusual circumstances surrounding your parents' car accident.

The car that hit them was a Chevy Suburban registered to a Tony Lafora. But he wasn't in the car that night."

"So who was?" Ryan asked.

"Some burned out drunk with three prior DUIs."

Ryan felt an unexpected wave of relief come over him at the news that the accident had indeed been random.

"But I don't think he was driving either," Weinstien added after a dramatic pause.

"What? Why? Was he at the wheel or not?"

"He was at the wheel, but I don't think he was driving. His blood alcohol content was .45, and his tox screen also came up positive for pretty high levels of benzodiazepines – you know, like Valium and Xanax. I don't think he could've been conscious, much less driving, at the time of the crash.

"Also, a quick review of his arrest records revealed that on every other DUI charge, he'd been pulled over for driving too *slowly* and swerving all over the road. The police determined that the car that hit your parents was going close to sixty in a twenty-five mile an hour zone.

"Plus he'd never stolen a car in his life – much less *this one*."

"Well, he doesn't exactly sound like a model citizen. He probably passed out with his foot on the gas," Ryan said dismissively, stubbornly clinging to the hope that his parents were just in the wrong place at the wrong time.

"Maybe. But get this. It turns out Tony Lafora, the car's actual owner, had been working on tweaking driverless car technologies through a joint venture between Google and NASA's Glenn Research Center here in Cleveland. And the Chevy Suburban he was tinkering with at his house had suddenly gone missing from his garage three days before the accident. He'd actually called the police to report it stolen."

"So did they ever find out who stole it?"

"Not definitively. They blamed it on the drunk. I mean, I can't say I blame them; he *was* in the driver's seat when it crashed.

"Lafora ended up losing his job at NASA for having the car off campus. But off the record pretty much everyone knew he'd keep it in his garage for weeks at a time. They only fired him to protect their image. They hired him right back a few months later with a slightly different title to do basically the same thing."

"How'd you find that out?"

"I talked to him! He still lives in Cleveland.

"He says, beyond a shadow of a doubt, there's absolutely no way a career alcoholic with no education could've pulled this off. Whoever stole that car would've had to have known not only how to override the driverless feature, which requires significant programming expertise, but also how to disable the tracking feature, which is even more advanced.

261

"Lafora never even considered that the car would ever be stolen. He didn't even lock it."

Exactly three months before the opening of Avillage, Ryan could hear Dillon whispering in his ear. "Maybe he wanted it to be stolen," he thought out loud. "Maybe the guy who stole it *didn't* know how to disable the driverless feature. Maybe Lafora disabled it – temporarily. Then he took back over when he was fed my parents' location.

"Listen, I know for a fact that someone, who was later gifted shares of my stock by Avillage, knew where my dad's phone was at all times."

Ryan ignored a brief vibration from his phone indicating a new text. "You said Lafora still lives in Cleveland. Do you know where?"

"I do," Weinstien answered with no change in his tone. "In the same duplex he's lived in for over ten years. He's got no criminal record. He rides a scooter to work, and he still – ten years after the incident – works the exact same job. Doesn't exactly sound like the kind of guy who would get into murder for hire. Good idea though. I think you're probably on the right track – just not with him."

"Did anyone ever talk to the drunk?" he asked.

"Not possible. He's dead. Died in the accident. Or I guess I should say *near* the accident. He was unrestrained. Ended up 30 feet down the road from the crash site."

"So the case is pretty much closed?" Ryan asked, almost rhetorically.

"Afraid so. No one really seems to be satisfied with the answers, but there are no other leads. Sorry I couldn't give you better closure.

"Oh, and obviously I haven't looked into your grandfather's situation yet. Gimme some time on that. I have to take care of some things back in Jersey first."

"Thanks a lot, Mr. Weinstien. I mean it. I'm really impressed. And it means a lot that you'd do this for me."

"Don't mention it, kid," Weinstien said just before hanging up, clearly not comfortable with compliments.

Ryan set his phone down face up on his desk and stared blankly out his bedroom window. But before he could bury himself too deeply in thought, a tiny flash of green light from the corner of his phone drew him back to the present. He'd forgotten about the new text he'd gotten while he was on the phone.

But it wasn't a text message. It was a stock alert from his brokerage account. He'd set the account up to notify him if any of his stocks moved over 10% in either direction.

Comfortable in the fact he wasn't overexposed in any one specific holding, he tapped the link embedded in the message more out of curiosity than concern.

As soon as the page loaded though, his jaw dropped to his chest. *No! What did he do?*

DILN was down over 90%.

~~~

"Move!" Dillon demanded over the shrill screams of the other food court patrons, half running for their lives and half huddling pitifully under their tables.

"Alright! Alright! Just settle down," Bradford stuttered. "You're taking this way too far. I'm just a businessman. I didn't do anything to you or your friends."

"Bullshit. I know what you did. And you're going to admit it," Dillon said confidently, directing him through the double doors to the parking lot. The '72 Impala was still waiting at the curb.

"Get in the back!" Dillon shouted, trying to sound psychologically unstable and capable of anything.

Bradford opened the door and slowly lowered himself into the backseat.

"Now shut the door!"

Dillon got in through the front passenger side and slid himself across the vinyl bench seat to the driver's side with his torso corkscrewed to keep the gun trained on Bradford's forehead. He manually rolled the driver side window all the way down with his free hand and then fumbled with the key behind his back, finally blindly landing it in the ignition.

Slowly he backed the Impala out of the rest area parking lot and continued in reverse down the right-side emergency lane of the exit ramp, against traffic.

A few hundred yards after they hit the interstate, alternating focus between Bradford and the rear window, Dillon finally saw the "Welcome to New Hampshire" sign come into view. They'd made it back to Massachusetts.

Leaving the engine running, he threw the transmission into park and rolled his window back up. He then pulled a small machine about the size of a walkie-talkie out of his backpack, and switched it on. The digital display read, "100 PPM." *Perfectly safe*. Then he unfolded a sunshade and wedged it on top of the dashboard to cover the front windshield, effectively blocking off the only clear view into the car from the outside.

"Don't worry," he said to his stone-faced captive. "I'm not going to kill you. Not because I don't want to. I'd love to. But you're not worth the death penalty – which I'd probably be eligible for, you know, with this being premeditated and all.

"That's why I brought the twenty-two. If I do have to shoot you, you probably won't die."

Tiny sweat droplets began to bead on Bradford's forehead. "What do you want?"

"I want you to admit what you've done – to Ryan Tyler's parents, to J'Quarius Jones, to Annamaria Olivera," Dillon said, fidgeting with his phone.

"Fine. I'll admit anything you want," Bradford blurted desperately. "But that won't make it true. And you have to know that nothing I say would ever stand up in court. There's no evidence for anything. Because *I didn't do anything!*"

"I'm well aware that a simple admission wouldn't be any good in court. That's why I want details. And if they're not consistent with what I know to be true, there *will* be consequences."

Bradford's mind raced. How much could Dillon really know about anything? There wasn't much of any substance on the Avillage intranet.

Dillon held his phone up next to the gun. "Talk!"

"Ok! Ok! Where do you want me to start?" Bradford stalled.

"Start at the beginning – with Ryan Tyler's parents."

Bradford turned toward the side window to see a growing crowd of police cruisers congregating at a safe distance on the other side of the now roped-off interstate. From a distance he could hear the staccato "thwup-thwup-thwup" of an approaching helicopter. If he could just confabulate for long enough to give the cops time to figure out how to get him out, he might not have to give up anything incriminating.

"As you may know," he started, speaking very slowly and deliberately, "Ryan's dad was a cardiologist in training." *True and verifiable,* he thought. "Well, he'd been on call the night before the car accident, and, from what I understand, he'd gotten little to no sleep.

"You can check this out yourself. It's all in the police report from the crash." *A lie, but there's no way Dillon could know that.* "The investigating officers speculated that he must have fallen asleep at the wheel..."

"Wrong, asswipe," Dillon interrupted, frustratedly gritting his teeth. "One. More. Chance. And I'm serious."

"Alright. You're right. You got me. That's not true – or it might be. I don't know. Like I said, I had nothing to do with what happened to his parents!"

He paused as if to regroup, stealing another look at the police through the side window.

"But as for poor J'Quarius Jones, I do know about his death. Not a day goes by that I don't question how I handled that situation." Again he paused reflectively for as long as he thought Dillon would let him.

"When Dr. Bennett first called to tell me that he'd passed out on the basketball court, I had literally *just* landed in New York from Panama. I mean, I was still on the plane." *True.* "And I'd been seated next to some screaming baby, who never should have been let into first class by the way, who had kept me up the whole flight – except for the final half hour. I had finally just faded into a deep sleep when the plane touched down, and the stewardess shook me awake.

"With the change in time zone and having just been woken up from a sound sleep, yet still sorely sleep-deprived, could I have potentially missed some details in the medical jargon Dr. Bennett was rattling off at me a mile a minute? It's possible. But I don't think so.

"I don't know if you're aware of this, but the University of Chicago Children's Hospital actually chose to settle a malpractice case I brought against

Dr. Bennett rather than risk taking it to trial." *True.* "Personally, I was just ready to put the whole thing behind me, so I took their offer, and I donated..."

"Just shut up," Dillon sighed, shaking his head.

"I'm sorry if..."

"I said shut up!" Dillon lowered his phone back down onto the front seat. "I wasn't even recording. I knew you'd never admit to anything.

"But you weren't the only one stalling.

"The truth is I'm not after confessions. I know what you did, and you *are* going to pay."

He glanced down at the display on the device resting in the passenger seat. It now blinked, "400 PPM."

Dillon smiled as he turned back toward Bradford. "You like the '72 Impala? She's a bona fide classic." He rubbed the back of his free hand down the tattered top of the vinyl bench seat.

"Here's an interesting fact," he continued. "Did you know that prior to 1975, cars manufactured in the U.S. weren't equipped with catalytic converters?

"Interesting, huh? So if something were to block the tailpipe, like some kind of debris, or snow, or something like... I don't know... duct tape," he said, holding up a half-used roll, "the interior of the car could very well fill up with toxic levels of carbon monoxide.

"Don't worry. We're not there yet." He put the tape down and held up the carbon monoxide monitor just before it ticked up from 400 to 800 parts per million. He then pulled a long piece of 1-

inch PFA tubing out of his backpack and cracked the driver's side window, just enough to thread about a foot and a half of the tubing out into the clean outside air. "Sorry. I've only got one," he said sarcastically before sucking in a long drag of fresh air.

For the first time since he'd first pulled the gun, he could see true terror back in Bradford's eyes. And he relished it.

"If you try to get out of the car, I promise you I'll shoot straight for your spinal cord." The pure hatred in his eyes convinced Bradford he meant it. He took another series of breaths through the tube. "Or you can stay in here with me and take your chances; I'm not gonna let you die."

The monitor emitted an agitated series of beeps as the display ticked up from 800 to 1600 parts per million of carbon monoxide.

"You feeling ok?" Dillon asked pseudo-empathetically, unable to fully suppress his smile. "Because you're not looking too good."

Bradford tried his best to stay stoic, but he couldn't quite fight off an involuntary urge to swallow awkwardly as an unnatural rush of saliva filled his mouth.

Dillon gleefully sucked in a few more breaths through his tube. "You've probably got a little bit of a headache right now? Yeah, unfortunately that's gonna get quite a bit worse.

"By the time this thing ticks up to 3200, you'll probably be vomiting that eight-dollar latte you were so smugly sipping a little while ago all over the back seat.

"If you're still awake to see 6400, you won't remember it.

"But that's right around the time I'm gonna give myself up, and one of those heroes over there will rush in and save your life."

Not unexpectedly, Dillon's phone interrupted his soliloquy.

"Hello? What? FBI? No, I'm sorry. I don't know any FBI. You must have the wrong number." He switched his ringer to silent and dropped the phone to the floorboard.

Bradford's sallow complexion was lacquered with perspiration, his lips pressed firmly together, completely devoid of color, and he seemed to be concentrating intently on not vomiting. That could only last for so long.

~~~

Ryan anxiously turned on the TV and flipped to the news, where he found a field correspondent, just back from commercial, rehashing Dillon's story from the southbound lanes of the interstate, flanked on both sides by the flashing lights of more than a dozen police cruisers. Mind-numbingly repetitive aerial and ground shots of the green Impala offered no clue as to what was going on inside.

"CNN has now confirmed that the owner of the car is one Dillon Higley, a freshman at MIT," the correspondent reported as Dillon's high school yearbook photo flashed briefly on the screen. "And his hostage is believed to be Aaron Bradford, executive vice president of Avillage, Incorporated."

"Witnesses from inside the Southern New Hampshire travel plaza – just a few hundred yards north of us – state that Mr. Bradford had arrived at the food court alone but seemed to have been expecting Mr. Higley. The two men held a brief, but what some have referred to as 'intense,' conversation, after which Mr. Bradford stood, apparently with the intention to leave.

"It was at this point that Mr. Higley brandished a weapon – a handgun of some sort – and forcibly led Mr. Bradford out of the rest area and into his car. From there, for unclear reasons, he *backed* up the exit ramp and continued southward down the northbound emergency lane, just past the state line into Massachusetts, where the car you're looking at live still sits."

It all came together instantly for Ryan. A week earlier Dillon had told him he'd been reevaluating his priorities. And the last time he'd signed off on the walkie-talkie, there had been such an unmistakable finality in his tone.

Dillon didn't really have career goals or ambitions. He didn't care about money. He cared about two things in life – reuniting with his father, which was never going to happen outside prison walls, and getting some measure of revenge against Avillage. In his mind, he probably thought he'd come up with the best possible way to have a chance of accomplishing both.

His dad was in *federal* prison. He'd purposely transported Bradford across state lines to make the kidnapping a *federal* crime.

~~~

"You're probably asking yourself, 'why carbon monoxide?' Aren't you?" Dillon asked his hostage who now appeared terminally seasick. "Well..."

Bradford's eyes suddenly bulged and his cheeks puffed out as he squeezed his lips together even more tightly.

"Go ahead. I'll wait," Dillon said, backing away from the seat-back to take a few deep breaths through the PFA tubing.

Bradford lurched forward, temporarily disappearing behind the front seat. Sounds of choking and retching and splattering were followed by coughs and gasps, and then more gagging and splashing as the acrid odor of stomach acid and stale coffee filled the car.

Bradford's head eventually popped back up into view, his face now sheet white. Had it been anyone else in the world, Dillon couldn't have helped but feel sorry for him.

"So, as I was saying," he continued as if nothing had happened, "carbon monoxide is kind of the gift that keeps on giving.

"What you're experiencing now are kind of the typical signs of acute poisoning.

"But you'll eventually get to a hospital, and they'll probably treat you with hyperbaric oxygen, and it won't be too long till you're feeling considerably better.

"Then at some point down the road – it might be three days from now, or it might be three weeks – but at some point, it's going to come back." He looked Bradford right in his glossed-over eyes, wondering how much he was still comprehending. It looked like enough.

"You could end up with personality change (which in your case could only be a good thing) or possibly seizures, dementia, symptoms of Parkinson's Disease, or all of the above.

"You'll live. But my hope is that you'll wish you hadn't." Just as he concluded, Bradford's eyes rolled back, and he quietly slumped over to his left side.

The monitor let out a continuous piercing scream, as it detected an imminently lethal air concentration of 6400 PPM. Dillon reached over to switch it off and then turned the car's engine off to avoid raising the carbon monoxide concentration any further.

He sat in relative silence, breathing comfortably through his tube, for a couple of minutes. For the first time in years, he actually felt at peace. He then looked down at his watch. Time was up. With no further need for a gun, he threw it down to the floorboard and slowly opened the car door.

A swarm of screaming police officers charged toward him as he timidly tip-toed away from the car with his hands above his head.

~~~

Bradford's doctors had cleared him to go back to work in three weeks. It had been a week and half, and he was already right back micromanaging and making his underlings' lives miserable as if nothing had happened. Except for the occasional headache and a little fatigue toward the end of the day, he hadn't experienced any of the late effects Dillon had predicted after the poisoning.

He'd just finished hanging up on his secretary for neglecting to add something to his calendar when Corbett Hermanson walked in. "It isn't true is it?" Corbett asked.

"Ever heard of knocking?" Bradford sneered. "And could you please give me a shred of context before you start spouting off stupid questions."

"The email you sent out this morning. It isn't true is it?"

"I didn't send any email out."

Corbett looked confused – and then terrified as it occurred to him for the first time: *Maybe Dillon hadn't been bluffing about planting something on their system.*

Bradford immediately cued into the change of expression. "Corbett! What is it?"

"Uh, there was an email that went out this morning..." he winced trying to work up the courage to continue. "And it was addressed to our entire internal mailing list... and CNN... and the Wall Street Journal... and the New York Times."

"What did it say?" Bradford shouted, his cheeks glowing fiery red.

"I think you should probably read it yourself. It was a lengthy and, I'm quite sure, dishonest resignation letter."

"Get out! I'll deal with you later. You're gonna take personal and public responsibility for this. Do you hear me?"

"Yes sir," Corbett whispered ducking his head as he backed out of the room.

Bradford opened his email and clicked on the sent mail folder. Thirty minutes prior an email had gone out to all of the addressees Corbett had mentioned and more.

Dear All,

Recently my life flashed before my eyes, and I didn't like what I saw. In order to begin the process of making amends, I feel that I must first start by taking some responsibility for my actions.

First, I would like to apologize to RTJ. At the time you were identified as a top prospect for our initial public offering, you had two young, healthy parents. And while you have turned out to be every bit as extraordinary as we had hoped, I would like to apologize for any role I may have played in the untimely deaths of your parents.

To J (may you rest in peace,) I'm sorry. I sent you into a basketball game knowing full well that you may not live through it because of a potentially lethal heart condition. I did this because I wanted to profit from a multi-million dollar contract you were set to sign after the game. After you died, I donated my own money to your charity, only to give the impression that I had received a large malpractice settlement from The University of Chicago Children's Hospital. I hadn't.

Although I know there are many others I've hurt, I'd like to conclude by apologizing to BUTY. I funneled cash directly to your orphanage's headmaster when you were only 13 years old, prior to your being adopted by Avillage, so that you could be subjected to a breast augmentation and tubal ligation without your knowledge.

I willingly accept the civil and criminal liability of my actions. I did all of this in the interest of generating profit. I hereby offer my resignation from Avillage, Inc.

Sincerely,
Aaron Bradford

Some of it was true. Some of it hinted at the truth, and some was off the mark, but the news outlets weren't going to sit on this. Investigative reporters were probably already chasing down leads.

Avillage's reputation to this point had never sustained a single blemish, and the company was viewed as a resounding success, even by most child-welfare advocates. Bradford kept his eyes trained on the end of the message, continuously shaking his head, contemplating how in the world he was going to deal with this.

When he finally looked up, still with no plan of attack, he started at the sight of his boss standing in his doorway. Prescott wore a disappointed but determined fatherly expression that read, "this is going to hurt me as much as it hurts it you."

Bradford opened his mouth to speak first, but he couldn't find the words.

"I'm sorry, Aaron. We've had a good run," Prescott said matter-of-factly. "You know I couldn't have built this company to where it is now without you. I will personally pay whatever legal fees you might run into."

"What?" Bradford gasped. "That's it? I didn't write that email. James, come on. You know me."

"I know you didn't write it. But I need you to tell me that none of it's true."

Bradford huffed and puffed like a philanderer who'd been caught in the act. "James, this is my life! I've got nothing else."

But he never said it was untrue.

"Put yourself in my position, Aaron. You know there's only one way out here. No one's bigger than the company." Although his voice was calm, there was an inevitability in his tone that sent Bradford into a panic.

"James, look, I don't know exactly what you're going through, but you're not gonna be around forever! There's nobody else qualified to run this place!"

"Aaron," Prescott sighed empathetically, knowing the day would come when he'd have to tell Bradford what he was about to say. "It was never going to be you. Avillage is my legacy. It was never going to leave my family."

Was that a joke? Prescott's kids had never set foot in the building – not even for social visits. Shocked, humiliated, devastated, Bradford's mix of emotion, for the first time in Prescott's presence, bubbled to the surface as pure rage.

"You've lost it!" he shouted. "Almost thirty years of service, and you throw me out like a piece of trash at the first whisper of misconduct? The cancer's gone to your brain! I'll have you declared incompetent!"

"I'm sorry, Aaron," Prescott replied steadfastly, with no change in his sympathetic expression. "This is a private company. You know there's no board to appeal to. My decision's final."

Bradford slammed his fists down on his desk and started to rise from his chair, but just as he did, his spine arched and his arms and legs stiffened like a frozen corpse's. His eyes remained open as his teeth clenched down involuntarily on his tongue, sending a rose-colored froth out of the corner of his mouth.

Prescott shouted for Bradford's secretary to call 911. Thirty seconds of forceful, rhythmic full-body jerks were followed by quiet flaccidity. Bradford's office chair slowly rolled out from behind him as his body sunk to the ground in a heap, his eyes still eerily open, his breath sounds sonorous, and his pants soiled.

Dillon couldn't have scripted a more undignified departure from Avillage.

CHAPTER 14

"I don't think I can do it," Annamaria whimpered into her phone from the backseat of an idling cab.

"Yes you can," Ryan shot back emphatically. "Trust me. I've seen the fire inside you. Let it out. You have *nothing* to fear. The fear, the shame, the regret – they all belong with him. Give them to him!"

She nodded her head and wiped the tears from her cheeks. "I know," she said, still sniffling. "I know." She took one last glance at the sign just outside her window that read, "Rainbow City 10 km," firmed up her expression and then gave her driver the go-ahead.

~~~

Nerves weren't an issue for Ryan, who calmly slid his phone back into his front pocket and leaned forward on the edge of his seat, resting his elbows on his knees and interlocking his fingers in front of him, staring determinedly out the plate-glass window of terminal A5 inside Boston's Logan International Airport. For him the hardest part had been waiting.

Traveling outside the United States without Prescott's permission had never been an option, until he'd turned eighteen six days prior. But it just so happened that the final spring break of his life conveniently fell within a week of his milestone birthday.

While he'd researched the trip obsessively, he hadn't whispered a word of his plans to anyone – not his parents; not even Annamaria – until the week before, when he'd legally become an adult.

The Cayman Islands were a perfectly reasonable spring break destination for an eighteen-year-old with more money than he knew what to do with, and it actually would be nice to escape Boston's subarctic version of spring. But this trip would be all business. Jared Ralston's reckoning was long overdue.

~~~

A rush of emotion flooded Annamaria's heart and mind, as she scanned the grounds of the orphanage. Everything was familiar. But different. The old dirt parking lot had been paved over with smooth asphalt; the uneven, muddy soccer field was now carpeted with lush green grass with real goals and bright chalk boundary lines; and the cage-like chain-link fence had been replaced by a white-washed wooden fence, accented with the children's brightly colored handprints. She couldn't see the children as she approached, but she could hear their telltale squeals and laughter.

After slowly making her way to the orphanage door, she paused for a full minute, her heart in her stomach, waiting for the surge of emotion that would compel her to throw the door open and storm inside. But it never came. And gradually, thoughts that she really might not be able to do this began to creep in.

She considered calling Ryan again, but he was probably in the air by now. And her cell phone wasn't picking up any signal anyway.

She then thought about retreating to the parking lot, where she could see the cab driver napping in the front seat – all the windows down, his head leaned back against the headrest, mouth wide open and nose twitching perturbedly at a swarm of gnats.

But she was suddenly struck with a trivial curiosity. The sidewalk she was standing on used to end at the door. She remembered that distinctly. Now it continued on to the back of the orphanage.

Convincing herself that solving this puzzle was a valid alternative to barging through the front door, she decided to follow the path and see where it led. Surely she'd find the courage to burst through the door afterward.

As she tiptoed quietly toward the back corner of the building, ducking as she passed by the headmaster's window, she was startled by a man's voice behind her.

"May I help you?" the familiar voice asked in Spanish.

She froze, still a few paces short of the back of the building, every fiber in her body tensing.

"Ma'am," the headmaster said a little louder. "May I help you?"

Annamaria straightened up her posture, threw her shoulders back with a deep breath in, and slowly turned to reveal her identity, staring directly in the headmaster's eyes.

Carlos Villanueva gawked at her as if she'd just returned from the dead. "Annamaria!" he gasped, falling to his knees under the weight of her glare.

"How could you!" she screamed, her trepidation replaced by rage.

"I'm sorry. I'm so sorry," he blubbered, making no attempt at denial, shamefully covering his face with his hands.

"I was just a little girl! I trusted you! And now I can't trust anyone!"

He offered no excuses and no defense, as he sobbed on the ground in front of her.

"Get up, Carlos!" she demanded. "I want answers!"

Slowly he rose to his feet keeping his head down, trying to regain some semblance of composure. "Of course, of course," he finally whispered. "Just not here. Not where the children might hear. Please, follow me."

He led her into his cramped office, seemingly the only part of the grounds left unchanged from the day she'd departed six years earlier, and offered her a chair and a glass of water, both of which she hastily refused.

"I've thought about the day you might come back everyday since I sold my soul to the devil," he started, his voice trembling. "First of all, let me say that what I did was wrong, and I will continue to pay for the decision I made for as long as I live.

"Now, you want answers, and you deserve them. Please, sit."

Annamaria kept her glare on him, her face still flushed with anger. "Damn it! I don't want to sit down!" she screamed.

"Ok, ok. I'm sorry," Carlos continued nervously, "It's been six years now since the earthquake. I took this place over just six months before that. I was only 24 years old at the time.

"After the quake hit, in the span of two days, our occupancy rate shot up from 25% to 200%. You were here. You remember." Every memory he had of her was fond. He wasn't aware that a smile had started to form on his lips as he took a moment to reminisce.

"Up to that point, I had always been more of a romantic than a realist. I took this job with dreams of cleaning the place up, filling it with light and laughter. Making something that felt like a home for the homeless. I converted the old headmaster's huge office into a gameroom and moved my stuff into this cramped little space. I fenced in the yard, so the kids could play outside more. I spent every cent the state gave me on enrichment projects and lobbied for more.

"But I was learning on the job. When the earthquake hit, I was overwhelmed. I had no money in reserve. Then half our staff either cut back their hours or couldn't work altogether because of injuries or damage to their homes.

"The government increased their allocation to the orphanage by 50%, but it wasn't even close to enough. We were barely keeping food on the table.

The kids with injuries were getting essentially no medical care, and we didn't even have time to think about child enrichment. You were a godsend, Annamaria. I'll never forget..."

"Don't!" she warned. She didn't want him toying with her emotions, and she wasn't there for flattery.

"I'm sorry," he stuttered, not entirely sure what he was apologizing for this time, and then continued on with his story. "One morning I was in my office, desperately trying to make the finances work when I came across a letter I'd actually meant to throw out from an American company by the name of Avillage. They said they were looking for orphans with 'exceptional skills or talents.'

"These children, they said, would be adopted into hand-selected American families. And the referring orphanages would be eligible for a finder's fee of sorts. They made it sound like a win-win situation.

"I was desperate. And you were the only child who came to my mind – beautiful, confident, responsible – so I sent off some pictures.

"I had just about forgotten about it when, after hearing nothing for months, Aaron Bradford showed up, on less than twenty-four hours notice.

"He was very slick. And pushy. Clearly adept at preying on the hopeless. An evil man. I should have sent him out immediately, but he understood how dire our situation was, and, in his brief encounter with you, I think he picked up on your compassion for the younger children.

"He told me what would need to be done to complete your adoption – and what the orphanage would get in return. I immediately refused, shocked and disgusted! But he persisted.

"Then he asked me a question that I've never stopped wondering about. He asked me, 'What would she do?'

"I thought I knew the answer.

"So, reluctantly, I consented.

"I hurt you. I damned myself... And *you* saved the orphanage." His voice trailed off, as he considered stopping there. But he couldn't stop himself from trying to satisfy his curiosity. "If you *had* been given the choice... what would you have done?"

"I'll tell you this," she said, the fire in her eyes reduced to smolder. "If my family had been on the verge of starvation and my dad had asked me, at thirteen, to have surgery and be taken permanently from the only home I'd ever known to save my family, I would have done it in a heartbeat.

"But he never would have asked.

"He was a man. A leader. A protector. A father." She shook her head disgustedly. "You aren't any of those! You don't deserve these children."

"You're right," he said softly, too ashamed to raise his head to make eye contact with her. "I was your only defense from the Aaron Bradfords of the world, and I failed you. I'm so sorry.

"But if I were put in the same hopeless position again, I can't honestly convince myself I'd do things differently."

"Then I hope you enjoy your last day," she said, turning for the door.

"Annamaria, wait! I understand if you never forgive me. I've got no right to ask for that. And I'll accept whatever consequences come my way for what I did. But can I at least show you the good that has come from your success? You deserve that."

~~~

Toward the end of the prior summer, Weinstien had called Ryan, and in typical fashion, was speeding through his third sentence before Ryan was entirely sure who it was.

"Your grandfather died of hypoglycemia – low blood sugar," he'd blurted into the phone. "His blood sugar was eight! Under seventy-five's abnormal! Anything under sixty is dangerous! I mean, he was essentially D.O.A.

"Anyway, he wasn't a coroner's case because he was a diabetic and generally didn't take great care of himself. So, no autopsy. Cause of death on the death certificate: diabetes-slash-hypoglycemia. No foul play suspected. Case closed, right?

"Well, maybe not," Weinstien teased after a dramatic pause. "I had a retired doctor friend of mine look over his records, and a couple of things jumped out to him. One: the only prescription he'd ever filled for his diabetes was a medication called metformin, and your granddad was only picking it up about every other month – i.e., he wasn't taking it regularly."

"But if he wasn't taking his medication, how'd his sugar go *low?*" Ryan had asked. "Seems like it should've been through the roof."

"Exactly! And on every other blood test he'd taken in the past three years, it had been! Three hundred, three-fifty, four hundred, three-eighty. Every one sky high. So the conclusion I came to was that he must've accidentally taken too much of his medication.

"But my doctor friend said his bloodwork didn't really support that. Plus he tells me that metformin usually doesn't tank your blood sugar – at least not to that degree.

"Now here's the kicker: turns out his potassium had bottomed out along with his blood sugar. There's really only one thing that saps your body of potassium *and* glucose at the same time."

"Insulin," Ryan had interjected, disappointed but not at all surprised at the ending of Weinstien's story.

"How the heck do you know this stuff?" a flummoxed Weinstien had asked, mildly deflated that he hadn't gotten to drop the bombshell he'd been building up to.

"It's pretty basic human physiology," Ryan had answered, before filling Weinstien in on the full details of J.R.'s state-license probation over a prescription he'd called in. For insulin. To a Seattle pharmacy. The day before his grandfather had died.

A week later, Weinstien had called back with J.R.'s address in Grand Cayman, and Ryan had begun planning his trip.

Now it would only be a matter of hours – a day at the most – before Ryan could confront him face to face, finally confident in the whole truth. He still wasn't sure what he was going to say – or do – when he found him. But he hoped when the time came, he'd be able to summon a reasonable level of restraint

~~~

"You've got ten minutes!" Annamaria huffed, showing herself out of the headmaster's office. Carlos scrambled closely behind her. As she exited, it dawned on her that the interior of the building was utterly unrecognizable. It no longer looked like a warehouse that stored children. A long central hallway with doors coming off either side every dozen feet or so led to the cafeteria at the other end of the building.

"No more barracks-style living," Carlos said with a smile, feeling suddenly unburdened – and resigned to his fate.

"The kids are all outside right now. Go ahead. Take a look," he said with the casual pride of a realtor showing off a prime property, nudging one of the doors open and flipping on the overhead light to reveal a set of wooden bunk beds and two small desks with chairs. A couple of hand-sewn stuffed animals were poking their heads out from under the sheets of the bottom bunk, and a bulletin board on the near wall was adorned with some of the kids' artwork.

"We've got eight rooms just like this on each side of the hall. Two kids in each room, so we can handle up to thirty-two kids, but our census usually runs in the mid twenties."

"The two rooms in the middle on each side of the hall are for the nannies to stay in at night, and the rooms right next to those are nurseries. There's a door connecting them, so the nannies don't have to go into the main hall if the babies cry at night."

Nothing was fancy. The drywall that partitioned the space was thin and roughly cut with no molding, the floor was polished concrete, and the doors were made from flimsy particle board, but it was a remarkable upgrade from what had been there six years earlier.

"We've got *two* bathrooms now – a boys' on the right, and a girls' on the left. No more shifts for showers in the morning and evening."

Annamaria involuntarily chuckled at the memory before quickly straightening her smile and continuing on down the hall toward the cafeteria.

"The kitchen's closed off now," Carlos continued. "The older kids still get the opportunity to work in there, but I never liked the idea of the kids going through a line with a tray. It felt so... institutional. We eat family-style now. The plates, cups and silverware are set up ahead of time. We have one adult at each table; we even distribute the little tikes in the high chairs at different tables. We talk, we laugh, we argue over who gets the last empanada. It really feels like family."

Carlos gazed around the room sadly. "I eat here every night," he said, missing his dinners with the kids already, trying to maintain the strained smile on his face.

"There's one more thing I want to show you," he said, doubling back down the long central hallway. They exited the main door next to his office and took a right, heading down the new section of sidewalk that had originally piqued Annamaria's interest, this time making it all the way to the back of the building.

Annamaria's heart nearly stopped as her eyes filled with tears. Two dozen kids, who looked like they could've been the exact same group she'd shared three months of her life with, were joyously splashing and bobbing in a full-sized swimming pool. Off to the side, a nanny was doting over a blissful dark-skinned toddler outfitted in nothing but a swim-diaper, wading in a small circular baby pool, as a teenaged lifeguard, probably one of the older orphans, dutifully prowled the perimeter with a whistle around his neck, never taking his eyes off the water.

"None of this would've been possible without you," Carlos whispered.

"This isn't fair!" Annamaria shot back, her voice trembling. She turned and stormed out of the pool area, determined not to let him see her cry.

Why couldn't he just have been the pure evil she was expecting? He had no right to make this even harder on her. What he did was inexcusable, and he had to pay for it!

Standing in the middle of the empty soccer field, she squeezed her eyes shut, losing the battle to hold back her tears. It was clear the children were happier now than when she'd been there. The facility was far superior in every way. Carlos was contrite, and he'd obviously used every cent of the dividends her stock had paid out on the kids, keeping his own office in the tiny supply closet. He'd even provided the kids with two computers that were several years newer than the one he used himself.

"Annamaria," Carlos said, hesitantly approaching. "You have a right to be angry. Don't feel guilty for that." He paused to give her the chance to vent if she wanted to.

"But you also have the right to feel proud. That's all I wanted for you."

She squeezed her eyes and lips together even harder, to the point that she was dizzy. "I can't have children because of you!"

"But look at all the children you've helped. You have a good heart. Nothing that happened to you was your fault, Annamaria. You'll make a wonderful mother some day."

"I might *never* be able to have children!" she growled, trying to keep her voice down for the children's sake. "What? You think the reversals are a hundred percent? They're not even close!"

"Reversals?" Carlos asked, genuinely confused.

"Getting my tubes untied!" she hissed. "What do you think?"

"Getting your..." Carlos stopped mid-sentence, bringing a trembling hand up to his mouth. "Annamaria, I had no idea. I never would have..."

"Don't try and deny it now. I had a private investigator track down the consent forms for my procedures, and your signature is all over them."

"They promised me the procedure would be purely cosmetic. The forms were all in English. I didn't..."

"You said it yourself, Carlos," Annamaria said resolutely but with an aching heart. "You were responsible for protecting me from people like Aaron Bradford. And you failed."

His shoulders drooped, as she brushed past him on her way back to the cab, knowing that there was nothing he could say at that point to make things any better.

~~~

A blast of heat and humidity hit Ryan as he walked through the sliding doors of the George Town airport on an uncharacteristically breezeless day, wearing a plain white T-shirt, navy blue athletic shorts, a pair of aviator sunglasses and flip-flops, carrying a backpack half full of the winter clothes he'd been wearing at the start of his trip.

His "garden view" hotel room half a mile away had no frills, no character, and certainly no view, but it was the only place he could find that, one, had availability and, two, was close to J.R.'s address. And, he reminded himself, he wasn't there on vacation. He threw his backpack onto his double bed and turned right back toward the door to start his search.

J.R.'s apartment was a third of a mile inland up a slight incline. Keeping up a brisk pace, his eyes constantly darting side-to-side behind his shades, Ryan noticed a gradual increase in the state of disrepair of the neighborhood (and the road itself) as the street numbers inched upward toward J.R.'s address. By the time he was halfway there, there wasn't a tourist in sight. But he'd been over the route so many times on his computer, he almost felt like a local himself.

As he approached a dilapidated two-story apartment building, he squinted to confirm the faded number 616 painted on the curb out front. J.R. certainly didn't appear to be living a life of luxury, sheltering millions in one of the Caymans' famous banks.

The probably-once-stately building's soiled white paint was cracking and peeling off of the brick façade, and it seemed every third shingle on the roof was missing. A couple of window-mounted air-conditioning units outlined in thick layers of duct tape jutted out conspicuously from the windows on the far side of the first and second floors, while every other window had been left wide open, the thin white curtains inside lying perfectly motionless in the still, tropical air. A vacancy sign that looked like it hadn't been removed for years was planted in the middle of the parched lawn, next to a cracked front walkway.

J.R. was in apartment 2C. The idea that there could be a "C" at all, implying that there were at least three separate domiciles crammed onto the second floor of the compact building, was in and of itself remarkable.

With his heart rate rising, more from anticipation than anxiety, Ryan strode confidently through the front door and bounded up the steps two at a time. Without pause, he knocked confidently, loudly, on the green door marked 2C, which from the orientation of its entryway seemed to overlook the street.

"Restraint," he whispered to himself.

No answer. The door had no peephole, and Ryan was pretty sure he hadn't been spotted on his way in. He gave the door one more good knock, jiggled the handle for good measure, and yelled, "Dr. Ralston?"

Again no answer. Ryan checked his phone – 6:15. Maybe he was out getting something to eat, which didn't strike Ryan as a bad idea. He hadn't eaten since Miami six hours earlier, and he'd noticed an English pub across the street. Maybe he could even pick up a little info on J.R. from the locals.

On his way out, Ryan stopped at the base of the stairs and pulled a solitary letter halfway out of 2C's mail slot. The postmark was recent, and it was addressed to Jared Ralston. This was definitely the right place.

Ryan seated himself in a booth in a back corner of the sparsely-populated, entirely *un*authentic English pub. A glass display case featuring large plastic bottles of well liquor hung above the bar, while spigots for the low-budget American and Caribbean beers on tap peeked up from underneath. Against the far wall, one patron had apparently called it an early night, already face-down on the bar.

Ryan ordered a can of Coke, no ice to be safe, and a basket of fish and chips, which all came out together in less than five minutes.

Too hungry just to walk away, he doused the limp planks of fish with malt vinegar and salt, more to ensure they were sanitized than to flavor them, and managed to choke down about half his order.

"Anything else?" his waitress asked briskly as he finished up, hoping he'd take the hint to ask for the check.

"No, I'm all set," he answered, handing her his credit card without asking to see the bill, equally anxious to get the hell out of there. He didn't want to miss an opportunity though.

"Actually," he called out, "there is one more thing."

The waitress, already halfway to the register, rolled her eyes before effortfully faking a smile and spinning back around.

Ryan waved her over closer to the table, which seemed to strain her insincere smile even further.

"I'm looking for an old family friend," he whispered. "You wouldn't happen to know an American by the name of Dr. Jared Ralston?"

The waitress politely shook her head no and started to turn back toward the register.

"Or he might go by the name of J. R.?" Ryan added. "I was told he lives right across the street."

With that, the waitress's smile widened, and she threw her head back, cackling loudly. "You mean *him?*" she howled, pointing to the drunk at the end of the bar. "Hey *doc!*" she shouted mockingly. "Wake up! You got company!"

He didn't budge. "Paging Dr. Cuervo!" she yelled, delivering a swift kick to the back leg of his barstool. By now everyone in the pub was laughing, except Ryan and the passed-out drunk.

The drunk yanked his head up off his folded arms, his lids only half open, and took a clumsy swipe at the waitress, nearly falling off his stool in the process.

"That him?" the waitress called out.

He seemed to have aged a good twenty-five years in the eleven years since Ryan had last seen him. But his face was unmistakable. This was it – the moment Ryan had been waiting for for years.

His gut reaction was to take a quick survey of the room to see if there was anyone in the place who would be physically able to prevent him from picking up a pool cue and bludgeoning him to death with it. His best guess was no. But he forced himself to take a deep breath and count to five – just as he'd rehearsed.

He stood slowly from his seat, stretched out his arms and clenched and unclenched both fists a couple times, cracking his knuckles in the process.

The rest of the pub disappeared, as he narrowed his sights on J.R.

Taking slow, controlled breaths through his nose, he strode slowly but confidently across the bar area, never taking his sights off his target who had just warily turned his head in Ryan's direction.

Stopping a few paces short, Ryan dropped his jaw. "J.R.! Is that you?" he exclaimed, feigning a smile.

"Who wants to know?" J.R. slurred, squinting and shielding his eyes from the dim overhead lights.

"It's me. Ryan Ewing – Ryan Tyler."

"Ryan?" J.R. gushed. "Little Ryan? You've grown up, kid! You're bigger'n I am now!" He struggled to his feet and leaned in to give Ryan an awkward hug, slapping him on the back a few times. He reeked of alcohol.

"Yep, all grown up," Ryan said, trying to keep up his chipper tone and pretending not to take note of any of the glaring stigmata of chronic alcoholism staring him in the face. He yelled down to the waitress to add J.R.'s tab onto his card. "I'm down here on spring break from Hah-vahd. You still on faculty at the medical school? I didn't see you on the website last time I checked."

"Nah, I'm done with that. I gave up my twenties and thirties to the practice of medicine." He brought his closed hand up to his mouth as he ducked his chin, futilely trying to suppress a belch. "And even when I wasn't at the hospital, I was answering their stupid pages all day and night. I finally said, 'Enough!' and checked out for good."

"Wow. We need to catch up! So, what, you live down here now?" Ryan asked.

"Me?" J.R.'s mind was moving too slowly to lie effectively. "Nah – I mean not yet. I'm just watching a friend's place for awhile, till the construction on my cozy little beachfront bungalow's finished."

Ryan looked up at the waitress, on her way back over with his credit card, rolling her eyes and shaking her head, having heard J.R. tell that same lie countless times.

"Hey, whaddya say I go buy us a bottle of something and I meet you over at your place – I mean your friend's place – in a couple minutes?" Ryan offered, guessing that someone who looked like J.R. probably wouldn't be able to resist the prospect of more alcohol.

"Yeah," J.R. slurred right on cue. "Let's do it. I'm up in 2C across the street.

"Oh, and why don't we drink a little Beefeater tonight? British island, British drink?"

And with that, J.R. stumbled out of the pub ahead of Ryan and wobbled across the street to his apartment, while Ryan ran two doors down to a small liquor store to buy his host a gift. J.R. was already well beyond drunk. Ryan wouldn't have considered buying even a single serving of alcohol for a real friend. But for J.R., Ryan left the store carrying two one-liter bottles of 94-proof Beefeater gin.

J.R.'s second-floor apartment was stifling, obviously not one of the units blessed with air-conditioning. The space was sparsely furnished with a card table and two folding chairs next to a small galley kitchen, a futon in the main living area, and an unmade double bed in the tiny lone bedroom. The walls were bare, painted a sterile white, and the white-tile bathroom looked like it may have never been cleaned. Despite the open windows, a stale smell hung in the air, giving the not-too-far-off impression that the unit had been abandoned months ago.

After letting himself in, Ryan closed the door and headed straight for the kitchen, pouring J.R. a ten-ounce glass of straight gin and himself a glass of water. "Still not 21," he smirked to J.R. who was watching him intently from his seat at the card table.

Ryan took the other seat at the card table opposite J.R. and endured several minutes of his absurd confabulation over his past, present and future, studying his burned out appearance as his hollow words evaporated into the ether.

He looked even worse in the fluorescent light of the apartment than he had at the bar, his greasy, stringy hair framing a ruddy complexion, underlain by delicate spiderwebs of red and blue veins. His shifty eyes, blood red around the dull hazel of his irises, faded to a rusty yellow near his sagging lower lids. He hadn't shaved in several days, and his gray teeth were stained by some combination of coffee and tobacco. Clearly chronically malnourished, his swollen ankles and protuberant belly only served to draw added attention to his otherwise rail-thin frame.

Ryan found himself so entranced by J.R.'s appearance that he almost failed to notice that his glass was empty. And his slurred speech had started to slow.

"I just found out my grandfather was murdered!" Ryan blurted out, hoping he hadn't overshot with his more-than-generous pour of gin. Directness was all he had time for at this point. "J.R., did you call in a prescription for insulin to a Seattle pharmacy the day he before he was killed?"

"What? No!" J.R. said, exaggerating a shocked expression but coming off looking like a chocolate-faced four-year-old, denying he'd seen the missing cookies.

"Look, I'm not accusing you of anything. You were the best friend my dad ever had." If there was an ounce of humanity in J.R., that lie would have to add to his guilt, which was the only thing that made telling it bearable. "But I know why your training license was put on probation.

"I know you wouldn't have done anything intentionally." Again, Ryan cringed at his own words. "But I think Avillage might've been behind this. Did they put you up to it?"

"They tricked me, Ryan," J.R. said, his eyes now welling with tears – not of contrition or sorrow but of self-pity. "They offered to pay off my student loans if I just called in one prescription. I didn't know what it was for!"

And you didn't question why someone would be willing to pay off your loans for calling in one prescription? He was clearly lying. "But you worked with them again, J.R. You fed them my parents' location the night of their accident. Why?"

Ryan demanded, as if he knew it as fact. J.R.'s lids were drooping. "J.R.! Why?"

His eyes snapped back open. "They told me if I didn't help them out one more time, they'd rat me out to the police for what happened to your grandfather."

"J.R., who is 'they?' Who told you to call in the prescription? Who told you he'd call the police? Who wanted my parents' location?"

"I don't know! Somebody at Avillage!"

"Was it Aaron Bradford? J.R.! Listen! I promise I'll make sure you're taken care of. Just tell me."

"I don't know!" he blubbered with a woe-is-me moan, emotionally incontinent from his drunkenness. "I swear. I'd tell you if I knew."

It was pointless. He probably truly didn't know, but there was no way Ryan could trust a single word that was coming out of his mouth either way. One thing *was* clear though. J.R. had clearly benefited directly from his actions – twice.

"J.R., listen to me," Ryan said placing his hand on J.R.'s trembling bony shoulder, still intent on getting a good measure of revenge. "You look tired. I'm gonna let you go to bed. And don't worry. I can see life has dealt you some bad breaks, but I'm going to make sure you're taken care of." And with that, Ryan walked out of the apartment, not stopping to look back.

Before heading back to his hotel, he made one last stop back at the liquor store, just before close.

As the owner jotted down his credit card information, Ryan placed a unique order. "I want you to deliver a liter of gin everyday to Jared Ralston in apartment 2C across the street," he said. "If he asks for more, I want you to deliver more. As much as he wants. Understood?"

The man behind the counter looked at him suspiciously. "You're gonna have to pay up front – a month at a time. Plus delivery."

"You can put a thousand dollars on the card now and a thousand more every thirty days. Call me if it's not enough. I'll pay more if I have to," Ryan said flatly.

The confused owner just nodded his head silently as he slid Ryan's card through the reader, still somewhat skeptical but not willing to risk blowing the biggest single deal he'd ever been offered.

There were fates worse than prison. Fates worse than death. And there were a few souls rotten enough to deserve them.

~~~

Ryan arrived back in Boston, three days early, to a stack of thick envelopes he guessed were probably job offers. They were too substantial to be rejection letters. And those usually came later in the interview season, after the employers were sure all their slots had been filled.

He rifled quickly through the envelopes, considering which one to open first: Goldman

Sachs? McKinsey? Maybe one of a handful of silicon valley firms?

But his attention was drawn to a shiny square envelope toward the bottom of the stack with his name hand-written in ornate calligraphy on it. The letter contained no return address but had been postmarked in New York. Probably an early invitation to a graduation party from one of his exorbitantly rich classmates, he thought.

He ran his finger underneath the flap of the envelope and pulled out another smaller envelope inside. If he'd known anyone who was planning to get married, he would have sworn it was a wedding invitation. The second envelope contained a small reply card, a frivolous bit of translucent tissue paper, and a hand-written invitation.

Dear Ryan, it read. *I would ask respectfully that you not formally accept any job offer prior to discussing your options with me. I would be happy to arrange transportation and lodging for you here in New York at my expense.*

The simple invitation on otherwise blank stationery was signed, *Sincerely, James Prescott.*

CHAPTER 15

"James Prescott."

Ryan's mind went blank. The last thing he'd expected was that Prescott would answer the phone himself – on the first ring.

Prescott smiled at the silence; his ploy, one he'd used countless times on less-experienced business associates to gain an early psychological advantage, seemed to have worked. Ryan had initiated the call, yet somehow he was the one back on his heels, as Prescott calmly spoke first. "Thank you for calling, Ryan. I presume you received my invitation?"

"Uh, yes. Yes I did," Ryan stammered, cursing himself for blowing his one and only chance to make an assertive first impression.

"I do hope you'll accept. As I mentioned in my note, I'd be happy to arrange transportation and lodging. Unfortunately, the one thing I can't offer is a lot of flexibility on dates."

Ryan already felt like he was playing catch-up in the conversation. As a legal adult, he had no obligation to Avillage, other than the appropriations from his income. So while he was intrigued by the vague invitation, he had no interest in making this too easy on Prescott. "What is this concerning?" he asked flatly.

Prescott paused for several seconds, as Ryan's mind raced to figure out why. Was Prescott unprepared for the simple question? Insulted by the tone? Was it a politician's pause to make sure he worded his answer correctly? Was he still considering just how much to reveal? Or, probably most likely, did he simply want Ryan to fret over why he was pausing?

"I thought you might be interested in joining your board of directors for our next meeting," Prescott finally answered, speaking with a deliberate, measured cadence. "We'll be convening this coming Monday at 4:00 just after market close."

Board of directors? "Is it standard for orphans to meet with their boards when they reach adulthood?" Ryan asked, quite sure the answer was no.

"I didn't say *meeting* with your board. I said *joining* it."

Ryan's jaw dropped slightly. That certainly wasn't standard.

"We can talk more in person. I can assure you, the trip will be worth your while."

"Well, I've got a lot to get done over the coming week," Ryan hedged. But his mind was already made up. "I guess if I could get some work done on the ride over there, I *might* be able to... Do you think you could get me a limo with reliable Wi-Fi access?"

"How about I send one of our executive Escalades? It's essentially a mobile office – far superior to a limo."

"And I have a stop I'll need to make in Northern Pennsylvania on Sunday."

"Not a problem," Prescott said without hesitation. "Our driver will be at your disposal. And our guests are usually quite comfortable at the Ritz-Carlton Battery Park. Will you be staying Sunday and Monday nights with us?"

"I'd plan to be there both nights, yes. But I'd prefer to stay in Midtown."

"Not a problem," Prescott said, still unfazed. "Any specific hotel we can book for you?"

"The Peninsula" flew off Ryan's tongue. "I've got a friend in the building."

"The Peninsula it is then," Prescott said, impressed by the teenager's decisiveness and poise throughout most of the conversation. "I've followed you very closely for over a decade. I look forward to finally meeting you."

"Likewise."

~~~

"Higley!" an armed guard shouted from halfway down the long hall of locked cells. "You got a visitor!"

Dillon popped his head up from a paperback book with a puzzled, mildly annoyed expression on his face. *A visitor?* Since he'd been sentenced to the Federal Penitentiary in Canaan, Pennsylvania six months earlier, he'd had visitors on precisely four occasions. Each time his adoptive parents. And each time he'd sent them away without seeing them.

Shouldn't they have learned their lesson by now?

"Who is it?" Dillon asked disinterestedly, reclining on a folded pillow on his cot.

"Some kid named Ryan Ewing. You wanna see him?"

A smile cracked Dillon's countenance. "Yeah. I do."

Dillon's smile persisted all the way up to the visitation area, where he quickly spotted Ryan grinning right back at him, seated behind a plexiglass window, holding a corded phone.

Dillon picked up the phone on the other side. "So how's life on the outside?" he asked, still just as skinny and ghostly white, with the same mop of disheveled black hair atop his head. He still looked young, but he didn't look like a kid any more. And not from some hardened-prison-inmate transformation. He looked wiser. Relaxed. At peace.

"Aah, life's about the same out here," Ryan said. "How about you?"

"Not bad. You're gonna think I've completely lost it, but I think I might actually like it better in here. My dad was pretty pissed off at me at first, but I think he's glad I'm here now. And he won't admit it, but I know he loves how I got here."

"You see him much?"

"A few hours a week usually, which is obviously a lot better than before."

Dillon had vigorously fought the charges against him for two solid months, using the highly-publicized trial to get as much dirt about Avillage out into the press as he could. Then, when he ran out of ammo, he'd made a shocking one-eighty and

308

offered to change his plea to guilty in exchange for the prosecution's allowing him to choose which maximum security federal facility he'd be sent to.

Prescott had successfully deflected all of the blame, most of it rightfully, onto his executive VP in order to protect the company. And Bradford, who was wasting every lucid moment between seizures in mortal fear of the next one, was too preoccupied to try to defend himself. In the end Avillage's sterling reputation had come out of the fiasco only slightly tarnished.

"So, was it worth it?" Ryan asked.

"I don't know; that's a complicated question. I'm glad I did it, if that's what you mean. That shitbag definitely deserved it.

"I would've loved to have stuck around and fought alongside you – brought the whole operation down. But I figure, best case scenario, we were probably ten years away from that. Too much legislation to overcome. And too much money. I probably couldn't have slipped the insider trading charge anyway."

"Oh yeah! What in the world were you thinking with the insider trading?"

"I know, that probably wasn't a good move," Dillon conceded. "But I needed some extra cash. I was working on some stuff on the side. We anti-establishment hackers are a pretty tight group, but we can't all work for free."

Ryan nodded. "Alright. One more thing. You'll never guess where I'm headed from here," he said, bracing for Dillon's reaction. "I'm going to meet with the one, the only... James Prescott – in person. He asked me to join my own board of directors. Can you believe that?"

Dillon smirked, surprisingly unmoved, seemingly liberated from his rage by his inability to change anything from inside a maximum security prison. "Hmm. Never heard of anyone joining their own board," he said. "Just be careful. Make sure you go in knowing exactly what you are and aren't willing to negotiate."

"That's it?" Ryan said with a smile. "I thought you were either gonna hang up and walk away or try to beat your way through this glass with your phone.

"Do you at least have any last-minute dirt I could use?"

"Nope. Nothing. Seriously. I spent hours inside their system every week for years, and I couldn't tell you a single thing about him. Bradford's tracks were well-hidden. Prescott just doesn't leave any.

"Look Ryan, you're special," Dillon said, blushing slightly. "And you know it's not my style to give compliments, so you're never gonna hear that again. But don't forget it. And don't be intimidated. You should never be intimidated."

"Thanks, Dillon. It was good to see you again."

"Good to see you too. And feel free to stop back by after you've toppled Avillage," he smirked. "Maybe I'll change my plea."

Ryan laughed. "Sure. And say hi to your dad for me."

"I will," Dillon said straight-faced. "But just to let you know, I'm pretty sure he'd hate your conformist guts."

~~~

Ryan could've easily paid for a couple nights at the Peninsula himself, but rolling up to it in the back of a mobile office on someone else's dime, he felt like he'd arrived. Dillon's advice about never needing to feel intimidated was appropriate, but in a way, it was too late. Something had changed in Ryan over the past year. Perhaps it had to do with the fact that he was a senior in college; perhaps it was just a natural maturation process, but Ryan had grown to embrace his status as a leader on campus. He was no longer self-conscious of his gifts or semi-apologetic that he knew things other people didn't or couldn't.

A few individuals were capable of changing the world, and he had begun to see no reason why he couldn't be one of them.

But some things still got to him.

As he entered the hotel lobby, his mouth did dry just slightly at the sight of Annamaria waiting in a casual black dress near the front lobby. He wasn't sure if his heartbeat had slowed down or sped up, but it was there – oddly conspicuous in his chest. And it hadn't been just moments earlier. His hands, which had been resting comfortably at his sides, suddenly felt awkward and out of place, before he jammed them into his pockets just to get them out of the way.

He couldn't help but return the smile she flashed at him, as she tilted her head coyly to the side and whisked an errant strand of shiny black hair away from her eye with her little finger.

"So, how have you been?" Ryan asked, giving her a much more formal hug than he would've liked.

"We can talk over dinner," she said, still smiling. She hadn't wanted to talk about her trip over the phone. "I got something I think you'll like delivered to my suite."

Annamaria's corner suite was twice the size of Ryan's "standard room," and featured a well-appointed living room that was flooded with light from the north and west. A small dining table was nestled up to the north-facing window on the far wall that looked out over rooftops of the adjacent buildings and on to Central Park a couple of blocks away. The little table was dressed with a white tablecloth and set with two plates – no silverware – and two cans of Coke. Occupying the rest of the surface area was the largest silver cloche Ryan had ever seen.

"Come on over!" Annamaria squealed, kicking her shoes off and bounding over to the table on her tiptoes, her silky black hair magically bouncing and cascading with each stride. Ryan consciously slowed himself down, following in her subtly perfumed wake at a casual pace.

Just as he arrived at the tableside, she snatched the cloche up off the table to reveal a still-steaming 16-inch authentic New York pizza, its beautifully thin crust perfectly charred around the edges.

His sputtering attempts at stoicism, which had been faltering for some time, officially died next to that little table. He was almost dizzy, intoxicated by the swirling aromas of basil, mozzarella, and San Marzano tomatoes in the air.

But it wasn't just the pizza. It was the fact that she'd remembered. He'd mentioned that he hadn't been able to get a good Margherita pizza in Boston only once – in passing, about two months ago. And it had obviously stuck with her.

They sat together eating pizza and drinking Cokes like a couple of high-schoolers on a first date, albeit in an eighteen hundred dollar a night hotel suite, talking about anything and everything but Avillage.

But when the pizza had been reduced to a few slivers of crust and the conversation finally hit a lull, Ryan reluctantly asked Annamaria how her trip had gone. He knew it would wind up killing the mood, but he had to know everything before he met with Prescott the following afternoon.

She didn't know how to begin to answer. She'd been physically back in New York for a week, but she still didn't feel like her trip was over. Emotionally, her journey had started well before she arrived in Panama. She'd hoped it would have ended there. But it hadn't.

She stood up, took a long look out the window, and then turned back toward Ryan, as beautiful as ever but not quite as radiant. "It was even harder than I thought it would be," she said.

She told him about the headmaster and the one bad decision he seemed to have made in six years of service – in a spot where there was no right decision. She told him how the children seemed so happy, so well cared for, and, most importantly, loved. How the headmaster had given her a sincere apology. How he hadn't argued when she'd told him he'd have to resign, only requesting that the kids continue to be loved and well taken care of.

"I went to Panama looking for two things. Answers and revenge. I found my answers. But they weren't the ones I was looking for. And I never got my revenge. There was no one there to exact it on.

"I'd always just assumed the orphanage would be in even worse shape than when I left it. And I saw myself swooping in as the protector of the poor neglected orphans, exposing layer upon layer of corruption and having the evil headmaster thrown in jail."

Ryan nodded. He'd had it considerably easier on his trip to the Caymans. "I can tell you that revenge isn't as sweet as you might think," he said. "Yeah, there's some catharsis in it, but it isn't cleansing."

"Is anything?"

"I don't know. Forgiveness? Maybe?" he thought out loud. "But I don't think it can be at the expense of justice. I honestly don't think you could've handled it better."

"I don't know. The main emotion I left Panama with was guilt – overwhelming guilt." She leaned gingerly on the arm of the sofa, slowly shaking her head, as her gaze fell to the ground. "I decided to give Carlos a month to stay on as headmaster, while he looked for a worthy replacement – which I would have to approve. Normally, he said the government would appoint a headmaster, but he was pretty confident that he and I could pretty much hand-select their appointee."

She stood back up, took both of Ryan's hands in hers and led him over to the couch next to her. "From the day I lost my family, the only extended period of time I've really felt good about myself – the only time I've felt a sense of purpose – was in the three months I lived in that orphanage.

"And I felt it again when I saw those kids. Right away. It had been so long since I'd felt a pull like that, I didn't even recognize it at first." She looked down at Ryan's hands in hers and nervously tightened her grip. For the moment she was quiet, but she clearly had more to say. Ryan hoped she wasn't building up to a tearful goodbye. As he gave her hands a gentle squeeze back, she looked up to meet his gaze. The boundless depth of her onyx eyes was no less hypnotic than it had been when he'd first lost himself in them a year earlier in his dorm room. If she was working up the courage to ask him something – anything – the answer was going to be yes.

"I remember the four things you told me your parents asked of you," she said. "Make a difference. Love. Be loved. And be happy. Well..."

She paused.

"I could do all of those in Rainbow City." Then she demurely dipped her chin, keeping her eyes on his, her hands trembling slightly. "*We* could do all of them."

~~~

Ryan's head still hadn't stopped spinning. Twelve hours ago, he wasn't really sure how Annamaria saw him. Now she was essentially asking him to move to Panama with her? The mere thought of being with her everyday made his head spin. The thought of *being with her* had him on the verge of fainting.

But he was eighteen years old! Settling down wasn't even in his ten-year plan. And running an orphanage was a philanthropic retirement plan for someone like him – after he'd made his mark in the world. His whole life of top-shelf education had to have been leading up to something – and it certainly wasn't this.

On the other hand, what was he really planning on accomplishing that would be more rewarding than changing the lives of dozens of truly vulnerable children? For obvious reasons, orphans held a special place in his heart. And, like Annamaria, he understood them – better than most people possibly could. Plus, he would thoroughly enjoy sticking it to Avillage and all his shareholders. Maybe he'd float the plan out at the board meeting and see how it went over. His lips curled upward at the thought.

He decided to forego the mobile office and trek the four miles or so to the meeting on foot, with every intention of organizing his thoughts along the way.

He should have spent the time pondering why Prescott was gladly paying for what had become a pretty expensive trip from Boston just to allow Ryan to attend his own board's meeting. Or maybe why Prescott wanted him to join the board *before* he officially accepted a job. Or whether or not today would be the day he'd bring up all the dirt he and Dillon had dug up on Avillage – in what would very likely be his only meeting with Prescott. But his mind was stuck on Annamaria and a simple but impactful life in a small town on the Caribbean Sea. That had to mean something.

CHAPTER 16

Above the Avillage headquarters, a towering cumulonimbus cloud mushroomed heavenward in an otherwise cloudless sky, nearly black at the low-lying base, brightening to a vivid white at the pillowy top, with infinite shades of gray in between, each subtle tone intensified by the brilliant light reflecting off of it from a blazing sun that seemed out of place in the same sky.

Ryan paused just outside the building, running half an hour early, intent on not allowing Prescott to catch him off guard again. He had hoped he would have been able to scout the lobby from outside, but the mirrored glass of the first floor made it impossible to tell if anyone was watching from inside. And if he were being watched, he would've already been spotted, so he really left himself no other option but to head right in.

Pushing the revolving door through clockwise, he entered the lobby and immediately glanced over his right shoulder to make sure Prescott wasn't lying in wait behind him, ready to revel in Ryan's startled reaction as he called out his name. He wasn't. Where he was, clearly, was inside Ryan's head.

A young woman in a neat gray suit intercepted him on his way to the security desk, introducing herself only as Mr. Prescott's assistant. Without ever asking for his name, she invited him to follow her into the first elevator in a bank of six and pressed the "45" button, waving her security badge in front of a small black authenticator. A tiny light turned from red to green as the doors closed, and they rode up alone.

Prescott's assistant seemed perfectly comfortable with the silence in the elevator, but Ryan didn't want to waste an opportunity.

As the elevator raced through the thirties, Ryan casually asked, "So, how do you like working for Mr. Prescott?" focusing more on her expression than her answer.

"It's exciting to work for a man with vision," she said. Overall it came off as sincere, if somewhat rehearsed.

He would've liked the chance to ask a few follow-up questions, but a chime indicating they'd reached their floor kept him quiet.

The top floor was a little taller than the others, with fifteen foot ceilings dotted with recessed halogen lighting. The sterile slate floors along with the glass and stainless steel office furniture belied the fact that the corporation was essentially a holding company for children.

Prescott's assistant showed Ryan into the conference room and invited him to choose whichever seat he liked at the large oak table. He was the first to arrive.

"Mr. Prescott will be joining you at four," she said. "Can I get you a cup of coffee or a glass of water while you wait?"

"Water would be good. Thank you," Ryan said, wondering why she hadn't said, "*The board members* will be joining you at four." Maybe

Prescott was the only one she thought she could speak for.

The assistant returned shortly with a tall glass of water and placed it on the table in front of Ryan. "The restroom is just outside the boardroom to your left," she said. "Let me know if you need anything else."

Ryan nodded politely.

"Oh, and I apologize that you won't be able to get any cell phone reception in the boardroom. This is by Mr. Prescott's design. Feel free to use the phone on the wall if you need to make a call. And of course you're more than welcome to sit in the reception area if you need to check your messages."

"Thanks," Ryan said, suddenly wishing he were meeting with Prescott anywhere else but on his home turf.

At ten till four Ryan was still all alone in the boardroom. His nervous fingers unconsciously spun the empty water glass in front of him in a tight circle on the table, as his eyes raced back and forth between the window and the clock. Showing up early, it turned out, had *not* been the right play.

The bathroom was right next door, and his bladder, he decided, probably wasn't going to make it through an entire meeting. Whatever the case, in his current frame of mind, any change of scenery struck him as a good idea.

He paused in front of the restroom mirror for a silent pep talk before returning to the boardroom, focused and ready. He'd expected at least one other person would have arrived, but when he opened the door, all the chairs were still empty.

The meeting was supposed to start in less than five minutes! Where was everyone? Prescott was known for his punctuality. Maybe he was planning a coordinated grand entrance to give a daunting eight-against-one feel.

At three fifty-nine, Ryan was still sitting alone. By force of habit, he pulled out his phone to check for a message, perhaps that the meeting time had been changed, but he was quickly reminded that he had no service. He slid his phone back in his pocket and bounced his right leg nervously on the ground.

By the time he looked back up, Prescott had silently materialized in the doorway. Ryan's whole body jumped almost imperceptibly. Almost. Somehow Prescott had gotten him again.

He quickly rose to shake Prescott's hand, taking care to match Prescott's firm grip precisely. Their hands were similarly sized, but Prescott's felt thinner; Ryan thought he looked *generally* thinner than he ever had on TV. Then again, he hadn't been on TV much recently. Similar in height, they naturally looked each other straight in the eye. Ryan had to fight the tendency to break the handshake or eye contact first.

"It's a pleasure to meet you, finally," Prescott said with a cordial smile, finally releasing his grip. "Welcome to New York. And thank you for coming. Please, have a seat."

He turned to close the door.

"Won't the other board members be joining us?" Ryan asked.

"No, they won't," Prescott said nonchalantly.

What?! Ryan thought. *Is he trying to pull some kind of bait and switch?* Prescott was known for keeping his associates guessing, but he didn't flat out lie to them. "I was under the impression that there would be a meeting of my board today," he said, trying to keep a steady tone.

"That's because that's what I told you," Prescott said with a smirk, lowering himself into the seat directly across the table from Ryan.

Ryan was starting to boil inside. He briefly thought about how satisfying it would be, on so many levels, just to walk out of the room without another word, pick up Annamaria at her hotel and leave for Panama straightaway, never to be heard from again. But, he reminded himself, he may never get this opportunity again. "So what changed?" he asked.

"Nothing," Prescott said, sensing Ryan was tiring of his evasiveness.

Ryan looked at him as if he were speaking a foreign language. He didn't appreciate being played. "Mr. Prescott, please realize that my time is very valuable – if not to the board members, to me. I'm going to give you one warning. Atlas is seriously considering shrugging, and if I do, it'll send waves – not ripples – all through your market."

"I apologize. I promise, I'll explain everything to you. I'll stay here as long as you like and answer every question you have. It's not in my best interest to withhold information from you," Prescott said smoothly. "But first, I want to ask you a few questions."

"Shoot," Ryan said impatiently, struggling to keep his emotions in check.

"Have you accepted any offers for employment yet?"

"No, not yet. I've got some good offers on the table," he said, his mind sticking on the one he'd gotten one night earlier from Annamaria. "But I haven't formalized anything yet."

"How are you going to decide?" Prescott asked, his eyes narrowing as he leaned into the table toward Ryan. "What are you looking for?"

"I'm looking for something *impactful*," he said without hesitation. "I realize I'm only eighteen, and maybe my first job won't give me the opportunity to change the world, but I have to see it as at least a step in that direction."

Prescott nodded. That was essentially where he'd been when he was finishing college. Every decision he'd made was toward one ambitious goal. But his goal had been better defined. It wasn't clear that Ryan was working toward something specific. Changing tacks, he continued, "What do you care about? What are you passionate about?"

Again Ryan answered without pause. "I think people with cancer naturally care about cancer research. People with Parkinson's disease care about that. So it should come as no surprise that on a personal level I care about the plight of orphans.

"And while I think Avillage has done some good things to address the issue of orphan neglect, I think you've swung the pendulum too far the other way – toward exploitation."

Prescott nodded indifferently, as if he were collecting random survey data. "What did you do your senior project on at Harvard?"

"I did it on Avillage," Ryan said.

"I did mine on Avillage at Princeton," Prescott said, smiling. "Almost forty years ago."

Ryan's expression lightened. "You might not be smiling if you read mine."

"I'd love to hear your perspective some time," he said, unoffended. "I'll be the first to admit I've made some mistakes along the way. But I'm also very confident I've done much more good than harm – on a national scale."

"What about on an individual scale?" Ryan asked.

Prescott gazed over the long table and out the window. "That's difficult, if not impossible, to measure. And if I'm being completely honest, I don't spend too much time thinking about that. But we both know that people who are miserable are generally unproductive, and that's not in anyone's best interest.

"I can tell you that what most parents – good ones anyway – try to do is identify their children's strengths and nurture those. We have the opportunity to go a step further. We identify strengths and then choose the parents who can best nurture that child's specific gifts."

"Meddling along the way of course," Ryan chimed in.

"As little as possible actually," Prescott said. "You'd be surprised how much we leave to the adoptive parents. We just try to take some of the subjectivity out of the parenting process."

"That's not the perspective of the Avillage orphans I've talked to."

"That may be a function of your sample size," Prescott said. "And I think you'd find that most kids, adopted or not, think their parents meddle too much in their lives."

"Most kids don't end up in federal prison over their resentment for their parents, or die on a basketball court because they weren't told of their potentially fatal heart condition, or wake up scared and alone in a hospital after elective surgeries their parents signed them up for without their knowledge."

"Those are extreme examples – all tied to one person in the company. And as soon as I found out what he'd been up to, I fired him on the spot.

"We've been cooperating fully with the authorities in their investigation from day one. Everything so far is pointing to Aaron Bradford's having acted alone.

"J'Quarius Jones was a tragedy," he said, shaking his head dolefully. "There's nothing I can do to make that any better, except to try to prevent it from ever happening again. After he died, I changed our policy to make medical records immediately available to the adoptive parents and the entire board – not just the chairman.

"As for Dillon Higley, he made his choices, and he'll have to live with the consequences. But he's far too talented to spend the rest of his life in prison. The federal government needs people like him on their side. My bet is he'll spend some quality time with his dad, but as soon as he gets tired of being in prison, he'll cut some sort of deal.

"Parenthetically, it'll be interesting to see how the government compensates the shareholders if they let him out early to work for them. You know he's still listed on the exchange."

Ryan couldn't help but be impressed at how well he knew each of his listings, but these were certainly some of the higher-profile orphans.

"And as for poor Annamaria Olivera," Prescott continued, "well, she's an international star now. I'd say it appears she's come through her childhood trauma quite well."

"So it would seem from the outside," Ryan said. "Did you know that last night she asked me to join her in running an orphanage in her hometown in Panama?"

For the first time, Prescott's smile faded. He could see that Ryan was serious. "Well, that would be a shame if you did something like that."

"Giving hundreds of orphans a home? Teaching them the skills they need to escape a life of poverty? That would be a shame?"

"It's a low-risk proposition with modest reward at best," Prescott said, his voice rising just slightly. "Granted it would take dedication and compassion. Admirable. But millions of people can offer that. You could personally hire the best headmaster on the planet for a hundred thousand a year and have him report to you. Ryan, you're special! When are you going to accept the responsibility that comes with that?

"I'm not talking about donating a few thousand dollars to the red cross or tithing to your church or rescuing a neighbor's cat from a tree! *History books* are filled with the stories of men like you and me.

"Your advancing a few dozen kids from poverty to the middle class in Panama wouldn't just be a shame. It would be a waste!"

Prescott kept his gaze locked on Ryan's. "And you know it."

For thirty seconds they sat in silence, staring straight at each other from across the table.

Ryan no longer felt at a disadvantage in the conversation. Prescott clearly wanted something from him, and floating out the idea of escaping to Panama seemed to have rattled him. A pressure had arisen in Prescott's speech. An urgency.

"Why didn't you let me defend my title in the spelling bee?" Ryan asked, breaking the silence and dialing back the tension that had been building between them. He did legitimately want to know the answer, but they both knew it wasn't the question he really wanted to ask.

"You'd already proven you could beat kids four and five years older than you," Prescott said, relaxing back in his chair a little, reminding himself that if Ryan made this too easy, he was probably the wrong person. "What good would it have done to send you back there one year older? It'd be like arm wrestling the strongest girl in your class. Lose and your reputation is shot. Win and you've gained nothing."

"I wouldn't have lost," Ryan said confidently.

"I know," Prescott countered, glowing with a fatherly pride. "And the fact that *you* know it too was precisely why you didn't need to go back."

Ryan made sure his mildly dejected expression didn't change, but he got it. It did make sense from a big-picture perspective.

"Why did you bring me here?" Ryan asked.

"That's a direct question. So I'm going to give you a direct answer. I brought you here to offer you a job."

"I'm not interested," Ryan said without asking to hear the offer. He now clearly held the cards. "You said you'd answer any question I had. I want to know about my birth parents."

"I'll do my best," Prescott said, having figured the question would come up at some point.

"Dillon looked all through your early records. The date of the opening was planned three months, almost to the day, after they died. He said you had no plan B."

"Did he say we had a plan A?" Prescott asked, unoffended. "Did we ever make mention of you specifically in any of our voluminous internal records? Sure, we were waiting for the best possible orphan to come along, but in my wildest dreams did I think it would be you? No."

"You knew I'd aced the initial aptitude test. You had the list."

"We secured a list of all the kids who scored in the top fifth percentile. There were thousands of names on it."

"My parents were murdered. I know that for a fact," Ryan finally said, studying Prescott's reaction. "Did you have any role in killing my parents? That's a direct question. I'd like a direct answer."

"No," Prescott said convincingly. "But let's say I had," he challenged him. "Would that change the fact that I'm offering you an immensely impactful job?"

"I'm sorry, Mr. Prescott. I just can't see myself ever working for you," Ryan said.

"Call me James. And that's a knee-jerk reaction – a starting point. Don't worry. I'm not going to hold it against you," Prescott said with the smooth tenor of an FM deejay, as he reached into the inside pocket of his coat. "For thirty years I have been Avillage. You were the first orphan we legally adopted. In the eleven years AVEX has been open, you're the only orphan whose board I've chaired." He pulled out an envelope and slid it across the table to Ryan. "You may not see it this way, but to me, you're like a son."

Ryan opened up the envelope and scanned the papers inside. He comprehended what he was he reading, but he couldn't believe it. "What is this?" he asked.

"As I was trying to tell you before, the entire board is present and accounted for," Prescott said.

"How can you do this? You don't own these shares."

"All of the previous members signed off on my takeover bid at a 60% premium to your already inflated closing price today. And I would've gone higher."

"You took me private?" Ryan gasped.

"That's one way of putting it," Prescott said, his warm smile back in full force. "But those shares are all yours – if you accept my offer."

"And if I don't?"

"I don't know. I'd probably gift them to you anyway," he said, standing up and walking over to the plate glass window. "Ryan, I believe in you. And I believe there's a reason you were the first IPO. It had to be you. From the day you became an orphan – I'll never forget the day, March 16th eleven years ago – I've known this day would come. I never thought it would be this soon, but..." his voice trailed off, and he peered deeply into Ryan's eyes. "Ryan, I'm not offering you a job at Avillage. I'm offering you *my* job."

Ryan's eyes widened, as he pulled back from the table.

"I'm dying, Ryan. Soon. I've got a few more months at best. Avillage is my legacy, and you're the only one I trust leaving it to."

"But I'm eighteen years old!" Ryan said.

"So what! I was twenty-two when I started out with nothing but a vision," Prescott shot back defiantly. "And Silicon Valley was built by kids not much older than you.

"Ryan, I hire good people here. But I've never had an employee that was worth half of what I was at twenty-two. I have something they don't.

Something they'll never have. You have it too. It's undefinable, but unmistakable."

"But there's no way I could just step right into your job. I'm not prepared for this," Ryan protested.

Prescott's smile widened. "I'm not cleaning out my office tonight, Ryan. You'd learn under me for however long I can continue to work. It may be a few months; it may only be a few weeks. But you're closer than you think. I raised you to be prepared.

"Did you know that an only child has a 57% chance..."

"... of choosing a profession in the field as their same sex parent," Ryan interrupted. "Yes, I've heard that stat before – from you."

Prescott nodded proudly and walked over to take the seat immediately next to Ryan. "I've been prepping you for this job your whole life. There was a reason I chose the parents I did for you. Your father, the intuitive hedge fund manager – he wasn't selected to make sure you were taken care of financially growing up. He was chosen to impart his knowledge to you. I didn't choose your mother, the educator of gifted children with a background in child psychology, so she could use her skills to ease your transition from the orphanage to home or to teach someone like you more effectively. It was so you could learn her specific skill set."

Ryan hadn't blinked in over a minute. He did know how to analyze an investment opportunity, almost intuitively. And he did have a knack for identifying kids who were truly gifted from those who simply tested in the gifted range.

"You say you're passionate about orphans? If you run an orphanage in Panama, you'll affect the lives of what? Fifty kids at a time?"

"Thirty-two," Ryan said, with a twinge of embarrassment.

Prescott winced at his answer. "There are 500 kids on our exchange today, each one selected for extraordinary potential, and that number's only going up. You have a chance to develop tomorrow's leaders. What could be more impactful than that?"

Prescott stood up again and laid his hand on Ryan's shoulder. "Come with me. I want to show you something."

He led Ryan down a short hallway, through an anteroom, pausing briefly to introduce Ryan to his secretary, and into his vacuous corner office with views of the Manhattan skyline to the north and the Brooklyn bridge to the east. Prescott's L-shaped desk faced out toward both vistas from the back corner of the room. In the windowed corner across from it was a small round table with two leather chairs, also facing out toward the multi-million dollar views. Prescott invited Ryan to sit with him and picked up the Wall Street Journal lying on the table between them.

"Pick a symbol," Prescott said, handing Ryan the back page of the Markets section.

"JY," Ryan said, playing along

"He's a thirteen-year-old somewhat speculative prospect, who's been on The Exchange for four years now. He's average in every way – except for mathematics. That was clear from an early age. Currently, he's leaving his eighth grade class for a couple of hours everyday to take math classes at UCLA. We're in the process of trying to steer him into mathematically modeling financial and currency markets.

"If it works, his shareholders will be richly rewarded. If not, he'll probably end up a math professor at a top university. Either way, that's a win in my book. Of course I wouldn't tell that to his shareholders.

"Pick another one."

Ryan thought about it this time. "Any symbol?"

"Any one you want."

"SUZ," Ryan finally said, watching for Prescott's reaction.

Prescott sighed, keeping his gaze out over the city. "You've been following this a long time, haven't you?" He didn't turn to see Ryan's response. "Susanna Ko had one of the most beautiful voices I've ever heard from a little girl. And she was cute as a button. We'd set her up with the perfect parents – a voice coach and a really top-notch songwriter.

"At twelve she was on the verge of a major breakthrough. She'd sailed through the audition-phase of a nationally televised singing competition with a song her dad had written. America was going to love her.

"And then she was diagnosed with leukemia. Killed her in just a few months."

There was genuine sorrow in Prescott's tone, but Ryan couldn't be sure if it was for the death of a child or the loss of a can't-miss ticker symbol.

"How long have you known you were on the exchange?" Prescott asked.

"From day one. I watched you introduce me. I heard you describe my parents. And I saw you ring the opening bell that first day."

Prescott nodded, more convinced than ever that Ryan was the only one who could succeed him. Keeping secrets – from everyone – was a vital part of his job.

"There's one more thing I have to show you," he said, walking over to his desk. He keyed a lengthy password into his computer and swiped his left index finger over a reader next to his keyboard. "Come on around," he said to Ryan.

Ryan scanned the financial statement on the monitor. His bulging eyes stuck on the bold-type ten-digit balance at the bottom.

"As I was building this company," Prescott said, making no specific reference to the numbers on the screen, "I knew the one thing I needed that I couldn't come up with myself was capital. And not from banks. I never would have been able to manipulate the numbers to justify the risk to any bank. And I didn't want to have to waste my time giving status updates to lenders.

"I had to sell my idea more to *donors* than investors. I pitched it as an idea to save an exceptional but declining America. And it was genuine. That has always been my vision.

"Never forget, the investors are important – we couldn't survive without them – but the *mission* of this exchange is not to make the investors rich. It's getting this country's exceptional individuals back to realizing their full potential."

Prescott paused from his soliloquy and turned to Ryan. "Do you know anyone more successful than Dillon was? Or Annamaria is? Or you are?"

Ryan kept conspicuously silent.

"About five years after I started building this company, the day arrived that I knew I would no longer have to worry about money. You've probably heard of Bill Gates' and Warren Buffett's 'billionaire giving pledge?'"

"Yeah," Ryan said. "They convinced a bunch of billionaires to agree to give away most of their fortunes to a cause of their choice when they died."

"Well, I met with dozens of billionaires before I finally stumbled upon a reclusive, probably somewhat jingoistic Texas oil tycoon in his late eighties, who thought my idea was worth throwing his money behind. He eventually vowed to leave 95% of his fortune – a little over ten billion dollars – to Avillage. And the money was given 100% at the discretion of the CEO. I wouldn't accept it under any other condition.

"Whoever the next CEO is assumes full control of all those assets – roughly six billion dollars and, for the first time, rising. There won't be any legal fight for it from my wife or my children.   The money wasn't given to James Prescott; it was given to the CEO of Avillage.

"I've been perpetuating a rumor, essentially by not denying it, that I'll be leaving the company in the hands of one of my children.   And in my opinion I am. If you'll accept the offer."

~~~

In the end it wasn't the corporate mission or the money that led Ryan to accept Prescott's offer. It wasn't that he was all of a sudden convinced that Prescott was a genuinely good guy or that he wanted to grant a dying man the fulfillment of generativity over stagnation. It was something else – something Prescott had said just before Ryan left that evening.

Seeing that Ryan was still conflicted as they were preparing to part ways, Prescott had played his final card.   "I'm sure at some point, you've probably wanted nothing more than to wipe this company I've built off the face of the earth. I can tell you with certainty that that could never be accomplished from the outside.   It's too well-rooted. We have legislators and judges at every level who not only invest but sit on the boards of several of our holdings.

"When I'm gone, Ryan, this company will be yours. Yes, I want you to see my vision, but I can't make you share it. I trust your judgment. I trust that you'll take Avillage in the direction it needs to go – whatever that may be."

That had sealed it. The only dilemma left was how to break it to Annamaria that he couldn't go with her.

While she'd been disappointed on a personal level, she realized he had a unique opportunity to make a much bigger impact by staying in New York. And Panama was *her* dream; *her* home. She'd left a week later with no warning and no goodbyes, halfway through a shoot.

They'd both been so busy, they'd only spoken briefly a couple of times since they'd parted. The certainty that they'd never be together full-time separated them more than the distance.

Now, two months out, as Ryan walked to work in the quiet of the pre-dawn, he allowed himself a moment to consider what his life might have been like if Prescott's invitation had come a few days later. He probably never would have answered it.

But as things stood, the first "emancipated" holding in Avillage history was about to take over the reins for good.

For the first time since the building had opened, Prescott had failed to show up for work.

Ryan opened his email shortly after arriving at his desk at 6:15. An urgent message from James Prescott topped the list with the subject line "Succession."

Dear Ryan,

I composed this email the day after you accepted my offer, and I scheduled it to be sent to you automatically the following morning at 6AM. Every morning since, I have manually delayed its release by 24 hours. Today, I was obviously unable to do that.

My life's work is now in your hands. Remember the mission of Avillage that I shared with you. You WILL have to make major sacrifices and painful decisions. Never delegate those. And always make them in the best interest of the mission.

A letter is being sent later this morning to all Avillage employees informing them of the change of leadership, effective immediately. I will not be returning, even if I feel I'm able to, in the future. This company needs a strong, consistent, unquestioned leader.

And they have one.

I'm asking that you be the one to make the announcement public today by ringing the opening bell.

Make an impact.

James

A chill raced through Ryan's body as he read the familiar final sentence of the email. More goosebumps followed when he realized the date was June 18th – exactly eleven years since he'd watched the opening of The Exchange, huddled in the electronics aisle of a Cleveland Wal-Mart.

The realization that this was happening – today – was nearly overwhelming. He looked back over the letter, his eye drawn to the middle of the letter: "You WILL have to make major sacrifices and painful decisions. Never delegate those."

He leaned back in his chair, let out a deep sigh and closed his eyes, as Prescott's words from two months earlier crept back into his head.

Let's say I had. Would that change the fact that I'm offering you an immensely impactful job?

...There's a reason you were the first IPO. It had to be you.

...I remember it was March 16th eleven years ago.

His eyes popped wide open as he shot back up to his feet. The clock on his desk still only read 6:30. He dialed New York Presbyterian on his cell phone as he ran toward the elevators.

"Do you have a patient by the name of James Prescott?

"What room is he in?"

~~~

Ryan burst into Prescott's room, moist with sweat, to find him propped up in bed, alone, his eyes half open, concentrating deeply on each arduous breath he took. A pair of thin plastic tubes stretched from his right arm to the IV pole next to his bed.

He looked up and gave Ryan a weak smile. "Good luck today," he managed, in an almost inaudible whisper.

"Thanks," Ryan said, still catching his breath from his run through the hospital. "But there's something I have to ask you! You said that you clearly remembered *March 16th* eleven years ago.

"James, that was the day my parents died. But I was in protective custody of the state until the *18th*. *That's* when I went to the orphanage. *That's* when I officially became an orphan. Please, James. Tell me you just misspoke."

As Ryan finished speaking, Prescott's smile widened slightly as his thumb slowly depressed the red button on the top of the control in his right hand, sending a bolus of morphine into his system.

His eyes almost immediately drooped the rest of the way shut, and the world faded to black. When it reappeared, he could see himself, more than a decade younger, picking up an insulin prescription at a Seattle pharmacy. He watched himself overpower Ryan's sickly grandfather who had come to answer a knock at the door, and then jab the fatal dose of insulin into his stomach.

Next he saw the screen of his old laptop, his hand on the mouse closing a window displaying the location of Ryan Tyler, Sr.'s cell phone. Then he saw the headlights of a Honda Civic getting closer and closer to the camera mounted on the Chevy Suburban he was controlling remotely. Then finally, everything went black again.

"James!" Ryan yelled. Prescott's breathing was no longer audible. His chest motionless.

"Nurse!" Ryan called out, rushing into the hall. "He's not breathing!"

"I'm so sorry," the nurse said empathetically. "It was his wish that we provide only comfort measures. He signed an order last night that we not attempt to resuscitate him. Are you a family member?"

"No. I mean yes. Kind of."

The nurse smiled. "You favor him."

~~~

Ryan stood just outside the door to the floor of the exchange, expressionless and motionless, as an aide dabbed the shine off his forehead with skin-toned powder.

"Are you ready, sir?" another aide asked skittishly seconds before his first big public appearance.

Ryan nodded determinedly without saying a word.

At 9:27, he stepped through the door and up to a podium above a throng of tipped-off media members and a few dozen traders on the floor below.

"I was the initial public offering on this exchange," he started in a quiet voice. "I lost both of my parents in one tragic night eleven years ago." The content and the tone paralleled the speech Prescott had delivered from the same podium eleven years earlier, almost to the minute.

"I found myself languishing in an orphanage with no family, virtually no stimulation and, the sad reality was, no hope. But that changed when I became a part of the Avillage family!"

Again the room filled with applause, just as it had eleven years earlier.

"Today begins the second volume in the epic of Avillage. I will no longer be a character in this story. Today, I become its author."

More applause.

"It still takes money to raise a child. It still takes morals, ethics and intelligence. It will always take love. And, sometimes," he paused, almost choking on the words, "it takes Avillage."

Just as the clock hit 9:30, he raised Prescott's antique wooden mallet and struck the opening bell.

Acknowledgements

A big thank you to my brother Adam, whose input – from concept all the way through publication – was absolutely invaluable.

Thanks also to my dad, without whose encouragement I almost certainly wouldn't have completed this novel.

A heartfelt thanks to my wife for supporting me and being nothing but positive when I got the crazy idea to write a book out of the blue.

Finally to my pre-readers and secret-keepers-in-chief: Mom, Sis, Chuck, Linda, Maya and Hubert, thank you. Every single critique was helpful.

Want more information about *THE I.P.O.* or its author, Dan Koontz? Have a comment or a question for the author? Be sure to check out www.dankoontz.net.

CPSIA information can be obtained at www.ICGtesting.com
Printed in the USA
BVOW03s2220050515

399140BV00008BA/42/P